Praise for *SHRIVER*

"Chris Belden's *Shriver* is as hilarious and smart as Michael Malone's *Foolscap*, as wise and sympathetic as *Stoner*. Academic farces don't come any better."   —Richard Russo

"A send-up of academia and literary pretension, as well as a poignant exploration of writerly insecurity."
                    —Dani Shapiro, author of *Slow Motion* and *Family History*

"In *Shriver,* Chris Belden has written a fast-paced, wildly inventive novel that is somehow both hilarious and thought-provoking. In fact, I couldn't stop wondering when I last read a book so enjoyable. Zbigniew Herbert famously compared lit conferences to the tenth level of hell; well, if he could've read *Shriver,* he would've added a level."   —Philip Schultz

"A hoot; a farce about mistaken identity set at a writers' conference where facile poets and pompous novelists declaim, caroused, and, possibly, commit murder. In a style somewhere between Evelyn Waugh and Mel Brooks, Belden's satire lampoons all things literary but also, amazingly, convinces us to care about the fools that these mortals be."   —Alan Davis, author of *So Bravely Vegetative*
                                          and *Rumors from the Lost World*

"This picaresque and piquant satire of writers, academics, their quirky characters, and content-lacking conferences is reminiscent of David Lodge's satiric spins on academe. . . . Despite its ability to laugh at the writing world and its daffy denizens, *Shriver* nonetheless ultimately affirms the essential importance of the word."
                              —Joan Connor, author of *History Lessons*
                                          and *The World Before Mirrors*

"Chris Belden's *Shriver* delivers intrigue, a cast of bizarre characters who are also somehow bizarrely believable, and moments of slapstick comedy that are laugh-out-loud funny—all the while exploring the deeply human need for meaning and connection. Read this book!"
                    —Elizabeth Hilts, author of *Getting in Touch with Your*
                    Inner Bitch and *Every Freaking! Day with Rachell Ray*

SHRIVER

A NOVEL

Chris Belden

TOUCHSTONE

New York   London   Toronto   Sydney   New Delhi

Touchstone
An Imprint of Simon & Schuster, Inc.
1230 Avenue of the Americas
New York, NY 10020

A slightly different version of this work was originally
published in 2013 by Rain Mountain Press.

First Touchstone trade paperback edition September 2015

TOUCHSTONE and colophon are registered
trademarks of Simon & Schuster, Inc.

For information about special discounts for bulk purchases,
please contact Simon & Schuster Special Sales at 1-866-506-1949
or business@simonandschuster.com.

The Simon & Schuster Speakers Bureau can bring authors to your
live event. For more information or to book an event contact the
Simon & Schuster Speakers Bureau at 1-866-248-3049 or visit our
website at www.simonspeakers.com.

Interior design by Kyle Kabel

Manufactured in the United States of America

1   3   5   7   9   10   8   6   4   2

Library of Congress Cataloging-in-Publication Data

Belden, Chris.
Shriver : a novel / Chris Belden.—First Touchstone trade paperback edition.
    pages ; cm
    I. Title.
PS3602.E434S57 2015
813'.6—dc23
2015014441

ISBN 978-1-5011-1939-2
ISBN 978-1-5011-1940-8 (ebook)

For Melissa

A writer is always admired most, not by those who have read him, but by those who have merely heard of him.

—H. L. Mencken

Now that I'm enlightened, I'm just as miserable as ever.

—Japanese monk

DAY / ONE

Chapter One

Somewhere between takeoff and landing, Shriver had lost his ability to read. Floating high above the clouds in the American Airlines Dash-8 twin-propeller plane, row nine, seat A, he gazed down upon the handwritten pages from which he planned to read at the conference, and his eyes failed him. The words blurred and merged together, the little blue letters piling up into one thick mass of ink. He blinked, and blinked again. He took off his glasses, retrieved a handkerchief from his coat pocket, and wiped his eyes. He looked at the stitched letters embroidered on the handkerchief—*CRS*, clear as day—then back at the page. The words remained unreadable. He took another sip of whiskey and cola, let the sweet concoction glaze his throat. That's better. He peered out the window, and everything came back into sharp focus. The clouds shone white with highlights of pale blue. Miles below, service roads divided the flat prairie into vast brown squares. Shriver looked back to the page, but the words again began to collide with one another. He turned to the corpulent lady next to him, who sat sleeping with her head resting atop her voluminous bosom. The details of her fleshy face were clearly defined, down to the individual black whiskers above her lip. Back to the page: a blur. He grabbed the in-flight magazine from the seat pocket in front of him and opened to random pages. THE TEN BEST GOLF COURSES IN THE US . . . SHOPPING FOR

ANTIQUES IN SAVANNAH . . . MALLS OF AMERICA. He
shut his eyes and tried to breathe.

Six months earlier, there had been a letter. *Dear Mr.
Shriver*, it began beneath the letterhead of a small liberal-arts
college located in the middle of the country, *As coordinator
of ——— College's annual writers' conference, I would like to
officially invite you to attend this year's event as one of our featured authors.*

At this point, Shriver had had to reexamine the envelope
to make sure the letter was not intended for someone else.
But there was his name, his address, all correctly labeled. Very
strange.

> Though your work has been controversial, even divisive,
> my colleagues have decided that you would be a valuable
> addition to this year's event, especially since the theme
> of this, our thirtieth anniversary as one of the country's
> premier literary conferences, will be LITERATURE AS
> CONFRONTATION. The consensus is that few living
> writers would be more appropriate to grace our stage this
> year than you and the other invited guest authors.

There followed some details about the event, including
an outline of what would be expected of him: a one-hour
reading, a panel discussion, an informal meeting with students from the university. *Of course*, the letter continued, *in
between these scheduled events you will be free to attend readings
and panels by our other featured authors, and to enjoy the many
planned receptions.*

The letter had been signed, *Best wishes, Prof. Simone
Cleverly*, and was accompanied by a self-addressed stamped
envelope to be used for Shriver's reply. And there was a hand-

written postscript: *I understand you do not have a telephone,* Professor Cleverly wrote in a sensible, ruler-straight cursive, *and so we are left this old-fashioned, and somehow appropriate, channel of communication—namely, writing. Nevertheless, if you have any questions, please feel free to call.*

Shriver had immediately read the letter twice more, then again. He set the letter down on the bed, which was where he read all his mail, and stroked the furry neck of his trusty tuxedo cat, Mr. Bojangles. Who would take the trouble to play such a strange practical joke on him? he wondered. He thought of his old friend Cecil Wymanheimer, who had once arranged a date for him with a rather convincing transvestite—but wasn't poor Cecil dead? Or it could have been Chuck Johnson, Shriver's mischievous old college roommate. Though he hadn't spoken to Chuck in at least twenty years, this definitely was the type of tomfoolery his friend would go in for. There was the time, as a bachelor party gag, Chuck had ferried Shriver around town to various bars and strip clubs, getting him drunker and drunker, until some off-duty police officers Chuck had hired "arrested" Shriver on charges of lewd and lascivious behavior. Hilarious! Yes, only Chuck Johnson was capable of such chicanery.

The reason Shriver was so suspicious of the invitation was that he was not a writer at all. He had never written any books, had never written a page of fiction, nonfiction, poetry, drama—he had never even written a screenplay. The only writing he was capable of was the occasional fan letter to his favorite newscaster, Tina LeGros, of the Channel 17 Action News Team. *Dear Ms. LeGros,* he wrote just last week, *Just a brief note to express my admiration for the way you conducted yourself during last evening's interview with our less-than-forthcoming mayor.* He was very proud of these letters, some of which ran to several handwritten pages—one went on for seven, inspired by Tina's ill-conceived change of hairstyle from an attractive, shoulder-length shower of blond to one of those stiff, helmet-like do's that all the lesser female newscasters favored—but Shriver was definitely *not* a writer.

Nevertheless, to show he was a good sport, he scribbled his acceptance on a sheet of legal paper, stuffed it into the envelope, and mailed it off. *Dear Chuck*, he wrote, *It will be my pleasure to attend your prestigious conference. I only hope I do not disappoint you.* To his surprise, a few weeks later he received more information about the conference, as well as round-trip air tickets. *We are pleased that you will be able to attend*, "Professor Cleverly" wrote in an accompanying note. *And don't worry about disappointing us—your mere presence will be a great victory for the conference.* In a postscript she added, *I'm not sure who "Chuck" is, but we are absolutely thrilled about this.*

Would Chuck Johnson go to such lengths? Whoever was behind this, Shriver thought at the time, was certainly resourceful and determined.

When he opened his eyes aboard Flight 1010 and looked again at the sheaf of paper in his hands, the words once more crumpled and folded in on themselves. He finished his drink and rolled an ice cube around his mouth to suck up the last of the whiskey. He wiped his forehead with the handkerchief and gazed out the airplane window. Just a few feet away a propeller whirred invisibly. Down below, clouds floated on the air like shaving foam on water. Some resembled animals—a duck, a sheep, a sleeping cat. That one there looked like the face of his ex-wife, with her typical expression of impatience. He felt a deep, burning sense of shame as she glared at him from a mile away, mocking him. He had considered sending her a card, telling her about the conference—he even wrote one out, using a nonchalant tone to inform her that he had been invited as a guest to a prestigious literary event—but then he remembered he didn't know where she lived, and he threw the note away. Besides, she would never have believed him. *You're no writer*, she would say in that voice that could cut a diamond in half.

He pressed the overhead button, and moments later, a flight attendant arrived wearing an expression of amused inconvenience.

"May I order another whiskey and cola?" Shriver asked.

There had been little correspondence from Professor Cleverly in the intervening months. She wrote once to inform him that she had ordered copies of his book—a novel Shriver had never even heard of—to be sold at the conference, and expressed hope that he would make himself available to sign them. Then just last week he'd received a brief note from her reminding him that someone would be dispatched to pick him up at the airport, and that if he had any trouble traveling—any delays or other unforeseen problems—he should call her immediately at the number provided. That's when Shriver finally began to realize that this may not be a hoax at all, but some huge misunderstanding.

Somewhere in this world was a writer named Shriver who was expected at this conference, but it was not him. What should he do? He'd committed to attending, and had even been sent what looked like genuine airline tickets. He checked the date on the itinerary—just three days away!

At that point he'd decided to write a letter to Tina LeGros about this peculiar situation. As co-anchor of the Channel 17 Action News Team she had seen it all—political scandals, extreme weather conditions, serial killings; maybe she could help. He fluffed up his pillows and sat up in his queen-size bed. After shooing away the ever-curious Mr. Bojangles, he set a legal pad of yellow paper on his lap and stared up at the water mark on the ceiling. *Dear Ms. LeGros,* he started, *I seem to have found myself in something of a pickle.*

After a few more lines, however, he grew bored, and sat staring up at the water mark, which had been on the ceiling since the rainy day his wife walked out on him. He stared and stared, thinking about what a real writer—a writer expected to present his work to a large crowd, a writer like this Shriver fellow—would make of such a water mark. He crumpled up his letter to Tina LeGros. Then he wrote "The Water Mark" at the top of the next page. He stared at the ceiling some more. After a while, he wrote, "The water mark appeared on my ceiling on the rainy day my wife walked out on me." He went on to describe the unique aspects of the mark, surprised to find that he enjoyed setting down his thoughts and ideas on paper. He wrote tentatively at first, in small fits and starts, but after a while he found a rhythm and was unable to stop until many hours later, exhausted and hungry. He woke up the next day and the same thing happened. The words seemed to flow out of him, as if he were a natural writer. This had continued right up through yesterday, when he achieved a sort of fever pitch as his story raced to its climax. At midnight last night he'd scribbled the words *The End,* then collapsed. Mr. Bojangles, freed from his banishment to the far side of the mattress, climbed onto his chest, curled up, and fell asleep.

The next morning, at precisely six o'clock, Shriver awoke to a knocking at the door. He pulled on a robe, padded across the apartment, and peered through the eyehole to see a tall bearded man staring back at him.

"Yes?" Shriver, still half-asleep, said through the door.

"Airport," the man said in a strange accent. *Ear-porrit.*

"Airport?"

"Ear-porrit, sir."

Then Shriver remembered: the conference. He considered sending the man away, telling him he had the wrong address—the wrong *man*—but then he recalled the story he'd written. "The Water Mark." He picked up the stack of paper and stared down at the dense blocks of words, some of them crossed out, with arrows and asterisks and question marks scrawled across the pages. He had written this. And it had been *fun*. Exhausting too, but in a good way. He hadn't felt so consumed by something since . . . he couldn't remember. Was this what it felt like to be a writer? he wondered. What if he . . . ?

"Sir?" the man said from the other side of the door.

"Be right there," Shriver said, and before he could change his mind he quickly threw on some clean clothes and rummaged through his closet for the suit jacket he hadn't worn in . . . how long? Then he stuffed a few things into an old suitcase, poured a mixing bowl full of dry cat food, and lifted up the toilet seat for Mr. B. to drink from the bowl.

"Don't fret, my little friend," he said, patting the cat on his furry head. Shriver couldn't remember ever leaving Mr. B. alone. He got onto his knees and squeezed the cat close. Mr. Bojangles purred. "I'll be back before you know it," Shriver told him as he poured an extra layer of litter into the cat box.

Lastly, he folded the pages of his story and slipped them into his jacket pocket.

When Shriver opened the apartment door, the airport driver, whose dark bushy beard did not at all match the color of his graying hair, grabbed the suitcase and made for the elevator.

Meanwhile, Shriver searched in his pocket for his keys. He could not find them in his pants, nor in his suit coat. He went back inside and stepped over the cat, who sat at the threshold, already awaiting Shriver's return. He rummaged around the apartment, looking under the piles of clothes on the bed, peering into crowded drawers and cupboards, eventually tossing everything onto the floor in a fruitless attempt to find his keys. He sat in a chair and tried to recall the last time he'd used them. He could not remember, but it couldn't have been *that* long ago.

"Sir?" the bearded man said again from the hallway.

"Yes, yes," Shriver said, giving up. He would just have to leave the door unlocked.

As they waited for the elevator, he could hear Mr. Bojangles mewing behind the closed—and unlocked—door. He covered his ears against the sad and pathetic sound until the elevator finally arrived.

When they reached the ground floor, Shriver did not recognize the building's main lobby. Had that mirrored wall been there the last time he went out? That sofa and matching chair near the entrance? The night doorman, still on duty at this early hour, looked at him and the bearded man with his battered old suitcase as though they were burglars leaving the scene of a crime. He must be new, Shriver thought, never having seen the doorman before.

"When did they put up those mirrors?" Shriver asked.

"Those?" the doorman said. "They've been there for as long as I have."

"Really?" Shriver wondered how he could have missed them. "Oh, will you please inform Vinnie"—the afternoon doorman—"he need not bring me my mail for the next few days?"

The doorman continued to scrutinize him closely. "Your name?"

"Why, I'm Mr. Shriver."

The doorman, dressed in a shabby maroon uniform one size too large, peered at him quizzically.

"Six F!" Shriver clarified.

He debated whether or not to inform the doorman that his apartment door had been left unlocked, but given the man's suspicious demeanor, he decided against it.

"Oh!" the doorman exclaimed. "Mr. *Shriver*. Of course."

The doorman gestured dramatically, like a master of ceremonies on a stage, toward the revolving door. Through the glass Shriver could see a rusty old town car parked at the curb. The bearded man carried the suitcase out the door.

Out on the sidewalk a fresh predawn breeze cooled Shriver's face. The street looked very different compared with his view from his sixth-floor apartment window. Billowy trees blotted out the slowly lightening sky, forming a pleasant green canopy over the cars parked up and down the block. At this early hour, the only sound was the rustle of leaves and the far-off hum of highway traffic. The bearded man grunted as he hoisted the suitcase into the town car's open trunk.

"Have a nice trip, sir," the doorman said, tipping his cap.

The bearded man slammed the trunk shut, then opened the rear door with a flourish. Shriver climbed into the backseat. The driver stood on the sidewalk for several minutes, talking with the doorman. Shriver strained to hear them through the closed car window. The two men laughed and shook their heads, giving Shriver the distinct impression they were talking about him. Then the driver climbed in behind the wheel, started the car, and pulled into the street. Moments later, they merged onto the heavily trafficked highway.

Shriver sat back and watched the city flash by, lit by the red-orange rays of the rising sun. He could not recall the last time he'd been in an automobile speeding down a highway like this. After a while, he noticed that the vehicle seemed to be moving independently of the steering wheel. The driver constantly turned the wheel left, then right, just to keep the car going in a straight line. Nevertheless, he was able to maneuver the decrepit vehicle like a getaway driver, weaving in and out of traffic with only inches to spare.

At the airport the driver refused to accept any money for the ride, not even a tip. "All taken care for," he said several times in his thick accent, bowing reverently, then he climbed back in behind the wheel and tore off, leaving Shriver amid a swirl of travelers with their huge piles of luggage and golf bags. Car horns blared; airplanes shrieked overhead. It was all a little overwhelming, but with the aid of a uniformed steward he managed to check his suitcase and receive his boarding passes. He then proceeded to the security checkpoint, where a guard asked him to remove his shoes before waving him through a metal detector. As Shriver walked through the machine a bell went off. He was ordered to go back, take off his belt, and place any keys or coins in a little plastic bowl.

"What's that?" The guard pointed at the bulge in his jacket.

"That's just some papers." Shriver pulled out the story he had written. The guard ordered him to place the manuscript in a plastic tub for X-raying.

"But it's just paper."

"I don't care if it's the Bible," the guard said, holding out the plastic bowl.

Shriver set his story down and watched as the guard pushed it through the machine. He then stepped through the metal detector. This time no bell rang. He stood off to the side and watched as two security agents peered at the ghostly image of his story on the little monitor. One of them pointed at the screen, and the other one laughed.

From there the first leg of his journey progressed fairly smoothly, except for some alarming turbulence during the ascent. Once the plane had reached its cruising altitude, Shriver downed two cocktails in quick succession and managed to relax and catch up on his sleep, resting so soundly that he did not wake up until the plane had landed and parked at the gate. Then, in order to make his connecting flight, he had to navigate the enormous Airport of America from Terminal B to Terminal F. En route, he passed fast-food restaurants, bars, clothing stores, bookshops, a pet store, ice cream stands, toy stores, and a massage parlor. He found it difficult moving among so many people. At one point he had to sit down and collect his breath. But he managed to find the correct gate on time and board the second, much smaller aircraft without incident.

When the flight attendant finally brought his cocktail, Shriver shut his eyes and took a long, slow sip. A warm wave rolled down his throat and into his belly. He sighed, licked his lips, then glanced at the pages again. The words were a train wreck.

He turned to the lady beside him, who was now awake and eating from a container of chocolate-covered nuts.

"Excuse me," he said, touching her pudgy elbow. "Ma'am?"

She turned and took in the empty miniature bottle of whiskey on his tray table. "Do you need to use the lavatory?" she asked, and commenced the elaborate preparatory motions necessary to remove herself from her seat.

"No, thank you," Shriver said. "I was just wondering if you could do me a favor."

She stared at him.

"I was wondering," Shriver continued, "if you can read this." He held out the pages.

She looked at them suspiciously. "You want me to read that?"

"No, I don't want you to read it. I just want you to tell me if you are *able* to read it. Is it legible?"

She tilted her head to see the top page more clearly.

"Is it comprehensible?" Shriver asked.

She squinted. "Well, the handwriting is pretty sloppy."

"But you can decipher it?"

Caught up in the assignment now, she set the tip of a finger on the top of the page, leaving a tiny smear of chocolate on the paper.

" 'The Water Mark.' "

"Yes, that's right," Shriver said.

" 'The water mark appeared on my ceiling . . . on the rainy day my wife walked out on me.' Is that right?"

"Thank you very much."

"Can't you read it?" she asked.

"Oh, I'm just having some trouble with my eyesight. Getting old, I guess. Thank you again."

"Say," the lady said, her eyes narrowing, "are you that writer? The one who's speaking at the conference?"

The day had gone so quickly that Shriver had not had time to worry about the moment he would have to take on the role he'd so impulsively decided to assume, but here it was.

"Yes!" the lady exclaimed, all smiles now, her cheeks breaking into dimpled slabs of dough. "I recognize you from your picture!"

"My picture?"

"It's in the brochure. Here."

She reached under the seat into a large, bulky shoulder bag of the kind woven by Guatemalan peasants and produced an envelope-sized brochure for the conference. On the cover were photos of the various featured authors.

"That's you!" the lady said, pointing to a murky black-and-white photograph. "Oh, this is very exciting!"

"May I see that?" Shriver reached for the brochure. In the photo a man sat on an armchair in front of thick, pale curtains. The chair looked vaguely familiar, Shriver thought, but the man barely resembled him. He was much younger, with a full head of dark hair and a taut jawline.

"Must be an old photograph," the woman said. "But I can tell it's you from the eyes."

Shriver peered closely at the subject's face. The eyes, it was true, communicated a certain sadness.

"It's the only picture I've ever seen of"—and here the woman made dramatic air quotes—"the *mysterious Shriver*.

"I come to the conference every year," she went on. "I'm also a writer. Oh, not like you, of course, not nearly so talented and interesting. I write romance novels, mostly, but I have this one project, a memoir, that I'm trying to publish."

Shriver opened the brochure to the brief biographies of all the featured writers. Under Shriver's name it said:

> One of America's most controversial authors, Shriver burst onto the literary scene twenty years ago with his best-selling novel *Goat Time*. Though he has yet to publish a follow-up novel, he remains one of our most revered chroniclers of the American absurd.

"I have a very interesting story to tell," the lady continued as she searched through the many items in her bag. "I was once involved in a sort of harem with this biker from Utah. I spent a couple years there, doing drugs and participating in sex orgies."

"Yes," Shriver said, still reading:

His long list of honors includes the Federal Book Award, the Outer East Coast Inner Critics Circle Award, the Publishers Prize, and numerous others.

"I have copies of the manuscript, if you'd like to take a look. Maybe you could help me find a publisher."

She thrust a two-inch-thick bound manuscript into Shriver's hands. On the cover, in large letters, was the title, *Harem Girl: My Life as a Sex Slave, A Memoir by Delta Malarkey-Jones*.

"Don't worry," Delta Malarkey-Jones said, "it's a quick read. I would say I hope you're not offended by graphic sex, but I figure you're probably not, so . . ."

She pulled from her bag a beat-up hardcover book. On the cover was a crude drawing of a satyr. "I think it's refreshing to read your work," she said. "Hardly anyone writes about real stuff like you do."

"Real stuff?"

"You know—the *raw* stuff."

"May I see that?"

"Maybe you could sign it!" she gushed as she handed the book over.

Goat Time.

This was his first glimpse of the book written by this apparently famous Shriver fellow. He had not patronized bookstores or libraries for many years because the smell of all that slowly rotting paper produced in him the urgent need to go to the bathroom. It was an instantaneous reaction, and very unpleasant.

He opened the book to the inside back cover, handling the pages gingerly, in case the sudden urge to defecate came upon him. There was no author photograph. The brief biographical note stated, simply, that the author lived on the East Coast.

Delta Malarkey-Jones produced a fine-point pen. "I would really appreciate it."

Shriver turned to the title page. He thought it very odd that he'd never heard of this famous author with whom he shared a name.

"You can just put 'To Delta,' plus whatever you feel like."

Shriver wiped his brow and wrote, *To Delta, she of row 9, seat B, on this day in May,* then he signed his name with a flourish.

"Thank you so much!" She held the book aloft. "One of these days I'm going to finish it too. Hey—I can't wait for your reading day after tomorrow!"

"That's very nice of you to say." Shriver had hoped that no one would show up to his reading. Now it turned out this Shriver fellow was quite famous and sought-after. A tiny moth of anxiety fluttered inside his chest. He closed the book and handed it back.

"You can hold on to my memoir," she told him. "I have a bunch. My address is on the front."

"Oh, thank you." Shriver squeezed the thick manuscript into the seat pocket in front of him. "I'll read it later, if you don't mind."

"Are you staying at the Hotel 19? Most of the writers stay there during the conference. I take the same room every year. I reserve it months ahead of time. Room twenty. In case you need to find me," she added, winking.

"Uh, I'm not sure where I'm staying."

She grinned. "I'd love to discuss those scenes with you."

"Which scenes?"

"You know—the sex scenes in your novel. They were very . . . imaginative."

"Oh," he said. "Thank you."

After a moment, during which his neighbor settled back

into her seat with a series of contented sighs, Shriver turned his attention back to his story. He glanced quickly at the first page, then looked away. For that split second the words appeared to be arranged normally. He breathed a little easier. He had to get this situation under control. There might be a lot of people at the reading, if this lady was any indication. He looked back at the first page, this time for several seconds before turning away. Again, the lines of script were legible—poorly handwritten, perhaps, but legible. There was the title, "The Water Mark," and, below that, the first line: "The water mark appeared on my ceiling on the rainy day my wife walked out on me."

Up to this point the flight had been quite smooth, but now, as the airplane skimmed just above the clouds, the fuselage began to shimmy and rattle like an old jalopy. To distract himself, Shriver turned once more to the pages in his hand. Immediately the words appeared to melt, as if the ink were wax over a flame, dripping down the page and onto his lap. He checked his watch. The numbers were as clear as the clouds outside his window. Less than forty-eight hours until his reading. As if it wasn't going to be difficult enough to convince all those people he was a writer!

While the plane bumped over air pockets, the flight attendant weaved down the aisle collecting empty bottles and cans.

"May I have another?" Shriver asked, holding out the empty mini-bottle of whiskey.

"I'm sorry, sir," the attendant said. "We're going to be landing soon."

The airplane then descended right into the clouds, the window went white, and the cabin started to slide from side to side. Shriver gripped the armrests and concentrated on the VACANT sign outside the forward lavatory.

Then, as it emerged beneath the clouds, the plane ceased its shuddering. The ground below lay as flat as a door on its side, from horizon to horizon, spotted with ponds that reflected clouds and patches of blue. Off in the distance Shriver could make out a small town, not much more than a cluster of low buildings and a water tower. The airplane tilted toward a large asphalt X in the middle of the prairie. Shriver's ears ached from the pressure. He rubbed the tender spots where his jawbone attached to his skull and swallowed deeply. His throat burned as a whiskey belch made its way up his esophagus. Before he knew what was happening, a freshly plowed field and then a strip of tarmac rose up to meet the wheels of the plane, and with a bump and slide, they were on the ground. A pleased Delta Malarkey-Jones immediately began to collect her many articles from beneath the seat in front of her, including her bag, a jacket, a floppy hat, and a paper sack full of snacks.

"Don't forget my manuscript!" she reminded him, pointing to the seat pocket.

"Oh, I won't." He placed the epic on his lap along with his own papers.

The plane rolled toward the terminal and lurched to a stop.

"I hope to see you around," Ms. Malarkey-Jones said as she leaped to her feet and started to remove items from overhead. "Remember: Hotel 19, room twenty."

The exit door swung open and the passengers shuffled up the aisle. Shriver rose unsteadily to his feet and entered the line. All the whiskey had settled in his legs. Wobbling a little, he gingerly disembarked onto a metal stairway that led down to the tarmac.

Looking up, he saw that the sky here was enormous, dwarfing everything beneath it. The clouds seemed thousands of miles wide, with vast swatches of blue in between. As for the land, it stretched flat and unbroken all the way to the horizon. Even the little airport was squat and low to the ground. He waved away a mosquito buzzing at his ears.

Shriver wondered who would be at the gate to meet him. For all he knew, Chuck Johnson would spring out from behind a potted plant and shout, *Surprise!* But he had the feeling his old friend was nowhere near this place. The letters from Professor Cleverly, the free airline tickets, that woman on the plane—it was too elaborate even for Chuck. These people really thought he was Shriver the Writer! As he walked across the tarmac toward the doors, he concentrated on the task of becoming someone else, and wished for the first time that his gastrointestinal system were at least able to endure the library long enough for him to have read this Shriver fellow's work.

What had he been thinking?

Passing through a glass door into the air-conditioned gate area, where a crowd awaited returning friends and loved ones, he cursed his decision to come here, to leave the safe confines of his apartment, to leave the unconditional love of Mr. Bojangles, the dedicated service of Vinnie the Doorman and Blotto, the delivery boy from the local grocery store. He could have been home right now watching the afternoon edition of the Channel 17 Action News and napping on the patch of sun that fell across his bed at this time every day. Instead, he was in this strange, aggressively horizontal land, pretending to be someone else entirely, someone who was a genius, apparently, and infinitely more intelligent than he, albeit it with a dirty mind.

How can I worm my way out of this insane situation? he wondered. Perhaps he could avoid the person dispatched to retrieve him and exchange his return ticket for the next flight home. He decided right then and there that this was what he would do—he would go home to Mr. Bojangles—and so he started toward the main lobby and ticket counter.

But his path was blocked by a petite young woman wearing a shiny yellow slicker.

She offered her hand. "Mr. Shriver, I presume."

She had long blond hair, nearly the same color as her coat, and thin lips painted ruby red. He thought she was about eighteen years old until he looked closer and saw the crow's-feet at the corners of her large brown eyes. She looked the way he imagined Tina LeGros would look in person, without the stiff hair and pancake makeup and power suit.

"I'm Simone Cleverly," she said.

"Yes," he replied, taking her hand in his own. "And I am Shriver."

Chapter Two

When the luggage finally arrived, Professor Cleverly insisted on carrying Shriver's suitcase, though it weighed nearly as much as she did.

"Really, I can carry it," Shriver told her, trying to grab the leather handle, but she pulled the bag away and started out of the terminal. For a small woman, Shriver thought, she was remarkably strong. While the other passengers at the luggage carousel stared at him with disapproving expressions, he followed her outside, where she lugged the suitcase across the small parking lot to a massive car, a three-ton contraption of black metal and man-made materials. She opened the rear door and, with a grunt, heaved the suitcase onto the seat.

"Climb aboard," she ordered.

Shriver pulled himself up into the passenger seat as if into a tank.

The professor turned the key and the engine growled to life. With some effort she shifted gears and aimed the monstrous vehicle toward the parking lot exit. She looked like a child in her yellow slicker, her tiny hands astride the colossal steering wheel. She had to scoot herself forward in order for her feet to reach the pedals. The car's hood was so enormous that if a grown man walked directly in front of the vehicle, he would not be seen.

"Normally we have graduate students pick up the featured

authors at the airport, but your handler is teaching at this hour, so I took the job myself." She watched the road as she spoke, not turning at all to address him.

"I feel honored, Professor."

"It's very inconvenient, actually. I have so much to do."

"I'm so sorry."

After a pause, she said, "To be honest, I was curious."

"Curious?"

"To meet the infamous Shriver."

"Oh? I didn't realize I was infamous."

She let out a sharp laugh. "Have you read your book lately?"

"I can't say that I have."

"I read it in graduate school," she told him, as if recounting the time she ate a spoiled piece of meat. "I *almost* got through the whole thing."

They passed a paddock populated by enormous, shaggy bison. A wooden sign, lettered in the style of an Old West ranch, proclaimed EAT BISON—LIVE WELL!

"But everyone's very excited that you're able to attend the conference," Professor Cleverly said, straining to sound positive. "This is quite a coup for us."

Shriver watched her profile as she drove: slightly crooked nose, strong jaw, skin tan and smooth but not pampered looking. Apparently, she spent a lot of time outdoors. The yellow slicker remained buttoned. She could have been naked underneath there for all Shriver knew. He blushed at the thought, and just then she turned to glance at him. He looked away toward a field of sunflowers stretching off into the distance.

"Ever been out this way?" she asked.

"Only to pass through. On a military train. All I can remember are the sunflowers."

Shriver was surprised that he remembered this. He hadn't thought about it in years. The train had been headed west, farther and farther away from home. He smiled, recalling the image, exactly like this one. "Millions of yellow-bonneted faces all turned to worship the sun," he said.

Professor Cleverly nodded, as if she'd expected him to say exactly that.

"The college is famous for its botany department," she said. "Did you know Native Americans used the oil for snake bites and wart removal?"

"I did not."

"Between the flowers, the seeds, and the oil, there are lots of uses for *Helianthus annuus.*"

Her voice sounded a little tight, he thought—the voice of someone trying to impress. He wondered what the real Shriver would say right now. Probably something erudite about agriculture, but he felt it was better at this point to keep his mouth shut. So far she had not suspected him of any fraudulence, and he didn't want to push his luck.

"We'll swing by the hotel first," she said, "so you can drop off your bag and freshen up a little. Then I'll take you over to the College Union, where you can see what we have planned for you."

She drove with great concentration, her knuckles white on the steering wheel. Perhaps she was simply nervous around such an "infamous" author. In any case, she did not seem to like him very much—or, actually, she did not seem to like the *real* Shriver. At the very least she disliked *Goat Time.*

He noticed that she didn't wear a wedding band. Instinctively, he covered his own with his right hand. For the first time he felt ashamed that he still wore the ring after all these years. He hadn't removed it partly because he simply couldn't pull the thing off his pudgy finger, and partly because he had never had any reason to. In fact, he'd forgotten he wore it at all; it had become invisible—until now. He vowed to take it off as soon as he was alone.

"There's quite a lot of interest in your reading," Professor Cleverly told him, working hard to keep the conversation afloat. "Everyone is wondering if you'll be sharing something new."

Shriver reached into his jacket pocket to pat the pages there. "Actually, I *am* hoping to read something new."

"That *is* exciting." Her words, on paper, would imply excitement, but her face appeared locked in what Shriver interpreted as a struggle between pleasure and distaste. "This could turn out to be a huge literary event."

Again, the moth of anxiety—or was it now a butterfly?—beat its wings against the fragile casing of his heart.

Fortunately, they were now pulling into the parking lot of the Hotel 19, a dull, square, three-story building teetering on the very edge of the town. Looking out a window from the front side, one would see a small college campus with tree-lined streets and old stone buildings; from the back one would see only prairie and sky.

"This place used to have just nineteen rooms," Simone explained. "Hence the name. Then, a few years ago, they added on."

She parked at the front entrance, then jumped down and ran around the car. By the time Shriver set his feet on the ground, she had hoisted his suitcase from the backseat.

"Why don't I come back in about an hour," she said as she carted the bag toward the building. "That will give you time to catch your breath."

"Please let me carry the bag," Shriver said.

The front doors opened automatically and the professor dragged the bag behind her across the carpeted floor. "The room is our treat, but you'll have to spring for anything extra. Room service, pay TV, that sort of thing."

The lobby was furnished with what appeared to be secondhand chairs and sofas, all mismatched and faded by the sunlight that streamed in through the floor-to-ceiling windows fronting the hotel. At the far end stood a tall reception counter behind which Shriver could make out the top of a towering, copper-tinted beehive hairdo. Only when he and Simone had reached the counter was he able to see the receptionist's lean, well-powdered face.

"May I help you?" she asked between smacks of gum-chewing. The name tag on her blouse read CHARLEVOIX.

"Good afternoon," Professor Cleverly said in an authoritative tone. "I believe there's a room reserved under the name 'Shriver.'"

"Shriver, Shriver, Shriver." The woman examined a ledger until she found the name. "Here we are."

Simone turned to Shriver. "Then I'll see you in about an hour."

"Thank you, Professor."

"Please—*Simone*. Nobody calls me 'Professor,' not even my students."

She walked swiftly across the lobby and out the door, and ascended into the behemoth. As he watched her drive off in a cloud of smoke, it finally sank in to Shriver that this was, in fact, not an elaborate practical joke. No, he was here pretending to be someone else, and that lovely woman believed him. So far, anyway.

Charlevoix had him sign the register, then slid a long, thin skeleton key across the counter.

"What's this?" he asked.

"That's your key."

"This is my key?"

She stopped chewing her gum. The effect was dramatic. "You've never seen a key before?"

Shriver hefted the heavy key in his palm. It resembled something that would unlock a crypt. "Of course I have."

Charlevoix resumed her chewing. "Room nineteen," she said in a dull monotone.

"Room nineteen?"

Again, the chewing ceased. "Is that a problem?"

He thought of Delta Malarkey-Jones in room twenty. "Are there any other rooms available?"

"That's all we got, sir. Between the writers' conference and the cheerleading competition, the place is filled up."

"Well . . ."

"You could try the Dew Drop Inn, but I betcha they're full up too. The whole town is full up."

He pocketed the key and felt his trousers dip a little bit with the weight.

"Room service is six a.m. to eight p.m.," Charlevoix explained, "and there's the Prairie Dog Saloon, open seven a.m. to midnight." She gestured toward the saloon's entrance at the far end of the lobby. Inside, a denim-clad man in a cowboy hat sat perched on a stool at the long, dimly lit bar.

Charlevoix then directed him to the elevator around a corner. When he reached the second floor, he followed the arrows pointing to "Rooms 15–30." Just beyond room nineteen, he saw that the dull beige carpet abruptly changed to a brighter, obviously newer beige carpet, and the wallpaper became more vibrant as well, as if they'd simply stitched the new wing onto the old.

Just as he was negotiating the key into the keyhole, Delta Malarkey-Jones emerged from room twenty.

"There you are!" she called out. Amazingly, she loomed even larger in the hallway than she had in the confines of the small airplane. She had changed into a loose-fitting dress with a paisley pattern, inside of which her breasts swung like coconuts as she rolled toward him.

"I'm headed over to the Union," she said. "Need a ride?"

"No, thank you."

"I rented a convertible!"

"Hm?" He could not get the key to turn.

"Need some help with that?" She grabbed the key from his hand and reinserted it into the hole. "You have to turn these old ones to the *left*." She grunted and turned the key. "Voilà!"

"Many thanks," Shriver said, pushing the door open. He dragged his suitcase inside while Delta leaned against the door frame and peered into the room.

"They should have given you one of the newer rooms," she said.

"I'm sure this will do."

"You should complain."

"I'll be fine, thank you." He badly wanted to be alone but felt it would be impolite to shut the door while she continued to stand there.

"A writer of your stature should have the best," she said.

"Really, it's fine."

"I'm going to complain for you."

"Please, don't bother."

"Oh, it's no bother. They know me here."

"I'm sure they do. Now—"

"You could have my room!"

"No. I couldn't."

"It's much nicer than this. Look at that old TV! Criminy!"

The television was, indeed, very old.

"I'll be fine here," he said.

"It's no big deal, Mr. Shriver."

"Really. I mean it. I'll be fine." He put some steel into his voice this time, and it seemed to land.

"Okay," she said, her smile gone. "Suit yourself."

"Thank you, though."

"Sure. Just let me know if you change your mind. I wouldn't be surprised if that old TV didn't even work."

"Yes, I'll be sure to let you know."

She lingered at the threshold for a few seconds, inspecting what else she could see of his room, then waddled away. Shriver shut the door.

He went to the window and opened the curtains to see the prairie unfurl itself, acre after acre of it. Two hundred yards away a single railroad track bisected the dull brown land. He stared hard at the ruler-straight line where land met sky to see if he could detect the earth's rotation. He had once seen on a public television program that the earth turns at one thousand miles per hour. At the time he'd pictured himself flat on the ground, holding on to the grass like a stuntman atop a speeding car so as not to hurtle off into space.

Feeling a bit dizzy, he removed his jacket and lay across the double bed. He shut his eyes against the vision of the meringue-like stucco ceiling slowly lowering itself toward him. He knew that, before this day was done, he would be unmasked as an imposter. Surely there would be someone at the conference—one of the other authors, or a publishing executive, or just a fan—who would have met the real Shriver at some point, who would immediately see that he was not him, who would expose him in front of everybody. It was only·

a matter of time. He pictured an angry Professor Cleverly, ordering him to go back home. He had just met the woman, and she didn't much care for him, but already he did not want to disappoint her.

He opened his eyes to see Mr. Bojangles resting on the bed, then realized it was just his suitcase, and that his beloved cat was nowhere near. He pictured Mr. B. going from room to room in the apartment, searching for him, mewing pathetically.

He sat up and inspected the room. The old television sat atop a walnut chest of drawers. In the corner was a built-in table for writing. Next to the bed stood a nightstand, with lamp and telephone. On the eggshell-colored walls hung two framed prints, one of a cow in a field, the other of a windmill. The bathroom was situated near the door, opposite a small closet. He went to the desk and found a stack of blank postcards. On the front of each was a faded photograph of the original hotel, only half its current size. Maybe I'll send Tina LeGros a postcard, he thought. He sat at the desk and took up a pen with "Hotel 19" written on its side. *Dear Ms. LeGros*, he wrote, *You'll never believe what I've gone and done.*

He paused and looked around the room. He noticed the yellow papers bulging from the pocket of his jacket on the bed. He pulled them out and moved into the light near the window. With trepidation he gazed down at the title. "The Water Mark." He giggled with relief. He read on: "The water mark appeared on my ceiling on the rainy day my wife walked out on me." From somewhere out on the prairie a train blew its whistle. "At first it was just a spot, approximately the size of a quarter, directly above the bed where I lay weeping," he read as the train wheels clackety-clacked in the distance. "Listening to the rain fall, I watched the water mark grow, ever so slowly, to the size of a baseball." A freight train appeared at the edge of the window, creeping slowly along the tracks. "After a few hours, the mark was as big as a honeydew melon." The floor of the hotel vibrated almost imperceptibly as the train continued to roll past. Shriver's mind wandered to that long-ago train ride, the millions of sunflowers staring at the sun. But then he realized that, in fact, he'd never been in the military. Perhaps it had been a passenger train. No, it must have been a dream he'd been recalling. "By the time it got dark outside," he read, "the water mark . . ."

The words started to dissolve. Shriver squinted, but it did no good. The page was underwater. He looked up and watched the train rolling by, an endless line of rusty freight cars. The sky appeared to be made of blue metal. All this— the train, the prairie, the sky—was crystal clear. He went to the desk and picked up the room service menu. "Chicken Fingers . . . Fried Mozzarella Sticks . . . Chili con Carne de Buffalo . . ." He looked up to see the painted cow staring at him with dull, brutish eyes from his field. He picked up the postcard: *Dear Ms. LeGros . . .* Clearly legible. Then he looked back at the pages of his story and saw nothing but a series of meaningless squiggles.

He sat on the edge of the bed and tried to breathe. Could he have had a stroke? What kind of brain malfunction would prevent him from reading only certain words he had written? He felt his skin go cold.

The telephone rang. Startled, he fell off the edge of the bed and banged his left buttock on the wooden frame before thumping onto the floor.

He clambered to his feet and reached for the phone.

"Hello?"

"I'm downstairs, whenever you're ready."

"Who's this?" he asked, rubbing his throbbing rump.

"It's *Simone.*"

"Already?"

"It's been an hour," she said.

He must have fallen asleep earlier, when he lay down on the bed.

"Are you okay?" she asked.

"I'm fine, thank you. You?"

He cringed at his own stupidity.

"Is the room all right?" Professor Cleverly asked.

"The room is very comfortable, yes. I'll be down in a moment."

"Take your time."

He hung up and limped into the bathroom. When he switched on the overhead light the bulb flickered a few times, then died out. In the meager daylight from the open bathroom doorway he managed to wash his face and comb his thinning hair. He felt stupid about it, but, still thinking of what lay beneath that yellow slicker, he wanted to look good for Professor Cleverly. In the bathroom mirror, he saw a stranger: graying, jowly, a paunch pushing out above his belt. How did that Malarkey-Jones woman connect him with the thick-haired, trim fellow in the brochure photograph?

He wondered if he should change his shirt. He sniffed under his arm and wrinkled his nose. But he had only brought one shirt for each day he was to spend here, so he decided to stick with this one. If only he had time to take a long, leisurely bath. Mr. Bojangles loved to sit on the edge of the tub and watch him as he lay in the luxurious bubbles. There they would carry on lengthy conversations about the miserable state of the world. He straightened his tie and went to retrieve his jacket. Now that he felt reasonably put-together, he picked up his key and left the room.

When the elevator arrived a gaggle of teenage girls de-
barked like clowns from a toy car, one after the other, for what
seemed like minutes, amid high-pitched squeals of laughter.
They all wore identical uniforms of sleeveless red tops and
short pleated skirts with matching sneakers. Shriver watched
their trim, athletic figures as they skipped down the hallway.
One of the girls, a willowy brunette with feathered hair and
muscular arms, turned and smiled at him just before she disappeared into a room. The elevator door nearly closed before
he remembered to board.

Downstairs, as Shriver hobbled past the front desk, the
cowboy-hatted man rushed from the saloon on severely
bowed legs.

"Hey, Shriver!" the man called. "Hold up there!"

Shriver could see Simone waiting just outside the hotel
doorway, a patch of bright yellow against parking-lot gray.
The massive black automobile idled nearby. And he had forgotten to remove his wedding band.

"Hey there," the cowboy said in a rumbling, smoke-
charred voice. He grabbed Shriver's hand and pumped it like
the handle of a farmhouse water pump. "I'm Tee What's-his-
name. I teach here at the university."

"Tee Wha?"

"It's spelled 'W-Ä-T-Z-C-Z-E-S-N-A-M,' but it's pronounced 'Whatsisname.' Some Ellis Island mix-up with the
official papers back in the day, I guess."

"Oh."

"It's a terrific icebreaker at parties."

"Well, it's very nice to meet you, Professor."

"Call me 'T.'—as in the letter. I'm a writer like yourself.
And I teach, of course. I'm moderating the panel you're on
tomorrow." The man's breath reeked of whiskey, which made

Shriver thirsty. "At some point," Wätzczesnam continued, "I'm gonna need to talk to you a little about that. There's a theme to the panel and I want to make sure I don't ask something stupid."

"A theme?"

"Yeah. They always have some kind of theme. This year it's 'reality-slash-illusion.' How's that for profound?"

Simone peered in through the glass doors and, seeing Shriver's predicament, came running inside. Shriver thrust his left hand into his pants pocket.

"There you are," she said. She turned to the cowboy and smiled wearily. "Hello, T."

"Hello, Simone," Wätzczesnam said, his voice turning softer. "I'm just grabbing a quick lunch." He pointed back toward the saloon. "Care to join me?"

Simone's eyes narrowed. "No thank you."

"Are you handling Shriver here yourself?" the cowboy asked.

"For the time being."

"Well, well," he said, sizing Shriver up. "'Fame is the scentless sunflower, with gaudy crown of gold.'"

"Are you done, T.?" Simone asked, rolling her eyes.

Wätzczesnam smiled impishly and turned to Shriver. "Remind me to give you a copy of one of my books, Shriver, before this whole shebang is over."

"I'm sure Mr. Shriver has better things to do than read about your adventures on the farm," Simone said. She took hold of Shriver's elbow and began to usher him toward the door. "Now, if you'll excuse us, you can get back to your 'lunch.'"

Looking a bit wounded, the cowboy waved and called out, "We'll talk later, Shriver!" to their retreating backs.

Outside, near the entrance, tied to a light pole, stood a horse. It was a bluish-white color, with dark spots. A battered saddle rested atop its swayed back.

"That decrepit old thing belongs to Professor Wätzczesnam," Simone explained.

The horse looked over at them with sad eyes, as if it recognized her voice.

"T.'s not allowed to drive a car anymore, for obvious reasons," she added as she climbed into her massive vehicle.

With his bruised buttock, Shriver had a difficult time hoisting himself up into the passenger seat. Fortunately, Simone did not seem to notice.

"T. sometimes thinks he's running the show here," she said.

"From the Prairie Dog Saloon?"

"Exactly," she snorted. "That's sort of his unofficial office."

Shriver was himself dying for a drink but was even more hungry. As he tugged unsuccessfully at his ring, he realized he hadn't eaten all day. There had been no time this morning for his usual bowl of oatmeal, and he'd declined the airline peanuts due to anxiety. By this hour he'd have had his lunch, typically a heated-up can of soup. Every week, Blotto, the delivery boy, delivered multiple cans of soup, along with Shriver's other groceries. Shaped like a Bartlett pear, Blotto had narrow, sloping shoulders and wide hips, and a round face that always beamed with blissful ignorance no matter the situation. His smile reminded Shriver of a cartoon graveyard with tombstones poking out at odd angles. Rain, snow, broken elevators—nothing stopped Blotto from his appointed rounds. Into the apartment he would spill, sending Mr. Bojangles scurrying for safety from the deliveryman's large, flat feet. Thinking of his friend's odd face put Shriver in mind of a bowl of cream of mushroom soup.

"Simone, is there anyplace where I might get a bowl of soup?"

"Of course. You must be famished. There's a cafeteria in the Union basement."

"That would be fine."

"Or I could drive you to one of our nice local restaurants. Believe it or not, there are a few in town."

"I believe you, but the cafeteria will do."

"We're scheduled to have dinner with some of the other writers tonight at Slander's, which is probably the best place around."

"That sounds delightful."

"Some of our visiting dignitaries assume it's just buffalo burgers and sauerkraut around here, but we're not all yahoos, you know."

"It never helps to assume, I always say."

"I mean, it's not the Big City," she added with a sniff, "but we do have some taste."

"I don't doubt it."

From the hotel they drove into the campus area, with its odd mix of dreary modern dormitories and older, stone-constructed classroom buildings. Students walked the streets and pathways, textbooks clutched under their arms, looking insanely youthful and vibrant.

"These are the spring/summer students," Simone said. "Quite a lot take classes year-round. It's a nice break from our harsh winters."

As Shriver continued to wrestle unsuccessfully with his wedding band, forcing it around and around his finger, a mosquito settled onto his right hand. Without thinking, he squashed it, then flicked the corpse out the open window. As he did so, his gold band flashed in the sun.

"Mosquitoes are kind of an issue here," Simone said. "There's probably going to be a lot of them after the heavy rain we had this morning, and now this sun."

So that explained the yellow slicker. The rain must have been part of the same weather system that had caused the flight turbulence. A low-pressure front out of the west, as meteorologist Lance Boyle of Channel 17's Action News Team would call it.

Another mosquito landed on the back of Shriver's right hand. Keeping his left hand—and wedding band—out of sight, he watched the insect navigate the dark hairs on his knuckles, then insert its proboscis into a vein.

"I hope you know your wife could have come along."

"Excuse me?" Shriver jammed his left hand beneath his leg, as if burying his wedding band there would somehow counteract the question. Meanwhile, the mosquito on his right hand finished with its grisly meal and flew out the car window.

"I mean, we couldn't spring for the airfare, but she certainly could have stayed with you at the hotel."

"My wife?"

On the back of his right hand rose a small pink welt, where the mosquito had left its toxic saliva.

"Oh, I'm sorry." She covered her mouth. "I just thought . . ."

"The wedding ring?"

"I couldn't help but notice."

He removed his hand and waved it about. "It's just that I haven't been able to take it off."

She nodded. "Oh, I can appreciate that. I left mine on for a whole year after my divorce."

"Really?"

"Yes. I wasn't ready to be not married, I guess."

"No, that's not it," Shriver said. "I really can't take it off." He made a show of trying to yank the ring off his finger. "See?"

Simone laughed, her crow's feet dancing. "How long has it been?"

"Twenty years."

Shriver had always wondered what a guffaw sounded like, and now he knew as Simone nearly rear-ended the pickup truck ahead of them.

"I'm sorry," she said. "It's not really funny."

"No. It *is*."

"But it *isn't*. And it's none of my business."

"I don't mind."

"Divorce can be very traumatic," she said. "At least for me it was."

You too? Shriver was about to say, but Simone jerked the vehicle into a parking lot and, clearly relieved to change the subject, announced, "Here we are." She pointed to a three-story building made of gray stone. "The College Union. This is where all the readings and panels are held." She switched off the engine and glanced into the rearview mirror. "Ready, Edsel?"

Shriver turned to see a young man sitting in the backseat.

"Hello," the young man said.

"Goodness. I didn't see you there."

"This is Edsel Nixon," Simone said. "He's a grad student here, and your official 'handler.' "

"I know what you're thinking, Mr. Shriver," Edsel Nixon said. He was a handsome young fellow in his late twenties, with a lilting Southern accent and searching, sincere eyes. "You're thinking, 'This is the most unfortunately named individual I've ever encountered.' I guess you could say my parents have a queer sense of humor."

"Perhaps it's good luck to have such a name," Shriver said.

"That's a very positive outlook, sir, and I appreciate it."

"Edsel is in our MFA program and teaches a seminar on modern American lit," Simone said.

"We're in the middle of *Goat Time*," the graduate student said. "The kids find it very . . . interesting."

Simone grabbed a shoulder bag and climbed down from the car. Shriver limped after her into the building, where he followed her down a set of stairs to the basement level. Like a child unable to resist touching a sore, he kept rubbing his left buttock, hoping the ache would disappear.

"So, Mr. Nixon," Shriver said, trying his best to be sociable, "what sort of writing do you do?"

No answer. Somehow, en route, his handler had disappeared.

"Where did he go?" Shriver asked, glancing around.

"Edsel? Don't worry, he'll be back. He's a poet. Very mercurial."

Shriver followed her into a large student lounge furnished with pastel-colored chairs and low tables. Those students who had been sitting around chatting or reading—there were about twenty of them—suddenly turned, in unison, to stare. He nodded, and they all returned, again in unison, to what they'd been doing.

"Over here is the cafeteria," Simone said, directing him to the left. They entered through a turnstile into an ordering area, with different stations for sandwiches, pizza, soup, etc. While Simone poured herself a cup of tea, Shriver approached the pimple-faced student behind the counter.

"What soups do you have?"

The student swallowed, as if he'd been asked something personal. "Pea," he said in a trembly voice, "vegetable barley, plain old vegetable, cream of mushroom, chicken noo—"

"I'll take the cream of mushroom."

"Sorry, we're out of cream of mushroom."

"Oh. I thought you said 'cream of mushroom.'"

"Sorry, sir."

"Vegetable barley, then."

"Yeah, we're out of vegetable barley also."

"But I could swear you said you had vegetable barley."

"Sorry, sir."

Shriver sighed. "What *do* you have?"

Again, the student swallowed and chanted, "Pea, vegetable barley, plain old vegetable—"

"But you said you *don't* have vegetable barley."

Simone appeared at Shriver's side. "Hi, Charles," she said to the student.

"Hi, Professor Simone Cleverly."

"He has to go through the whole list," she explained to Shriver. "It's just the way Charles works."

"I see." Shriver turned to the student. "Do you have pea?"

"We're all out of pea."

"How about vegetable?"

"Yes, we have plain old vegetable."

"Are you sure?"

The young man looked hurt. "Of course I'm sure."

"I'll take plain old vegetable, then."

At the checkout counter Simone removed a manila envelope from her shoulder bag.

"Here," she said, handing it over. It was unexpectedly heavy, the bottom half bulging as if filled with pebbles. "Your per diem."

Shriver looked inside the envelope to see a mass of nickels, dimes, and quarters.

"It's thirty-one dollars and fifty-eight cents per day," she explained. "I don't know how they arrived at that figure, but anyway, it's all there. Three days' worth."

Shriver used the money to pay for his lunch, piling up the change for the seemingly unfazed Charles, who made sure to count every coin. From there they made their way to a booth in the corner.

While Shriver spooned up his soup, Simone set her over-packed shoulder bag on the table. She cursed softly and removed several small items, one at a time. Keys, lipstick, crumpled receipts, tissues, more keys, a small can of Mace. Finally, she managed to free a sheaf of papers.

"This is the schedule for the conference. It's for you to keep, so you know what's happening. This afternoon there's a reading by Gonquin Smithee, the poet. Tonight there's a reading by Basil Rather, the playwright. Are you familiar with their work?"

Shriver shook his head no. The soup was hot and salty, just how he liked it.

"They're extremely talented, and sort of controversial."

" 'Literature as Confrontation,' " Shriver said.

"Exactly. The readings should be interesting, anyway. A couple of the drama students are performing a scene from one of Rather's plays tonight. Then there's a Q-and-A."

"Am I to do a Q-and-A also?"

"Of course. We find that the audience is very interested. We typically get about seven hundred people."

A mouthful of soup erupted through Shriver's nose.

"Are you okay?"

He nodded, wiping his face. "That's a lot of people."

"Wait till *you* read," she said. "We expect standing room only."

The former moth in his chest, which had since grown into a butterfly, now inflated to about the size of a fruit bat.

Simone proceeded to remove her yellow slicker. She was not naked underneath. She wore a simple white blouse, with the top two buttons undone, revealing a splash of freckles across her collarbone area.

Shriver forced his eyes away, toward the schedule. Tomorrow at noon was the discussion panel, with the theme "Reality/Illusion," moderated by T. Wätzczesnam, featuring Basil Rather and Gonquin Smithee, as well as Shriver. In the afternoon someone named Zebra Amphetamine was to read. Shriver was also scheduled to meet with some creative writing students in the morning. Various receptions, book signings, and dinners were scheduled between events.

The soup roiled inside his stomach.

Still, he forced himself to continue eating. So far, Simone appeared to believe he was the real Shriver, but he would have to come up with some conversational topics—ideally, about himself—if he was to convince these people he was an actual writer.

Among the papers Simone had removed from her bag was a copy of the conference brochure.

"Can I ask where you got that photograph?" Shriver asked, then immediately regretted the question. What if she examined the photo more closely and found that its subject barely resembled the man in front of her?

"Sorry, but I'm unable to reveal my sources," she said with a cocky grin, clearly proud that she'd managed to uncover a candid shot of the elusive Shriver.

Shriver stared at the photo. Upside down, the man looked

even less like him, though those curtains in the background *were* familiar.

"If you're finished with your soup," Simone said as she returned the brochure and other items to her bag, "I can show you around upstairs."

/

She climbed the stairs gracefully, with the slicker draped over one arm, a slight but perceptible wiggle to her walk, her legs smooth and tan beneath a tight orange knee-length skirt. Shriver followed lopsidedly, feeling the pull of the envelope full of coins in his right coat pocket.

In the upstairs lobby, he stiffened at the sight of a long folding table covered with books for sale. People milled about, browsing and chatting. Several called out hello to Simone as she led him toward the table, where she introduced him to the various conference workers. They all appeared excited to meet him, smiling warmly, shaking his hand. So far the books seemed to be having no effect on his colon.

"And this is Ora Lee Sanford," Simone said, nodding toward a stout, spiky-haired woman behind the long table. "She's in charge of selling your books."

Ora Lee shook his hand rigorously. "Your book is selling like hotcakes, you'll be happy to know."

Shriver glanced down at the books laid out on the table: collections of plays by Basil Rather, books of poetry by Gonquin Smithee, and several volumes of stories by Zebra Amphetamine. At the end of the table sat a fanned pile of unsold books by T. Wätzczesnam, all with photographs of horses on the covers. But the tallest stack of books consisted of the paperback edition of *Goat Time*, with the same satyr on the cover that had graced the hardback copy he'd signed for Delta

Malarkey-Jones. Feeling bold, he picked one up. On the back, voluminous blurbs praised the novel for its "bacchanalian fervor." He opened the book to a random page. At first the words made sense—something about a blind woman on a subway train—but then the letters blurred.

Shriver felt his face go cold. His bowels gurgled. As the two women chatted ("Have you noticed the mosquitoes?" "I think they're going to be bad this week"), he set down the copy of *Goat Time* and discreetly excused himself, gesturing toward a nearby restroom. He somehow managed to reach the door without running, but once inside he scrambled into a stall and frantically lowered his trousers. He slammed himself down on the seat, yelping at the pain of his newly bruised rear end.

He would have to steer clear of the book table from now on, he decided.

When he emerged from the restroom several uncomfortable moments later, his face damp with sweat, the women watched him closely.

"Are you okay?" Simone asked.

He paused several feet shy of the table.

"Airline food," he said. "But I'm fine now."

"Simone says you're going to read something new?" Ora Lee said.

He hovered at this apparently safe distance, feeling the gradual return of blood to his face. "I'm hoping to."

"Gosh, that's exciting. This is going to be something else!"

"Don't make him nervous, Ora Lee," Simone said. "Here, let me show you the main room, where all the action takes place."

Feeling grateful, Shriver followed her past the table and into a vast ballroom. Hundreds of black folding chairs faced a long raised stage against the far wall. On the stage sat a table draped with crimson fabric atop a dais. At one end stood a pale wooden podium.

"This is where it all happens," Simone said. "But don't worry. We can bring in extra chairs if we have to."

The fruit bat caged inside his ribs had now transformed into a squawking, fluttering crow.

Chapter Three

At the afternoon reading by Gonquin Smithee, seated among the students toward the rear of the filled ballroom, Shriver found himself leaning to the right to take some weight off his smarting behind—easy to do, with all the change weighing down his right coat pocket. This position also afforded him a better view of Simone, who sat in the front row, her long yellow hair casually pulled over to one side and bunched at her shoulder, her head cocked as she took in Ms. Smithee's words.

The poet wore a man's tailored suit, complete with necktie, her chiseled face framed by graying hair cut short and choppy. She read her work aggressively, each line a stone hurled at the audience.

"'Your eyes like an ice-cold speculum,'" she read from the podium, "'pushing deep into the tender pink folds of my soul.'"

Earlier, just before his intestinal difficulties, while he was browsing through the books on the lobby table, Shriver had noticed the enthusiastic critical endorsements printed on Ms. Smithee's book jacket. "A painfully honest exploration of survival." "Gonquin Smithee plumbs the depths of emotional truth as she attempts to exorcise the demons that have possessed her." "These are gut-wrenching poems that do not flinch from the hard truths." Glancing through the pages, he'd noticed a number of poems concerned with rape and/

or blood. The author's bio, accompanied by a rather severe black-and-white photograph, broadcast the information that she had been sexually abused by her father.

" 'Your hand as big as a vulture's wing on my buttery skin,' " Ms. Smithee intoned. " 'Fingers long and hairy between the knuckles / their tips rough as a cat's tongue.' "

Simone, Shriver could see, took all this in like it was the Gettysburg Address. He wondered if she would do the same with his story—if he ever got to read it. Then she glanced over and caught him watching her. Surprised, he did not even bother to turn away. She looked at him for a moment with an impenetrable expression, then returned her attention to Gonquin Smithee.

"She's very intense," someone whispered into Shriver's ear. He turned to see Edsel Nixon beside him. Shriver had not even noticed the grad student sitting there. He'd been too busy watching Simone.

"Who?" Shriver asked.

"Why, Gonquin Smithee, of course. Who else?"

As Shriver attempted to digest the poetry—" 'Your cock,' " Ms. Smithee chanted, " 'tastes salty and smells of yeast / and baby powder' "—he was suddenly overwhelmed by the abrupt realization that he was in this strange room in a strange town full of strangers. Why on earth was he here? What business did he have consorting with poets who wrote openly about their fathers' genitals? His heart pounded. Icy sweat erupted on his forehead. He wondered how long it would take him to get back home—to get to the airport, to fly halfway across the country, to take a cab to his building—if he walked out of here right now. He was sure he would die if his heart did not slow down.

He shut his eyes and thought of Mr. Bojangles, who was

always able to comfort him at anxious times such as these. The cat would somehow sense his distress and leap daintily onto his lap. Shriver would then stroke Mr. B.'s silky head and ears, feeling the vibrations building up deep inside the animal. He had seen a program on public television about cats in which experts admitted bafflement about the origin of purring—how the noise is manufactured, and even where. Apparently, it remained a pleasant mystery.

"Are you okay?" Edsel Nixon whispered.

Shriver realized that he'd been miming the act of stroking a cat.

"Fine," he said, shifting in his seat.

He made an effort to pay more attention to the poet's words, in case he would have to speak with her later on, at dinner. He wanted to be able to say something intelligent and, hopefully, complimentary, and needed a concrete example of her work to talk about.

Ms. Smithee was now reading from her epic poem *Menstrual Show*: " 'You have finally killed me, I thought / when you pulled out your blood-drenched sword / but then disgust spread across your face like a shadow / and I knew it was I who had somehow done wrong.' "

Shriver wondered if perhaps he should compliment her vivid imagery but worried that this was not original enough for a writer as sophisticated as the real Shriver seemed to be. He rehearsed to himself various comments—"I particularly enjoyed your comparison of semen to wood glue," or "How did you come up with so many striking rape metaphors?"—as Gonquin Smithee brought her performance to a well-received climax.

" 'Remember this,' " she read. " 'Though I cannot murder you / though I will not yank the ragged fingernails from your hands / though I dare not take a razor to your dangling scrotum / my words will tear you limb from limb / and I / and thousands of readers / will applaud that some sort of justice has been served.'"

After a lengthy amount of justice-serving applause, during which Ms. Smithee stood tall and defiant at the podium, the poet asked if there were any questions. No one raised a hand. Shriver watched as Simone scanned the apparently stunned crowd. Seven hundred people, and no brave volunteers.

Simone stood and said, as loudly as she could manage, "Okay, I'll get the ball rolling."

How courageous she is, Shriver thought.

"Is it difficult," she asked, "to be so open about your personal story in these poems?"

Gonquin Smithee mulled over the question as if it had never been asked before. Then she leaned toward the microphone and said, "Yes."

There was a pause as the audience awaited further elucidation. None came. Shriver heard a few titters as people realized this. Simone, he could see, was worried. She now stood off to the side of the room, watching for any raised hands. Ms. Smithee, meanwhile, remained proudly at the podium, awaiting the next question.

"Come on," she said. "I won't bite you."

Several people coughed. Shriver felt sorry for Simone, who now seemed embarrassed. No doubt she had played up the audience-participation angle to the author. She wiped at the sheen of sweat on her brow.

Impulsively, Shriver raised his hand.

"Mr. Shriver," Gonquin Smithee said with an exaggerated nod.

How does she know who I am? Shriver wondered as murmurs spread through the crowd. He could hear his name being whispered all around him. He stood. Simone, obviously relieved and grateful, smiled encouragingly.

"What is the question?" Ms. Smithee asked. He thought he detected a hostile tone to her voice.

Shriver licked his dry lips and tried to think. He looked down at Edsel Nixon, who watched him with great anticipation. Out of the corner of his eye he caught the intense gaze of Delta Malarkey-Jones, who sat as if frozen in the act of taking a sip from a large soda. He said the only thing that came into his mind.

"Have you ever written a poem from the point of view of your father?"

During the long moment that followed, a truck could be heard backing up—*beep, beep, beep*—somewhere outside the building. Why he'd asked such a question was a mystery to Shriver. He knew nothing of literature, never mind poetry.

The poet looked down at him with an amused expression. "And why would I do that?"

Still standing, Shriver felt 1,398 eyes turn toward him. He cleared his throat. "I just thought it might be interesting."

The audience buzzed.

"Any other questions?" Ms. Smithee asked, looking around the room.

Shriver glanced over at Simone, who did not meet his gaze. A woman in the rear called out that she too had been abused by a family member, and she'd written six hundred poems about it. Ms. Smithee responded warmly to this information.

When the Q-and-A had ended, Shriver followed Edsel Nixon into the lobby, where hundreds of people now loitered. A few smiled at him; others looked away, embarrassed. One young man, tall and dressed in dark clothes, seemed about to approach him, then turned and hurried away, as if he'd been caught doing something illicit.

"Shriver!"

From across the lobby, a man's voice.

"Shriver, you old devil!"

A middle-aged man in a cheap suit squeezed his way through the crowd. Rather portly, he wore thick glasses and a gray mustache that contrasted sharply with his brown toupee.

"You haven't changed a bit, you mischievous old SOB," the man said, offering his hand. "Jack Blunt. Remember?"

Fate tapped a paradiddle on Shriver's heart. He tried to brace himself, but it was no use. This man knew the real Shriver. Here was the moment he was to be exposed.

"I interviewed you years ago," Jack Blunt said. "Your book had just been published. We went out and tied one on." He laughed. "Jesus, I think I'm *still* hungover."

He doesn't remember, Shriver thought. Relieved, he said, "Of course. Blunt. That was a long, long time ago. I hardly recognize you."

"You look the same," Blunt said, sizing Shriver up through cola-bottle glasses.

"I do?"

"Of course not," the reporter said with a laugh. "None of us do. Listen, how about an interview?"

"Oh, I don't know."

"This is a big occasion. Your first appearance in, what, twenty years? I flew all the way out here for this."

"I'm not really doing interviews, Mr. Blunt."

"And it's only appropriate you talk to *me*," the reporter said, "since I was the one who got to you first all those years ago, when you were a nobody. That article was a big deal for you, Shriver. This will make for a delicious bookend. Plus, I really need the break."

"But I don't have anything to say."

"Look, let's go to this little hole-in-the-wall around the corner, I'll buy you a drink or two, and we can just shoot the shit. Off the record. Then you can decide. How about it?"

He felt he was stepping deeper into a quagmire, but a drink sounded very good to Shriver, especially after that reading.

"I think there's a dinner thing planned," Edsel Nixon said. "With Gonquin and a few of the others."

"I'll have him back in time," Blunt promised.

"Will Professor Cleverly be there?" Shriver asked Nixon.

"Yes, I think so."

Shriver turned to the reporter. "I really must be back by—"

"Six," Nixon said. "At Slander's Restaurant."

"No problemo," Blunt said. "I'll have him there by then."

Nixon appeared troubled. "Mr. Shriver— Professor Cleverly will kill me if you get lost or anything."

"Time's a-wastin'," Blunt said, miming the tipping of a bottle to his lips.

"Don't worry, Mr. Nixon," Shriver told his handler. "Tell Simone—er, Professor Cleverly—that I'll be there at six." Poor Nixon looked stricken as Blunt led Shriver down the stairs and out the front doors.

"Goddamn, it's good to see you, old man," the reporter said as they crossed the street. "To be honest, I thought you were dead."

"Dead?"

"Where else would you be for twenty years? But the minute I heard you were appearing here, I made my plans."

Shriver had to skip to keep up as the fast-walking Blunt

rounded a corner. The change in his jacket pocket jingled with each step, and mosquitoes buzzed noisily around his head.

"And that question of yours," Blunt said. "Goddamn brilliant! How I despise the self-serving victim crap that dyke ladles out."

They came to a one-story cinder-block building, painted brown. On the metal door adhesive letters spelled out THe BLOoDY DuCk. Inside, thick, gray cigarette smoke fogged the room, though there was only the bartender and a waitress in the place, neither of them smoking.

Blunt led Shriver to a booth and called to the waitress for two double whiskeys. Shriver winced as he sat on the cushionless bench. Initials and names and slogans adorned the wood of the booth. Directly over Blunt's left shoulder someone had carved NOW THAT I'M ENLIGHTENED, I'M JUST AS MISERABLE AS EVER.

The waitress brought their drinks. She had skin the color and consistency of alabaster, and green-apple eyes. She set the drinks down and walked away with the sultry air of a woman in a black-and-white movie set in a tropical bar frequented by mercenaries.

"Look at the keister on her," Blunt remarked. "Cheers." He held up his tumbler and the two men toasted.

Shriver relished the heat that cascaded down his throat.

"What I want to know," Blunt said, "is what the hell you've been up to these past twenty or so years, besides living large off your royalty checks."

Shriver thought back over the past two decades. They were as hazy as the bar.

"This and that," he said.

"Have you been writing?"

Shriver patted the yellow pages in his jacket pocket.

"A little."

"A novel? Stories? What?"

"Not sure."

Blunt slapped his now-empty tumbler down on the table. "You're playing games with me, Shriver." He signaled to the waitress for another round. Shriver hurried to catch up with him, draining his glass and setting it down beside its companion.

"No games," he said.

"All right. So tell me why you've been out of the spotlight for so long. Is it the ol' sophomore slump?"

"I guess so."

"Writer's block?"

"Sort of."

"I mean, the first book goes nuclear, millions sold, a buttload of awards—who could follow *that* up?"

"Not *me*."

The waitress delivered two more glasses of whiskey. Shriver drained his in one gulp. He felt like a man in an airtight wetsuit slowly submerging into an icy lake.

"Still able to put it away, I see."

"What is it you want from me, Mr. Blunt?"

"Just *talk* to me. Tell me where you've been, what you've been doing."

"Why would I do *that*?"

"Oh, come on, Shriver. You *need* me now, just like you needed me then. You may be a star at this little dog and pony show, but out there"—he waved toward the wall and beyond, toward the rest of the world—"nobody remembers you. I had to explain who you were to my editor. The ignorant twit."

"Then why bother to talk to me at all?"

"Because as ridiculous and self-serving as these little events are, it is a big deal that you're coming out of the woodwork, and it's a great opportunity for me."

"You want a scoop."

"Hell yes! And I can help *you* while I'm at it."

"Help me how?"

"By getting your name out there! And your face too."

From his coat pocket Blunt produced a small camera, the kind a spy might use.

"No!" Shriver cried, covering his face. "Absolutely not!"

"Just one shot. No one remembers what you look like."

"Good!"

"They didn't even put your photo in your goddamn book."

"Honest to God, Blunt, if you take a picture of me I will not speak to you at all."

"Oh, all right." The reporter slid the tiny camera back into his pocket. "Still cranky. That hasn't changed."

As Shriver scratched at the mosquito bite on his hand, the waitress emerged from a wall of smoke with two more drinks.

"On me," she said. "I'm a big fan." Then she turned and wiggled away.

"Yum yum," Blunt said. "Play your cards right, Shriver, and . . ." His eyebrows flapped suggestively.

Shriver ignored him.

"I'm onto you, old boy," Blunt said, eyeballing him over the rim of his tumbler.

Shriver's adrenal gland pumped madly away. "What do you mean?"

"You're up to something."

"Such as?"

"It's some sort of stunt. I don't have it all worked out yet, but . . ."

Shriver's lips began to quiver a little.

"What I can't understand," Blunt said, "is why you would agree to attend this puny little conference."

"It's simple. They asked me."

"Is that all it took?"

Shriver nodded.

"So you've been hiding away for two decades because no one asked you out?"

Shriver finished his drink and peered through the foglike smoke at the clock on the wall.

"Sorry, Mr. Blunt, but I really must go. I am expected for dinner."

"You haven't changed much, Shriver."

"You don't know how pleased I am to hear you say that. Thanks for the drinks."

"Anytime. How about tomorrow? An on-the-record chat over lunch?"

"I don't think so. Have a nice trip back home."

"Oh, I'm not going anywhere. I'll see you around town, old boy."

Shriver squeezed himself out of the booth. "Bye!" the waitress called out with a wave. "Come again!"

Shriver walked stiffly from the tavern, trailing a wispy tail of cigarette smoke.

Chapter Four

Shriver stood outside Slander's Restaurant, peering in through the large plate-glass window. Located on Main Street between the Church of Pornocology and the Dusty Rose Rodeo Museum, the place looked elegant in an old-fashioned way, with dark wood tables and chairs, and sepia-toned historical photographs hanging on the wide-plank walls.

Mosquitoes buzzed madly around Shriver's ears. They were growing in number now that the sun had started to set. The clock near the entrance read six thirty.

"There you are!"

Shriver turned to see Edsel Nixon standing beside him.

"You have an unnerving habit of materializing out of nowhere," Shriver shouted over the pounding of his heart.

"Sorry, sir. I'll try to be more noisy from now on. It's just that Professor Cleverly is worried about you."

"I got a little lost."

It was true. Along the way Shriver had been forced to ask several people for directions, with mixed results. Fortunately, he'd stumbled upon a liquor store, Big Chief's Liquorarium, where the proprietor, a squat fellow of Native American descent, silently drew a detailed map on a brown paper bag. To thank him, Shriver used part of his per diem to purchase a pint of whiskey, which he now kept inside his jacket pocket.

Nixon led him through the restaurant to a back room

where the conference people sat at a long table—seven in all, plus Shriver. Simone sat in the far corner. Unfortunately, the seats on either side of her were spoken for.

"Shriver!" A hatless T. Wätzczesnam sat at the far end of the table, to Simone's left. He was bald, Shriver now saw, with a graying comb-over made sweaty from all those hours of dank confinement. "Where ya been, buddy?"

Shriver waved hello and sat at the near end of the table, to the left of Edsel Nixon. "Ouch," he hissed as his sore rump collided with the seat.

"We thought you got lost," Wätzczesnam said.

"Mr. Shriver was talking to the press," Simone explained to the group.

"Ah," the cowboy said with a chuckle, "fraternizing with the enemy, eh?"

The waiter—young, tall, with dark hair and deep-set eyes—arrived with a menu.

"I'll have a double whiskey," Shriver told him.

Simone took it upon herself to make introductions.

"This is Basil Rather," she said, indicating the gentleman to Edsel Nixon's right. The playwright sat ramrod straight in his seat, his face narrow and jagged, a thin, ink-black beard lining his jaw. He wore a maroon turtleneck beneath a houndstooth jacket.

"How do you do?" he said in a theatrical voice.

"And to his right," Simone continued, "is Mr. Rather's assistant, uh . . ."

"Lena," the young woman said. "Lena Brazir." A busty redhead, she was perhaps twenty years old, less than half the age of the playwright.

"You know T., of course," Simone said. The cowboy raised his tumbler in salute.

"I don't know if you've *officially* met Gonquin Smithee." Simone indicated the poet to her right, who nodded minimally. Up close her face appeared softer, unlined, with full, sensuous lips. "And her friend Ms. Labio," Simone added, gesturing toward the woman to Gonquin Smithee's right, directly across from Shriver. She closely resembled the poet, with erratically trimmed hair above a smooth, shapely face, except instead of a man's tailored suit, she wore a rather frumpy dress with a squared-off neckline.

"That was an interesting question you asked, Mr. Shriver," Gonquin Smithee said just before taking a sip of white wine.

" 'There are no other questions than these,' " Wätzczesnam intoned from the far end of the table. " 'Half squashed in mud, emerging out of the moment / We all—' "

"*Thank* you, T.," Simone said.

"Nixon?" Wätzczesnam shouted.

"Ashbery, sir," the graduate student answered.

"Very good."

"I've read your novel," Gonquin Smithee continued, aiming her green, laserlike eyes at Shriver. "Well, I didn't finish it, but from what I did read I was struck by the fact that you seem taken with writing from the point of view of villains and abusers."

"Er . . . ," Shriver started, as the mosquito bite on his hand began to itch.

The waiter appeared like a guardian angel with a tumbler of whiskey. Everyone watched as Shriver grabbed the glass and sipped greedily. The waiter removed a pad and pencil from his pocket and asked if Shriver was ready to order. The young man gazed down upon him intently, as if all the world depended upon the answer.

"Go ahead," Simone told Shriver. "We've ordered already."

"Do you have any soup?" Shriver asked.

"This evening we have a cabbage and smoked sausage soup, and a Peruvian lamb soup."

"Uh-huh. How about a sandwich?"

"We have a bison sandwich, sir."

"Bison?"

"Live well, Shriver!" Wätzczesnam exclaimed.

"Do you have anything less, uh, fleshy?" Shriver asked the waiter.

"A Caesar salad?"

"I'll have that."

"Excellent choice," the waiter said. Then, sotto voce, "I'm a big fan."

When the young man had retreated, Shriver turned to the group, hoping that a new subject had been introduced, but they seemed to be awaiting his response to the poet.

"Er . . . ," he repeated.

"I prefer to speak for the victims," Gonquin Smithee declared. "I think the violent, sexist patriarchy has had its time to speak, and now it's our time."

"Good Lord," Basil Rather said with a snort. "I've time-traveled to 1975!"

Shriver gripped the tumbler tightly and mumbled, "You're probably right about that, Ms. Smithee."

Ms. Labio sighed dramatically. "That is so patronizing."

"Tell me, Ms. Labio," Rather said, "what do *you* do for a living?"

"She's an artist," Gonquin Smithee answered for her friend.

"No kidding?" Rather said with a tight little smile. "And what is your medium?"

"Sculpture," the artist replied.

"Clay? Stone?"

"Cake."

"Cake?"

"I sculpt nudes made of cake."

"How delicious!" the playwright said.

"Male?" T. Wätzczesnam asked. "Female?"

"*She*-male," the sculptress answered with a satisfied grin.

"Well, I'll be," the cowboy said.

"How long do they last?" Edsel Nixon asked.

Ms. Labio shrugged. "A week or so, depending on the conditions."

"Sometimes we eat them," Ms. Smithee said.

"I find temporary art to be baffling," Rather said. "What do *you* think, Shriver?"

Shriver turned to Simone, who, recognizing his distress, piped up, "Well, this distinguished group of writers has certainly created some permanent art." She hoisted her glass of Chianti. "To a great conference!"

Everyone raised their glasses and drank. Then, amid more talk of the mosquito problem, dinner was served. Throughout the meal, the waiter hovered nearby, his focus primarily upon Shriver, it seemed. Conversely, Shriver couldn't help but notice that Gonquin Smithee and her sidekick would not look at him at all. Unnerved, he poked at his salad in silence, barely listening to the talk of literature and academics. Occasionally, inspired by a word or phrase, the cowboy would utter some snippet of poetry, then quiz poor Edsel Nixon as to its author.

"You have an impressive familiarity with poetry, Mr. Nixon," Shriver said.

"I have to. Professor Wätzczesnam is my faculty adviser. He says if I get any wrong he's going to torpedo my thesis."

"All the more impressive."

"Not really." Mr. Nixon leaned in and spoke quietly. "He

quotes from the same poems all the time. Usually he's too inebriated to realize it."

Professor Wätzczesnam did seem a bit sauced, Shriver thought. At the moment he was tilting toward Simone, talking animatedly, though she looked eager to get away.

Meanwhile, Basil Rather, in between chewing bovinely at a hunk of veal, asked Shriver if he was planning to attend that evening's reading. "It should be quite interesting," he said, "if I do say so myself."

"I'm sure I'll be there," Shriver said.

"You know, Shriver, your novel was quite important to me as a young man."

"Is that so?" Shriver felt himself blushing slightly.

"I can't remember much of it now—I'm not even sure I finished it—but I recall it made an impression on my soft, unformed intellect. Of course, I imagine it would not cast the same spell now that I am older and wiser."

"I can see the influence in your work, actually," Edsel Nixon told the playwright.

Through clenched teeth: "Really? How so?"

"In the transgressive nature of the characters. How they yearn for meaning so much, they destroy meaning in the process."

"Nonsense," Basil Rather said to the young man. "Did you hear that, Lena? My characters are transgressive! Wätzczesnam, what kind of claptrap are you teaching these students of yours?"

"Probably the deconstructionist element," the cowboy explained in a tone of grave seriousness. He cast poor Nixon a withering glance. "They're running rampant in the English department."

"God help us!" the playwright cried.

"And what's wrong with deconstructionism?" Gonquin Smithee asked.

"Ah-ah-ah!" The cowboy wagged a crooked finger. "Save it for the panel discussion tomorrow. Looks like there could be fireworks, eh, Shriver?"

Shriver signaled the hovering waiter for another whiskey. He dreaded the panel discussion. He knew nothing of deconstructionism or transgressive characters. He was just a man who liked to lie in his bed and watch the Channel 17 Action News. He missed Mr. Bojangles. He loved to rub the white cummerbund of fur on the cat's belly. Mr. B. never spoke to him about poetry or the meaning of literature. He never made any demands beyond regular feedings and the stroke of a hand.

When dinner was over, the waiter presented each guest with a separate check. Great piles of quarters and dimes appeared upon the white tablecloth. As Shriver added up his tip, the waiter knelt at his side.

"Mr. Shriver, it's a real pleasure to meet you. I've read your book three times."

"Three times?"

"And I'm reading it again for my writing class."

"You seem to be the only one to have finished it."

"I think it's fascinating."

The young man remained on one knee for a moment, his eyes watching Shriver from their deep sockets. For a moment, Shriver was convinced that he knew the boy somehow.

"I was wondering," the waiter said, looking away now, shyly. "I'm a writer too, and I was hoping maybe you could take a look at—"

"Be gone, young interloper!" Professor Wätzczesnam shouted. "Mr. Shriver has better things to do with his time than to read your juvenilia."

"Oh," Shriver said. "But I suppose I could—"

"Nonsense, Shriver. You're beyond that sort of thing."

The young waiter stood and gathered up Shriver's money. "Of course," he said. "So sorry." He walked off, dejected.

"Honestly," T. said. "The nerve."

/

Edsel Nixon ferried Shriver and T. Wätzczesnam back to the Union in a decrepit old army-issue jeep.

"Where's your horse, Professor?" Shriver asked.

"Walter? He's home resting, poor fellow. His battered hooves are destined for gelatin and postage stamps, I'm afraid."

"Sorry to hear that."

Shriver had hoped to catch a ride with Simone, but she'd promised a lift to Gonquin Smithee and Ms. Labio, so he thought it best to accept his handler's kind offer. He sat in the cramped backseat, among books and ice scrapers and teeth-marked pens, and rolled from side to side with every sharp turn. There was no roof, and the engine sputtered like a dying lawn mower.

"I like to ride with the top off," the graduate student hollered over the noise. "The wind keeps the mosquitoes away!"

" 'Insects do not sting out of malice,' " the cowboy quoted, one hand clasped to his fluttering ten-gallon hat, " 'but because they also want to live: likewise our critics—they want our blood, not our pain.' "

Poor Edsel Nixon was drawing a blank.

"Okay, I'll give you a pass on that one," his adviser said.

"Who is it?"

"Nietzsche, my boy! Don't you ever read anything but bullshit poetry?!"

They drove down a tree-lined street beneath dense, overhanging limbs. Gazing up through a blur of leaves, Shriver caught a glimpse of the nearly full moon.

"So, Shriver." Professor Wätzczesnam's rugged, sunburned face appeared between the front seats. "Any thoughts on the panel tomorrow? Or should I surprise you?"

"I'm not sure I have much to contribute, T.," Shriver said, hoping to lower expectations.

"Balderdash! You're one of this country's most revered novelists. A mystery man for twenty years! You must have a lot to say about reality-slash-illusion."

Shriver's hand began to itch. The bite had grown to the size of a quarter.

"People are coming from hundreds of miles away to hear your thoughts," T. continued. "I know this for a fact!"

Shriver removed the bottle of whiskey and, with some effort, unscrewed the cap. He offered it to the cowboy.

"Don't mind if I do." Wätzczesnam grabbed the bottle and indulged in a rather prodigious swallow. "Nixon?"

"No, thanks."

"Oh, right," T. said, handing the bottle back to Shriver. "Our man Nixon here is a teetotaler. Did you know that, Shriver?"

Shriver took a long slug and screwed the cap back on.

"I'm afraid I may disappoint Shriver fans tomorrow," he said.

Wätzczesnam laughed. "I know you're up to something, Shriver. I've never met a writer who didn't have something to say. I don't know what it is, but I'm *sure* you're up to no good!" He laughed some more.

"'If I had to give young writers advice,'" Edsel Nixon said in a dramatic voice, "'I would say don't listen to writers talking about writing or themselves.'"

The two older men looked at the graduate student.

"Lillian Hellman," he said.

/

The ballroom was once again filled to capacity, with many of the same faces as at the afternoon reading, including that of Delta Malarkey-Jones, who waved a candy bar at Shriver from her seat near the door. Simone stood up front, chatting with a group of graduate students, while Basil Rather waited off to the side, tall and imperious. Ms. Brazir skulked beside him, looking as anxious as her mentor looked calm. Perhaps Rather kept her at hand to absorb all the trepidation that came with being an award-winning playwright. Shriver wished he had such a sponge for his own unease, and then realized that, in fact, he did: Mr. Bojangles. Oh, if only the cat were here with him tonight.

Edsel Nixon invited Shriver to sit up front with him, but he declined, preferring a row toward the back, where he could imbibe more easily. He found a seat in the far corner, next to some undergraduates abuzz about the upcoming perfor-mance.

He settled in and surreptitiously sipped from the bottle. Even from far across the ballroom, he saw, Simone stood out in the crowd. Her face glowed pink from the wine; her blond hair cascaded down her back. She was not only lovely, but apparently also a revered teacher, for her students listened closely to her words, in thrall, before peeling away, one by one, to perform their duties. The last of them, a bearded young man wearing a gold hoop earring, stepped up to the podium. The crowd dutifully quieted down as he cleared his throat.

There followed an adulatory introduction of Basil Rather.

The graduate student spoke of a trip he once made to New York, where he took in one of Mr. Rather's many critically lauded plays. Watching the performance, he said, he was sucked into a vortex of language he had never experienced before. Or something like that. Shriver was much too busy watching Simone, who had returned to her usual seat in the front row corner, to pay much attention.

Despite her obvious popularity with the students and her colleagues, Shriver thought Simone seemed lonely and isolated. He'd been touched by her talk of divorce and how difficult it had been to remove her wedding ring. She seemed to be someone who, when she loved, loved deeply.

After the introduction, an attractive man and woman walked onto the platform and stood a few feet apart. Using voices trained in the college theater department, they proceeded to enact a scene from the playwright's canon.

"Cunt," the man casually began.

The undergraduate students near Shriver snickered.

"Coward," the woman responded.

"Twat."

"Weakling."

"Bitch."

"Mama's boy."

Shriver heard a groan behind him and turned to see T. Wätzczesnam, who rolled his eyes toward the sky.

As the play continued, Shriver resorted repeatedly to his bottle. Eventually, both of the characters turned to the audience and recited monologues about the pointlessness of relationships and the impossibility of connecting.

"Can you ever know someone," the young man wondered, "when you don't even know yourself?"

"We are just bundles of neuroses," the woman said. "Each

of us a jigsaw piece with its own distinct bulges and crevices. What are the chances of finding the perfect match?"

Shriver heard T. grunt and say, "Mixed metaphors."

Up front, Simone sat leaning forward, as if hanging on every word. But as Shriver watched her, he hoped she was thinking of other things—the progress of the conference so far, the meaning of life, or (dare he think it?) the genius of the author Shriver—anything, he hoped, but the play being enacted onstage.

After about thirty very long minutes, the actors abruptly stopped speaking and, amid smatterings of applause, took their bows. Shriver felt a tapping on his shoulder and turned to see T.'s sweaty visage.

"I could sure use another slug of that there hooch, Shriver, old buddy, after that sorry display."

Shriver handed the bottle over, and the cowboy took a long pull.

Meanwhile, Basil Rather bounded onto the stage and leaned against the side of the podium, twisting the neck of the microphone to point it closer to his face. His mouth moved but no sounds emerged. He continued with this pantomime until several audience members began shouting, "The sound is off!" and "Turn the mic on!"

"Oh, what a blessing," T. said.

Rather's face reddened. He turned to look at Ms. Brazir, who was standing off to the side of the stage. Ms. Brazir, in turn, looked toward Simone, who was already rushing to the podium. She examined the microphone, pushed a button, but still there was no amplification. The playwright's face grew more and more crimson as poor Simone scurried up a side aisle to the back of the room.

Shriver watched as she conferred with the obviously confused young technician behind a large soundboard. Knobs were turned, cables extracted and replaced. Still no sound. The audience became restless, their whispers like rustling paper.

"Shriver," Wätzczesnam said, "what say we adjourn to the Prairie Dog Saloon to discuss the profound piece of *thee-a-tah* we were just subjected to?"

But Shriver was distracted. Directly above the area where the soundboard was located, he saw for the first time a large screen hanging against the room's back wall. Projected onto this screen was the photograph of the author Shriver from the conference brochure. One of the students sitting next to him, a young girl in dark pigtails and a halter top with a sunflower design, looked from the projected photo to him and back.

"Hey, that's you," she said.

"No, no," Shriver said, but the girl had already turned to her friends and shared the news. They all smiled and said hello. "We're reading your book in our class," one of them said.

Meanwhile, the image had faded and the face of Gonquin Smithee had appeared on the screen. After a moment this photo dissolved into a professionally lit publicity shot of Basil Rather.

"Can you hear me?" Basil Rather called out from the lip of the stage.

"No!" someone barked back.

At this point, an earsplitting shriek of feedback rocked the ballroom. It went on so long and so shrilly that Shriver had to cover his ears.

When the noise finally faded, Shriver looked around with one open eye, half expecting to see the room in tatters. On the stage, Basil Rather stood bowed with his hands still over his ears, his face twisted into a grimace.

The gaping silence was broken by T.'s rumbling voice: "'All the heavens / Opened and blazed with thunder such as seemed / Shoutings of all the sons of God,'" followed by a more timid utterance from the front of the room: "That would be Tennyson, sir."

Meanwhile, Simone had run to the podium, where she tapped tentatively at the microphone.

Thump thump thump.

A few people applauded, Shriver among them.

"I am *so* sorry about that," Simone announced. She then made room for Basil Rather at the podium. The playwright approached the microphone as if it might bite him. Ms. Brazir stood nearby, ready to administer first aid.

"Well, that was *interesting,*" Rather said.

He then apologized, not for the technical difficulties, but for the blunt language of his play, which, he said, was necessary to bring home the point of the piece. He did not elaborate on that point. Instead, he wondered if there were any questions.

Again, the audience was reluctant to pose queries. Wishing to avoid any temptation to leap into the fray, Shriver stood up and sidled past the young students toward the aisle. He would go out to the hall and relax, sit on a couch, have a drink. As he crossed the back of the ballroom, he glanced at Simone beside the stage. She was scanning the audience, clearly hoping to see some upraised hands. There were none. For a second their eyes met, and Shriver stopped in his tracks. He did not want her to see him leave.

"Come, now," Basil Rather said. "Someone must have a question."

Simone looked at Shriver with imploring eyes. *Please don't go,* she seemed to be thinking. For some reason, perhaps to convince her that he was not actually going anywhere, he waved.

"Mr. Shriver!" Basil Rather shouted.

Heads turned. Shriver froze, hand still in midwave.

"First into the breach again?" the playwright asked.

Shriver looked back toward Simone, herself equally stationary, the two of them statues on either side of the curious throng.

Basil Rather leaned forward, awaiting Shriver's inquiry. The playwright's steady breathing could be heard over the sound system. In the sea of heads between them, Shriver made out the artificial coloring of Jack Blunt's hairpiece. The reporter smiled mischievously. Shriver scratched at his itching hand.

The noise seemed to come from underneath them at first, like the shifting of tectonic plates miles below the surface of the earth, but then it rapidly grew in intensity until, after welling up deep inside the bowels of the sound system, a volcanic blast of feedback erupted, making the previous disaster seem like a minor annoyance. Shriver watched as seven hundred people pressed their hands to their ears and shut their eyes—all except Simone, who ran onto the stage, straight to the podium, grabbed the microphone, and switched it off.

The noise ceased immediately, trailed by an echo that ricocheted around the room like an errant bullet. People seemed reluctant to uncover their ears, understandably worried that there might be another brain-frying aftershock. Basil Rather stood crimson-faced on the stage with Simone, speaking quietly but with many gesticulations.

Shriver took the opportunity to exit the ballroom. He could always claim ear damage as an excuse. Out in the hall, side by side on a couch, sat Gonquin Smithee and Ms. Labio.

"I don't know which was worse," the poet said. "The feed-back or the play."

"Such claptrap," her companion added.

"I mean, I don't mind confrontational—*I'm* confronta-tional; *you're* confrontational, Shriver—but at least he should have the talent to back it up."

Shriver wondered if this meant Gonquin Smithee thought he had talent. Or that the *real* Shriver had talent. An olive branch, or at least a leaf, seemed to be in the offing. He sat down a little too hard on a couch opposite the two women.

"Would either of you like a snort?" he asked, removing the pint of whiskey from his pocket while, with his other hand, he rubbed his sore bottom.

"What the hell," Ms. Smithee said, reaching for the near-empty bottle.

Ms. Labio watched with a disapproving expression as her friend downed a considerable amount.

"Gonky," she said in a tone of warning.

The poet swallowed, shook her reddening head from side to side, and flapped her arms. "I can handle it," she squawked, handing the bottle back. Her eyes were pink-edged and a little crossed. "So where do you teach, Shriver?" she asked.

"Teach?"

"Harvard? Princeton? Must be an Ivy."

"I don't teach."

Her eyes bulged. "You don't teach?"

Shriver shook his head.

"You mean you just write?"

"Is that good or bad?"

Ms. Smithee sat back in her chair and snorted. "Oh, it's good, it's very good. You're the genuine article. I wish I had the guts to do that."

"How would you make money?" her friend asked.

"I could wait tables. Work in a bookstore. Whatever."

Ms. Labio rolled her eyes at this. Shriver got the impression she rolled her eyes quite a lot.

Ms. Smithee gestured for the whiskey and took another long pull.

"You know, Shriver, I've been thinking about what you said earlier."

Shriver took a serious drink himself.

"What *I* said?"

"You know—about writing from the point of view of my father. I may have been hasty in my assessment of that suggestion."

"It wasn't so much a suggestion as a question," Shriver said, anticipating another assault.

"But the question suggests that there is this other approach, and I've never really considered it."

Relieved, Shriver said, "I bet it might be interesting."

"What do you think, Majora?" Gonquin asked her friend.

"I think you've had enough to drink."

"Aw, bullshit! I'm tired of being the frickin' victim. I wanna be the bad guy for once. See what it feels like. What does it feel like, Shriver?"

"How should I know?"

"Oh, c'mon. All those pervs and nasty-ass characters in your book. That guy cut off his wife's head, for Christ's sake."

"Oh," Shriver said, detecting a far-off rumble inside his bowels. "Him."

Gonquin Smithee laughed. "You know, Shriver, you're not at all what I expected."

"Is that so?"

"I thought you'd be this stooped-over goat man or something, leering and slobbering at all the girls, all full of yourself with your awards and shit."

"Is that my reputation?"

"You don't *have* a reputation. That's the amazing thing. I asked around about you but got nowhere: not a word for twenty years. You're a mystery, Shriver."

"More than you know."

"You're actually much more complicated, I can see that now."

"Thank you. I think."

"I'm fascinated by your divided nature."

"Oh?" Shriver felt uncomfortable under the poet's piercing gaze.

"It's like there's two different people inside you, wrestling. There's the *real* you, gentle, sensitive, genuine. Then there's the liar, the imposter, the villain—the *writer*."

Shriver tried not to gulp, but his Adam's apple moved of its own accord. "Must one be an . . . imposter to be a writer?" he asked, trying desperately to engage rather than turn and run away.

"Depends what he writes about." Gonquin leaned forward. "Tell me—what's it like to inhabit those people? To crawl inside their skin and walk around doing such bad things?"

"I never thought about it," he told her. "I suppose it must be sort of liberating."

"Exactly! I need to be *liberated*!"

"You need some coffee," Ms. Labio commented dryly.

"I need to be a liar! An *imposter*!"

"We shouldn't have come. This happens every time."

"That's right," Gonquin said. "Every time we come to one of these conferences, I meet real writers and have a *great time*! *That's* what you can't stand, Majora."

Shriver stood up. "Excuse me, ladies."

"Aw, look what you did," Ms. Smithee said. "You drove him away."

Feeling woozy from the whiskey and all this literary talk, Shriver walked in a jagged line across the lobby and into the men's room. As he relieved himself, he became aware of a presence in the nearby stall. He heard a groaning sound, followed by impressive flatulence. He washed his hands at the sink and, staring at himself in the mirror, saw that he'd never looked so old. Bags hung under his bloodshot eyes; gray whiskers dotted his sagging chin. He dabbed some water on his scalp and tried to comb his wiry, thinning hair into submission. Then he pulled down his trousers and examined the rather alarming purple bruise that had formed on his left buttock. It was shaped like something, but he wasn't quite sure what.

"Good God Almighty, Shriver!" T. Wätzczesnam cried out as he emerged from the stall. "Looks like you got kicked by a mule!"

Shriver quickly pulled his trousers up and buckled his belt. "It's nothing."

The cowboy vigorously washed his hands. "A vinegar compress'll help that, ya know. I used to get whacked all the time back when I was in the rodeo." He dried his hands with a paper towel and tossed it away.

"I didn't see you leave the ballroom," Shriver said, changing the subject.

" 'By stealth she passed, and fled as fast / As doth the hunted fawn . . .' "

With that, the cowboy made his exit. Shriver lowered his trousers and took another glance in the mirror. The bruise was shaped like an animal—an opossum, say—or maybe a small

Eastern European country on a map. Moldova? Slovenia? He would have to consult an atlas later.

Out in the lobby people were now emerging from the reading. Shriver swam against the tide and squeezed through the doorway. He scanned the room for Simone. Up near the front, Basil Rather was holding forth for several audience members. Nearby, Edsel Nixon spoke to some of the under-graduates, and Blunt, still sitting in his seat, scribbled in a little notebook. Over in a corner, Professor Wätzczesnam had been trapped by Delta Malarkey-Jones, who pressed a copy of her manuscript into the cowboy's hands.

Simone stood at the back of the room, Shriver now saw, conferring with the sound technician, who appeared to be explaining something to her. She seemed on the verge of tears. Shriver loitered nearby, hoping to speak to her. He felt awful about deserting her earlier. He should at least have been able to come up with a question for Basil Rather.

Nearby, in a shadowy corner of the ballroom, stood a tall young man dressed in black, fidgeting as if trying to decide on an action to take. He kept looking at Shriver, then looking away. Finally, he appeared to make up his mind and headed toward Shriver just as Simone broke away from the sound technician.

"What a disaster," she said to Shriver. She looked much older now, aged by stress and the unforgiving glow of the fluorescent ceiling lights.

"I'm sorry."

"I don't know what happened. Some sort of technical snafu that I don't understand."

"Can I help?"

"Most definitely not."

She moved off, the little wiggle in her step canceled out by the speed with which she walked.

"Going to the reception, sir?"

He turned to see Edsel Nixon. Had his designated handler noticed him staring at Simone's shapely derriere?

"The reception? Of course. Can you lead me there, Mr. Nixon?"

As he followed the graduate student Shriver turned to look for the tall man in black, but he was gone.

"This is going to be interesting," Nixon said as they crossed the street. He did not appear to be bothered by the mosquitoes that were busy dive-bombing Shriver.

"How so?" Shriver asked, waving his arms to ward off the insects.

"Well, Mr. Rather is really upset about the sound. He thinks someone sabotaged his reading."

"Sabotaged?"

"He said he might not come to the reception, even though it's for him."

The St. George Café was a roomy coffeehouse with high, arched ceilings and a huge cross hanging on the wall. Several of the graduate students stood around drinking coffee and snacking on small pastries that the conference had supplied. A man with a shaved head tuned up an acoustic guitar on a small stage at the far end of the room.

"I'm going to get a latte," Edsel Nixon said. "Do you want something?"

"Just get me an empty coffee cup, if you can." Shriver opened his jacket to show the whiskey bottle. Nixon nodded and went to the counter.

On the café stage the folksinger, flanked by two public address speakers, stepped up to a foam-covered microphone. "This is a song by Jackson Browne," he said, and started strumming.

"I'm going to rent myself a house," he sang, "in the shade of the freeway . . ."

Meanwhile, Edsel Nixon returned with an empty coffee cup, into which Shriver poured himself a finger.

"Shriver!" came the now-familiar rumble. "Got any of that hooch left?"

Shriver offered a slug to the cowboy.

"What did you think of the reading, Professor?" the graduate student asked.

"Not my cup of whiskey, to be perfectly frank about it," Wätzczesnam said before downing a significant portion of Shriver's booze. "I'm more of an *Our Town* kind of guy."

"Too bad about the sound," Edsel said.

T. grunted. "We'll see if that haughty old queen Rather shows up."

Right on cue, Basil Rather, closely followed by Ms. Brazir, entered the café. Wätzczesnam started clapping and ran up to them, showering the playwright with praise. Rather thanked him, but his face remained stern.

"And don't fret about the sound," the cowboy told him. "It didn't make any difference. Everyone was very happy with the performance."

"Where did you go, Shriver?" the playwright asked. "Didn't you have a question?"

Shriver took a deep sip of whiskey.

"My ears," he explained. "That last blast of feedback."

Rather nodded dismissively. Ms. Brazir hung on to his arm, gazing up at the man's bearded chin.

"You didn't miss much," Rather said with a wrinkled nose. "These yokels don't have a brain between them."

"Perhaps they were simply stunned by the profundity of your work," Wätzczesnam theorized.

"Yes," the playwright said. "Their expressions did resemble those of cows at the abattoir."

The cowboy glanced over at Shriver and fluttered his eyelashes.

"Where is Professor Cleverly?" Rather asked.

"I hope you know how awful she feels," Shriver said. "It wasn't her fault."

"And how awful do you think *I* feel, Mr. Shriver?"

"I'm sure you feel—"

"Let's see how *you* react when someone deliberately sabotages *your* reading."

"But who would do that?"

"Yes," the cowboy piped up, "that's quite an accusation, Basil, ol' buddy."

"I will leave you to your whiskey," Rather said, walking past them with his nose in the air. Ms. Brazir followed, but not before giving the two whiskey drinkers withering looks.

"'A vile conceit in pompous words expressed / Is like a clown in regal purple dressed.'"

"Alexander Pope," Nixon said.

"Damn straight," the cowboy muttered before weaving off on his increasingly bowed legs.

"I'd better go make sure Professor Wätzczesnam doesn't get into trouble," Nixon said. "Let me know if you need a ride back to the hotel." The student then ran to catch up with his wobbly faculty adviser.

Shriver stood near the door sipping at his whiskey. Did this sort of sniping go on at all literary conferences? he wondered. Who knew that a gathering of writers could be such a viper's nest?

After a few moments the door swung open and Simone stepped in, her eyes sweeping past him to take in the whole café.

"He thinks it was done on purpose," she said, watching Basil Rather across the room.

"By whom?" Shriver asked.

"Does it matter? The man's paranoid."

"Does he think *you* did it?"

"Who knows? I wish I didn't have to be here."

She was standing close, using him as a shield. She smelled like citrus and flowers. Looking down at her face, he could not help but peer past to see her freckled chest and the edges of the pale blue brassiere she was wearing.

"Are you having a good time?" she asked.

Was she being sarcastic? Had she caught him glancing at her underwear? No doubt she could smell the whiskey. She probably thought of him as just another booze-drenched writer. *But I'm not!* he wanted to tell her. *I'm not a writer at all!*

"Yes," he answered. "But I'm very anxious."

"Don't be," she said in a weary voice. "I promise we'll have the sound problems ironed out before your reading."

"No, it's not that."

He wanted to tell her about how he couldn't read the words of his story, how he couldn't even read them to himself, never mind amplified in front of seven hundred Shriver fans. Then he wanted to confess to her the whole abysmal situation, to tell her she'd made a titanic mistake by sending him that invitation, that he was a fraud. To hell with how she would react.

"There's something I need to tell you," he began, not knowing how to explain it.

"Oh, God, here he comes." She bravely stepped out from his shadow to meet Basil Rather head-on.

"Professor Cleverly," Rather said.

"Mr. Rather." Simone's eyes tilted upward to meet those of the lanky playwright. Behind him, of course, came his mistress.

"Have you found the source of the technical difficulties?" he asked.

"I was assured it was accidental. Something about a power surge."

"How apt," Rather snipped. "Whose power was surging, I wonder."

"I'm told it affected the entire campus."

"The timing was certainly interesting, don't you think?"

"Who would do such a thing, Mr. Rather?"

"Perhaps there are those who are envious," he replied, his eyes focused on Shriver. "Where is our friend Ms. Smithee?"

"I wouldn't know."

"And her sidekick, Betty Crocker?"

Simone narrowed her eyes into steely bullets. "Surely you don't think one of the other writers tampered with the equipment?"

"Stranger things have happened."

"Not here."

"No, of course not," the playwright sniffed. "Not at your precious writers' conference."

"Now, see here, Rather," Shriver started. He wanted to belt the man in the mouth, but he was fairly certain that, with his superior height and reach, the playwright could amply defend himself. "Don't speak to Professor Cleverly like that. She's doing her best to make this conference a success."

Shriver was surprised to see that the playwright seemed a bit intimidated. Then he realized that, as far as Rather was concerned, he had just been upbraided by the legendary Shriver. Who knew literary eminence brought with it a certain amount of authority?

Emboldened, Shriver added, "You owe Simone an apology."

Rather's face turned pink. "Of course," he said meekly. "I'm sorry, Professor. It's just that I was a bit . . . thrown off by the whole incident."

"And I apologize to *you*, Mr. Rather," Simone said. "I look forward to seeing you at tomorrow's panel."

Rather nodded, then he and his assistant turned like two dancers in a choreographed movement and, side by side, disappeared through the door.

Simone looked back at Shriver, and he knew, somehow, what it was she needed.

"Yes, please," she said, accepting the offered cup. She drank greedily. "Thank you."

"I am at your service."

The singer had started another tune, an upbeat number with a welcome perky rhythm.

"Trying to be too bad," he sang, "trying to be too tough . . ."

"It's been a long day," Simone said.

"For both of us."

"Yes. I think it's time for me to head home."

His heart sank. The whiskey, the defeated look on Rather's face, the memory of Simone's pale blue brassiere—all had combined to lift his spirits, and now she wanted to go?

"Can I give you a ride back to the hotel?" she asked.

Chapter Five

They ran to her car, zigzagging to throw off the relentless mosquitoes.

"The nightmare continues," Simone said once they were safely in the massive vehicle.

Though it was a warm night, they had to keep the windows rolled up. But Shriver didn't care about the bugs. He couldn't even feel the bruise on his rump anymore. Illuminated by oncoming headlights and other ambient light, Simone looked incandescent.

"I just want to say," he told her, "I think you're doing a great job."

"Oh, I'll be fine. It seems every year there's some sort of controversy."

"I guess you get a bunch of writers together and . . ."

"Exactly. Last year, for example, there was this poet who did his best to seduce everyone in the department. Women, men—he'd have had his way with a bison if there'd been one on the faculty."

"Wow. How successful was he?" Shriver asked pointedly.

She hesitated. "He was a seductive character. He was short and I was not a fan of his poetry, but there was something about him. Self-confidence? Cockiness? I don't know."

Shriver tried to think of something cocky to say but came up with nothing.

Simone braked at a red light. "What is it about writers? Why are they so self-absorbed? Is it because they spend all that time alone? Is it because they're so used to playing God? Is it something in their genetic makeup? I don't get it!"

With each question Shriver's heart wobbled. This woman had obviously been hammered by some blunt instrument.

"I'm sorry," he said.

Simone laughed and said, "Oh, no, *I'm* sorry!"

"For what?"

"Here I am running down all writers, and meanwhile you . . ."

"What about me?" he asked.

"Well, you're sort of the ultimate example of the species."

Is that how she saw him? As the ultimate self-absorbed writer? Then he remembered that he wasn't a writer at all, and his hopes perked up.

She turned into the hotel lot, pulled up to the door, and shifted into park. The behemoth's engine purred.

"Well, I hope your first day wasn't too terribly traumatic," she said.

"Not at all."

"I'm sorry if I burdened you with my personal drama."

"I honestly don't mind."

"Tomorrow you're speaking in Teresa Apple's writing class, remember."

"Have I met her?"

She snorted. "You'd have remembered, believe me."

"Oh?"

"She'll pick you up at nine or so."

"I'll be here," he said, disappointed that Simone would not be driving him in the morning. "Though I don't know what I'm going to tell her students."

"Just tell them what you know."

"That won't take long."

She laughed, almost reluctantly, and feeling as though he'd hit a bull's-eye, he opened the door and climbed down onto the pavement.

"Thank you, Mr. Shriver," she called down to him.

He turned back. Simone's face was lit a rose color from the hotel's neon sign. "For what?"

"For what you said back there, to Mr. Rather."

"That was my pleasure."

She gazed down upon him from her high perch. "And sorry about that crack about writers," she said.

"Writers are trouble," he told her.

"Yes, they are. Truth is, I kind of forgot you were one of them." She blushed and quickly added, "Good night."

"Good night, Simone."

He slammed the door and she roared off, leaving him in a mini-twister of exhaust and swirling mosquitoes. As he ran inside he wondered if he should have asked Simone in for a nightcap at the saloon. Had she wanted him to? She seemed to be softening toward him. It had been so long since he'd had to read the subtle signals of a woman, he felt like a man raised by wolves. He wondered if someone was waiting for her at home, and was surprised at how sad that thought made him.

As he made his way through the lobby, Shriver spotted Gonquin Smithee sitting by herself on a corner stool in the Prairie Dog Saloon.

"Good evening, sir," the clerk called out to him from behind the front desk.

He paused to take in the beehive hairdo, the lean face, the gum chewing.

"Are you still here?" he asked.

The clerk's face crinkled in confusion, then she grinned.

"Oh, you probably mean my sister, Charlevoix. I'm Sue St. Marie." She pointed to a homemade name tag.

Shriver stared, amazed at the resemblance.

"I'm three minutes older," she said, "in case you're wondering."

Just as Shriver was walking away, the clerk called out, "Oh! I almost forgot. There's a message for you."

"For me?"

"You *are* Mr. Shriver, correct?" She handed over a folded sheet of paper.

He opened the note: *I'm in bar. —GS.*

For a moment he considered meeting with the poet but decided there had been enough drama this evening and headed to the elevator.

As he waited, he heard high-pitched laughter from the arriving car. The doors opened and half a dozen teenage girls fell out, dressed in bathing suits with towels tossed over their slender shoulders, the braces on their teeth flashing. Among them was the girl he'd seen before, the willowy brunette. She smiled coyly as she passed by, then ran to join her friends on their way to the pool.

Shriver boarded the elevator and rode to the second floor. There, he inserted the key to room nineteen. Again, the key would not turn. Then he remembered to turn it to the left. He heard a click, and he pushed open the door. He switched on the light and sat on the edge of the bed. Outside a train crept by, its wheels clanking rhythmically.

He rose and went into the bathroom. He flipped the light switch, but the room remained dark. He'd forgotten about the burned-out bulb. Oh, well. He would take a bath anyway. He searched in the dim room for the faucet and turned on the bathwater. He poured in some of the bubble oil provided by the hotel. If only his old friend Mr. Bojangles were here, he would not feel so lonesome.

As he started to take off his jacket, he remembered the story he'd written and removed the pages from the pocket. He sat on the bed near the lamp and looked down at the words on the page.

"The Water Mark."

His eyes were tired but they seemed to be working properly as he read the first few lines.

"The water mark appeared on my ceiling on the rainy day my wife walked out on me. At first it was just a spot, approximately the size of a quarter, directly above the bed where I lay weeping. Listening to the rain fall, I watched the water mark grow, ever so slowly, to the size of a baseball. After a few hours, the mark was as big as a honeydew melon. By the time it got dark outside, the water mark had elongated to roughly the shape of a two-foot-long oval. All night I lay there, wide awake, wondering what the water mark would look like when daylight started creeping in the next morning—"

Then came a sharp knock on the door. Startled, Shriver threw the pages onto the bedside table and stood up.

"Who's there?"

"House detective!"

"*What?*"

"Please open up, sir."

"What's the problem?"

"We've had a complaint from one of the cheerleaders, sir."

Oh my God, Shriver thought. The brunette. What had she told them?

"Are you sure?" he asked.

"Please open up, sir."

He unlocked the door, and T. Wätzczesnam came crashing into the room, accompanied by several others, including Edsel Nixon and Gonquin Smithee.

"Fooled ya!" The cowboy tipped up the front lip of his ten-gallon hat. "Brought some replenishment, Shriver, ol' buddy." He set a substantial bottle of whiskey on the writing table, along with a full ice bucket and some hotel cups wrapped in plastic.

Shriver turned to Nixon, who shrugged. Gonquin Smithee unscrewed the bottle cap and poured herself a generous drink. Her eyes appeared shellacked over.

"Didja get my note?" she asked.

"I thought I'd freshen up first."

"Izzat so?"

"Where's Ms. Labio?" he asked.

"Aw, she's back in our room, sulking, as per usual."

Delta Malarkey-Jones reeled through the door, her doughy arm around the folksinger from the café.

"This here is Christo," she announced.

The singer, not quite as inebriated as his companion, grabbed Shriver's hand and shook vigorously. "I am a major fan."

The other stranger in the room was a tall African-American woman with closely cropped hair and long, pendulous earrings that looked painfully heavy.

"Oh," the cowboy said, "let me introduce you to the last, but not least, of our featured authors. This is Zebra Amphetamine. She flew in tonight."

The woman nodded to Shriver with heavy lids.

" 'A Nubian girl,' " Wätzczesnam recited, " 'more sweet than Khoorja musk, / Came to the water-tank to fill her urn . . .' "

Zebra Amphetamine laughed like a hyena at this, as did the cowboy, who wrapped his arm around the much taller woman's waist and pulled her close.

"Was that Aldrich, sir?" Edsel Nixon asked.

"Nixon, you are most impressive."

Someone handed Shriver a plastic cup filled nearly to the brim. He peered down and saw his face, tired and defeated by gravity, reflected in the brown liquid. Then he took a sip.

"Listen to that train!" Zebra Amphetamine shouted as she ran to the window. "It's the sound of America! We could be Lakotas in our skin teepees listening to the clackety-clack of White Death rolling toward us!"

"Never mind that," the cowboy hollered. "Look down there!" He cranked open the window and shouted, "Ahoy, girls!"

On the back lawn of the hotel, lit by the moon and fluttering underwater swimming pool lights, several girls in bathing suits lounged on deck chairs while bubblegum music percolated from a nearby radio.

"Watch out for those mosquitoes, girls!" the cowboy warned, but the cheerleaders appeared impervious to the attack of insects.

"Come on down!" they shouted. "Let's party!"

Among them, Shriver saw, was the willowy brunette, dancing provocatively with one of her fellow cheerleaders.

"We would be fools, gentlemen," the cowboy said, "to pass up such an invitation."

"I don't think it's a good idea, Professor," Edsel Nixon said.

"Poppycock! These nubile young things are more experienced than all of us put together. Who's with me?"

"I'll go!" Zebra Amphetamine said.

"Capital. And you, Shriver?"

"I think I'll stay put, T. I'm tired."

The cowboy held his face just inches away, his breath flammable. "I'm very disappointed in you."

He grabbed the bottle and left with his new friend. Meanwhile, the shaven-headed singer strummed his guitar in the corner, with Delta at his feet.

"Well," Shriver said after the singer's second tune, "I'm a bit tired, so—"

He was interrupted by a deep-throated braying that could be heard from outside. On the lawn the cowboy danced lewdly with the brunette, his hat held high in one hand as he waggled his bowed legs to the sugary music. Zebra Amphetamine stood nearby, doubled over with laughter.

"They're on their own," Edsel Nixon muttered, shaking his head.

"Oh my gosh!"

Delta Malarkey-Jones jumped up and pointed toward water flooding underneath the closed bathroom door. Shriver pushed inside and splashed his way through the dark to the tub, which was full of overflowing bubbles. As he attempted to turn off the water he slipped on the soapy floor and crashed onto the froth-puddled tiles.

Delta cackled at the sight of Shriver struggling in vain to climb to his feet, his face now bearded with foam. Edsel Nixon attempted to help him up but also succumbed to the slippery floor and dropped with a great upheaval of bubbles. Delta, still hooting, entered the room despite pleas for her to remain outside, and immediately lost her footing. She proceeded to teeter like an oak on the edge of collapse, first in one direction, then the other, all in tortuous slow motion, until finally the momentum was too much and, as Shriver and Nixon covered their heads, she plunged backward into the tub. A tsunami flooded the bathroom and sent a small wave out into the hotel room proper, where Christo the Folksinger stood strumming in accompaniment.

Somehow, Shriver was able to reach up and twist the faucet handle into the off position. He then pulled the lever that opened the drain. Nixon got quickly to his feet and tossed dry towels onto the floor. Meanwhile, Delta Malarkey-Jones lay in the tub, held tight by the suction from the draining water.

"I'm stuck," she chortled, holding out her hands for anyone brave enough to come to her aid.

The task required all three men and nearly sent them to the floor as their feet slipped on the soapy tiles. But after a few moments of tugging and grunting, they finally pulled Delta free, and she gave them each a sudsy, smothering hug for their efforts.

The ever-efficient Nixon ran to the front desk to get some more dry towels, as well as a new bulb, and in fifteen minutes the floor was relatively dry and the light fixed.

"Thank you, everybody," Shriver said, sitting down on the commode in exhaustion.

"Well, I've had about enough for one evening," his handler announced. "I'm headed home. If Professor Wätzczesnam shows up again, tell him I'll see him tomorrow."

The dripping graduate student departed, leaving behind Delta and her folksinger friend.

"Listen," Delta said, "Christo and I have been talking it over, and we'd really like it if you came back to my room for a bit."

"What for?"

"Okay, we could stay here, if you prefer. But my room has a king-size bed. There's room for all of us."

The musician smiled throughout this exchange, his hands gripping the guitar.

"Thank you," Shriver said, "but I think I'll pass."

"You sure?"

"Very."

"Okey-doke. Don't say we didn't try. C'mon, Christo." She grabbed the musician by the wrist and pulled him out the door.

Shriver stood by the window and removed his wet shoes. Out on the lawn the cheerleaders were in the process of forming a human pyramid, with the cowboy and Zebra Amphetamine on their hands and knees among those at the base. The group had reached the third level, comprised of three girls atop the backs of the four girls below them. Two more girls clambered up like monkeys to form a fourth level. Then the willowy brunette ascended the pyramid to her solo spot at the apex, where, tall and lithe in her aqua-blue bathing suit, she stood perfectly poised atop the backs of the two girls beneath her, her angelic face level with Shriver's. The confident cheerleader smiled at him with dazzling teeth and asked, "Are you a writer too?"

While Shriver pondered this question, the girl shouted down to her teammates, "One . . . two . . ." On three, the entire pyramid collapsed, like an imploded office building, and the brunette landed in the arms of two of her huskier teammates while the other squealing girls rolled off one another onto the grass. The cowboy and Zebra Amphetamine were the last to emerge from the pile, their skin wet with perspiration, the grins on their faces speaking of some secret ecstasy.

Shriver cranked the window shut and removed his sopping clothes. From his jacket pocket he retrieved the manila envelope and set it down on the desk with a metallic clank.

After toweling himself off, he climbed into bed. There, he took up the pages from the bedside table and continued to read his story.

"All night I lay there, wide awake, wondering what the water mark would look like when daylight started creeping in the next morning. As dawn broke, I saw that the spot had grown even more, now to the general size and shape of an adult person, complete with arms and legs, and at the top, a head. Furthermore . . ."

Here his eyes failed him again, scrambling the words into meaninglessness. He turned to page two, then three, but found only a jumble of inky symbols. Perhaps it was just fatigue this time. He set the pages down, turned off the light, and lay listening to the sound of a seemingly endless train, broken by the occasional bark of laughter and high-pitched squeals from outside, or maybe next door, he couldn't tell. Either possibility was unpleasant to contemplate.

After a while, when the train had finally passed and the cheerleaders had gone inside, he slipped toward the ether of slumber. Reaching out to stroke Mr. Bojangles, Shriver heard only the sound of rhythmic breathing, which gently lulled him to sleep.

DAY / TWO

Chapter Six

When the telephone rang, waking Shriver from a deep sleep, he did not recognize his surroundings. Where was his mahogany bureau? Where was his signed portrait of Tina Le-Gros of the Channel 17 Action News Team? Where was the water mark over his bed? Most alarming of all, where was Mr. Bojangles? Normally his friend's whiskered face, always so charmingly neutral in its expression, hovered inches away from his own as the famished cat awaited his morning bowl of cottage cheese.

The room was dark but for a bright strip of sunlight between the heavy window curtains. The bed felt strange, the sheets crisp with starch, the pillows thin and hard. Not his usual soft cotton sheets and thick, fluffy pillow.

And that irritating sound? It had been so long since he'd heard the close-up jangle of a telephone, he assumed it must be emanating from somewhere else. *Answer the damn thing!* he wanted to shout to his annoying neighbor, the one who played his television so loud every night until two in the morning. But no, he now realized. The offending telephone was right here, beside the bed.

"All right, all right," he said as he reached for the phone. "Hello?"

"Mr. Shriver?" came a chirpy, singsong voice.

"Yes?" he croaked through dry lips.

"Hi. This is Teresa Apple."

"Yes?"

"You're speaking to my class this morning?"

"Yes?"

"I'm here to pick you up."

"Uh-huh."

"I'm down in the lobby."

As his eyes grew accustomed to the dark, he could make out the old television set and the painting of a windmill on the wall.

"Oh! Of course! I'll be right down!"

He jumped to his feet, hobbled to the bathroom, and turned on the light. The sudden brightness scalded his eye-balls. He grabbed his skull and, forgetting about his bruised backside, sat down hard on the commode.

"Ow!" he cried, his headache momentarily gone.

The whiskey-tinged taste of bile floated up into his throat and it all came back to him. As if watching a Channel 17 Action News summary, he saw a briskly edited montage of yesterday's events, from his ride to the airport—it seemed so long ago—to last night's debauchery on the hotel lawn.

Then he recalled a vivid dream in which he'd been awakened by the sound of snoring only to find Gonquin Smithee passed out in the bed beside him. He remembered touching her shoulder, but she did not wake up. He shook her, to no avail. Her face, so hard and defended when awake, seemed to him soft and open, and so he'd decided to let her be. The dream was so real it seemed more like a memory to him.

Gasping, he ran out and checked the bed, but Gonquin Smithee was not there. Thank goodness—it *was* a dream.

A dull throbbing returned to the space behind his eyes. More than anything in the world he wanted to take a long bath, but he had no time. He splashed some water on his stubbly face and under his arms. He brushed his teeth. He took a moment to lather up his left hand with soap and attempted to pull off his wedding ring. He felt some give, but he was unable to force the gold band past his knuckle. For the first time in years, he wondered what his ex-wife had done with *her* ring. Had she pawned it? Thrown it away? Was it sitting in a dark drawer somewhere?

He unzipped his bag and dug around for some fresh socks and underwear. He threw on a clean shirt and trousers and checked his jacket, which was draped over the curtain rod, still damp from last night's Keystone Kops routine. He would have to go without.

He went out into the hall, and only after the door had slammed shut behind him did he remember that the key was still in his jacket. He tried the knob. Locked. Now he would have to go through some big rigmarole with one of those beehived clerk twins. He hoped this was not an omen.

A horde of uniformed cheerleaders had gathered at the elevator. They seemed so small and young now, fresh as the proverbial daisies, all corn-fed innocence. He thought of the half-nude vixens of the night before and wondered if these could possibly be the same creatures. And here was the willowy brunette, looking like a Sunday school student but for the gum she chewed extravagantly as they entered the elevator. Shriver squeezed in beside her and as the elevator descended the girl smiled and blew a bubble that covered half her face. The doors opened, and the cheerleaders poured out into the lobby, erupting into their usual squeals and giggles as they scurried toward the saloon for their eggs and cornflakes.

Coming around the corner into the lobby, Shriver noticed Ms. Labio at the front desk. She looked even more agitated than usual as she spoke shrilly to one of the twins behind the counter. Staying out of her line of sight, he tiptoed past the desk toward the door.

"Shriver!"

T. Wätzczesnam sat on his usual stool in the saloon, his hat beside him on the bar, drinking what appeared to be a tall glass of milk. The cowboy waved him over.

"I believe I may have discovered the fountain of youth last night!"

"Please, T.," Shriver said, mentally blotting out visions he did not want to have.

"Ever hear of the 'low-hitch stunt,' Shriver?"

"Can't say that I have."

"How about the 'Swedish fall'?"

"Nope."

Shriver noticed a young woman waiting near the door. Tall, curvy, with straight reddish hair, she seemed tense as she glanced at her wristwatch.

"Excuse me, T.," he said.

The cowboy lifted the glass of milk in a toast, his hand visibly trembling.

" 'Youth, large, lusty, loving—' " he chanted. " 'Youth, full of grace, force, fascination.' "

Shriver started toward the door.

"There's a whole uncharted world out there, Shriver," the cowboy called after him. "These gals today are capable of almost anything!"

As Shriver made his way toward the door, Ms. Labio waved him over to the front desk.

"Is something wrong?" Shriver asked, noticing the sculptress's pink eyes and puffy face.

"Fucking A, something's wrong. Gonquin is missing."

"Missing?"

"Mr. Shriver!"

The redhead rushed to meet him with an outstretched hand. She wore tight, faded jeans and a clingy red blouse that showed off her pert bosom. Though perched upon preposterously high heels, she seemed perfectly balanced as she jogged across the lobby.

"Teresa Apple," she said.

"Hello," Shriver said, shaking her hand. Her face was lightly freckled, her eyes a piercing blue.

"What am I going to do?" Ms. Labio cried. "I don't know where she is!"

"What's the matter?" Teresa Apple asked.

"Ms. Smithee is missing," Shriver said.

"*Missing?*"

"That's what *I* said."

"Maybe we should call the police," the clerk suggested.

"The police?" Ms. Labio screeched.

"What's the ruckus?"

T. Wätzczesnam approached the desk, the tall glass of milk sloshing in his shaky hand.

"Gonquin Smithee is missing," Ms. Apple told him.

"*Missing?*"

"She never came back to our room!" Ms. Labio bellowed.

"How strange," Wätzczesnam said. "Well, let's see. Wasn't she in your room last night, Shriver?"

"*Shriver's* room?" Ms. Labio said.

"Yes," Shriver said, then quickly added, "Along with everybody else."

He tried to recall the poet leaving his room but remembered only his dream about her passing out in his bed.

"I didn't notice when she left," he told them. "But I'm sure there's some explanation."

"What do you mean," the sculptress asked, "you didn't notice when she left?"

"There was a lot of chaos last night," Shriver explained. "People in and out."

"You were all *drunk!*"

"Ms. Labio," the cowboy said, "I resent the implication."

"I'm sorry," Ms. Apple interrupted. "But we have a class to get to." She turned to Ms. Labio and added, "I'm sure Gonquin will turn up."

"Where could she be?"

"Maybe she went for a walk," Wätzczesnam offered.

"A walk? Where to? There's nothing here!"

"I think we should call the police," the clerk again recommended.

"Mr. Shriver," Ms. Apple said, taking him rather firmly by the elbow, "we're going to be late."

Shriver looked back as they made their way through the lobby. Ms. Labio and the cowboy continued conferring with the clerk, the sculptress's arms wheeling about in distress.

"I wonder what happened to her," Shriver said as he followed Teresa Apple into the parking lot.

"She probably met someone nicer than her current companion. Here's my truck."

She led him to a worn-out pickup, faded red in the spots not covered by rust.

"I apologize for my tardiness," Shriver said as he climbed up into the cabin. "I overslept."

"You had a long day yesterday," Ms. Apple courteously replied. She proceeded to stomp on the gas pedal, and the truck shot out of the hotel parking lot.

The vast sky shone bright and cloudless, and as Teresa Apple steered the rumbling pickup toward campus, there came a refreshing breeze through Shriver's open window. The throbbing blood vessels in his head had quieted down.

"Did you sleep well?" Ms. Apple asked.

"Like a baby."

"The helicopter didn't wake you up?"

"Helicopter?"

"They sprayed early this morning. Some sort of synthetic pyrethroids."

"Pyre-what?"

"Insecticide. It works pretty well, but the mosquitoes will be back at dusk. Trust me."

"Oh dear."

"*Aedes vexans.* The bane of our existence. They migrate up to twenty miles for a blood meal."

Shriver scratched at the raw lump on his hand. "Sounds gruesome."

"I hate the little fuckers," Ms. Apple said as she accelerated to beat a yellow traffic light. "You're younger than I expected," she said after a moment.

"Really?" It hadn't occurred to Shriver that the real Shriver might be older.

"Your novel strikes me as having been written by a cranky old man."

"I hope you're not too let down."

"On the contrary," she said with an enigmatic smile. She made a sharp right turn into a parking lot behind one of the university buildings and screeched to a halt. "Here we are."

Feeling dizzy from the ride, Shriver gingerly set foot on the ground.

"This is Custer Hall," Teresa Apple said, swiftly leading him to a back entrance. He followed her up a flight of stairs and down a long hallway. Students scurried past on their way

to class, their faces screwed up into serious academic expressions. Oh dear, Shriver thought. This class would be the big-
gest test yet of his ability to fool people into thinking he
was the real Shriver—but it was just a warm-up for the panel
discussion to come.

As Teresa was about to enter the classroom, Shriver grabbed
her elbow and pulled her aside.

"I want to ask you," he said, feeling the now-familiar flutter
of the black crow in his rib cage, "in all seriousness: what do
these students expect of me?"

She patted him on the arm. "You're nervous, aren't you?
That's sweet. But they've all read your book. Some of it, anyway. They think you're a genius. You could fart in there and
they'd worship you. Okay?"

"Okay," Shriver said. "I guess."

As she turned on her considerable heel and sashayed into
the classroom, Shriver again scolded himself for accepting the
conference invitation. He wished he'd been discovered right
away as an imposter and sent back to his comfortable home.
But then he remembered Simone. He recalled shards of another dream he'd had last night, in which she had figured
prominently. She'd been wearing a cheerleading outfit and
was bouncing on an unseen trampoline outside his sixth-floor
apartment window. Each time she arced up into view she per-
formed a different acrobatic maneuver, bright red pom-poms
in her hands, and asked, "Are you a writer?"

Shriver took a deep breath, swallowed yet another upsurge
of bile, and entered the classroom.

Inside, a dozen or so students sat at their desks and gazed
up at him as though he were about to hand out one-hundred-
dollar bills. The windows had been thrown open, letting in
fresh air and the musical chirping of birds. Shriver stood

abashedly to the side while Ms. Apple introduced him. She utilized a range of superlatives to describe Shriver's talent, creating a weird, almost disembodied experience for him, since after all she was not actually speaking of *him*, even as she and the students thought she was.

"I encourage you to ask Mr. Shriver anything at all," she continued, "but since this is a creative writing class, you may want to know about how he works—his process, his writing habits. Anyone want to dive in? Or," she said, turning to the guest of honor, "do you have anything you'd like to say first?"

Shriver's mouth, already parched, became a veritable desert.

"Well," he squawked, his dry lips clicking, "as you probably know, I haven't been writing so much lately."

"Twenty years," Teresa Apple helpfully reminded him.

"Yes. So, I'm a little bit out of the loop when it comes to technique and that sort of thing." He was hoping this would excuse him from having to answer any technical questions about writing.

"You haven't written anything *at all*?" a young man asked from the front row. "Not a word?"

"No, I have written a little," Shriver said, thinking of his story.

"When are we going to see it published?" someone asked.

"I have no idea."

"What's it about?"

"It's hard to describe."

"Are you going to read it tomorrow?"

Shriver leaned back against the front edge of the teacher's desk. "I hope to."

The students murmured excitedly.

A hand shot up. "Why is your book so misogynistic?" a pigtailed young lady asked. The rest of the class sniggered.

As Shriver tried to come up with an adequate response, another student—a young man sitting far in the back—said, "I don't think it *is* misogynistic. I think he's just telling it like it is, ya know?"

"But it *is* misogynistic," the young lady said. She opened a copy of *Goat Time* and, in a clear voice, read aloud: " 'He stroked his cock furiously, remembering the night he'd spent with the dark-haired waitress from the saloon—the way she had writhed atop him, her knees up, both feet flat on the motel room floor, her green eyes rolling backward, her breath catching in her throat, her small breasts flopping in counterpoint to the rest of her body . . .' "

Shriver's face turned red. "I wrote that?"

"I think it's kind of erotic," another girl said.

"It's just *dirty*," the pigtailed girl countered.

Shriver found himself agreeing with her.

"What's wrong with 'dirty'?" Ms. Apple asked. "Is there room for dirtiness in literature? Are our lives so clean? Do we have to limit ourselves as artists to those clean moments, those corners of our lives that are not shadowed, or *dirty*?"

Shriver thought she might have a point.

"Not if we're going to be honest," the boy in the back offered.

"I don't know," the young lady said, feeling outnumbered. "It just seems excessive to me."

True, Shriver thought. That bit about the flopping breasts was over the top.

"*Life* is excessive!" a chubby young man in a tight T-shirt shouted. "We have a responsibility to show that."

"You *would* say that, Cornelius," the pigtailed girl shot back. "All you write about is fellatio."

The other students chuckled in recognition.

"Yeah, well, fellatio can be important."

Cheers from the others.

"Okay, you guys," Ms. Apple interrupted. "Let's get serious."

"I *am* serious," Cornelius said.

Another hand went up. A pale young man with a wispy mustache asked Shriver where he'd gotten the idea for his novel.

He had rehearsed this one. "I don't remember."

"Why is the novel partly written in the second person?" someone asked.

"Second person?"

"Are you indicting the reader?"

"Uh, I'm not sure."

"What about your new story?" the pale student asked. "How'd you come up with *that*?"

"Well," Shriver began, thinking back to last week, "I was lying on my bed, and there was a water mark on the ceiling, so I thought I'd write about that."

The students hummed.

"Fascinating," Teresa Apple said. She turned to the class. "You see how art can be inspired by the mundane, the little details that are right under our noses?"

"And we all know what's under *Cornelius's* nose," the pigtailed girl said.

An alarmingly thin girl raised her hand. "Why did you name your protagonist after yourself?"

"I did?"

A few students laughed.

"Was it because the story is so autobiographical?"

"I suppose I couldn't think of any other name," Shriver said.

"And why'd you give the other characters such funny names?"

"What happened to his wife?" the thin girl asked. "How can someone just up and disappear like that?"

"Did she really disappear?" Shriver asked, curious now.

"Hm," Ms. Apple said. "Interesting question."

"He killed her, didn't he?" someone asked.

"More misogyny," the pigtailed girl said.

Shriver, feeling a blood vessel vibrating in his head, was relieved when the boy in the back row responded. "Why do you have to have all the answers? Why can't a novel be ambiguous?"

"Yeah," Cornelius said. "Sometimes you're not *supposed* to know."

"But what's the point of that?"

"*Life* is ambiguous!"

The discussion continued in this vein, with Shriver happily unable to get a word in edgewise. He leaned against the desk with a tightly constructed smile on his face, and as the students debated the merits of ambiguity, metaphor, and post-structuralism, he thought: I have no idea what these young people are talking about. When he'd written his story about the water mark he had simply come up with the words that described what had happened to him. His wife had left him. It was raining outside. He lay on the bed. The water mark grew and grew. Then he had gone a little further because what had really happened beyond that point was not so interesting to him anymore, and probably not interesting to anyone else either. He had to make things up. Then he had to come up with a proper ending. He needed to feel like this had all led to something. He did not once think about deconstructionism, or whatever it was called. He didn't even know what it meant.

He had never heard of those French people who apparently invented it.

Before he knew what had happened, Ms. Apple interrupted to announce that the class was over. The students applauded and lined up to have him sign copies of his book.

First in line was the pigtailed girl, whose name, she informed him, was Cassandra.

"Sorry I gave you a hard time," she said. "The truth is, the book is totally hot."

Inserted at the title page was a card with her name and a telephone number.

"Oh, you can keep that," she said. Her face, with its healthy complexion and youthful shine, betrayed no indication of her motives.

He wrote, *To Cassandra, My book may be dirty, but I, alas, am not. I predict you will be a fine writer someday. Best . . .*

He then placed the card back in the book and handed it to her. She shrugged good-naturedly and, still smiling, walked out of the classroom.

As he signed the others' books, using the same signature he penned on his checks to the electric company, he wondered what the real Shriver's autograph was like. Was it florid, or jagged? Did the letters lean forward, or backward, or rise straight up and down? Was he left-handed? Was he clever with inscriptions, or did he make do with "Best wishes"?

Last in line was the student from the back row. He plopped a well-worn copy of *Goat Time* onto the desk and told Shriver, "Please make it out to Vlad."

"Vlad?"

"As in Vladimir."

"That's an exotic name."

"I think my father was really into *Pale Fire*."

The student stared at Shriver as if he expected a reaction.

"*You* know," he continued, "the one where the narrator pretends to be someone he isn't?"

Little pearls of sweat formed on Shriver's brow. "Yes, of course," he mumbled as he quickly signed the young man's book.

Vlad stared down at Shriver. "You don't remember me, do you?"

Shriver looked up at the long, pale face, shadowed by budding black whiskers, the eyes small and almost as dark as his clothing. He *did* look familiar.

"Have we met?" Shriver asked.

Vlad's face drooped in disappointment, and then he loped out of the room. Only then did Shriver recall where he had seen the young man before: he was the waiter at the restaurant last night.

"Well, that was really great," Teresa Apple said. "They loved you."

"I'm not sure I helped them at all," Shriver said absentmindedly. He kept thinking of that boy, Vlad, and his comment about the narrator who pretends he's someone he isn't.

"Sometimes it helps," Teresa said, "just to know that books are written by real flesh-and-blood people."

"Yes, I suppose you're right."

He followed her down the stairs to the front door of the building. "I could use a drink," she said.

"A drink?" It sounded good to Shriver. Vlad had unnerved him, and the panel discussion loomed like an impending rock slide. But then he needed to keep his wits about him, if only to convince Simone that he was not a complete lush. "I'm afraid I can't," he said finally.

"That's cool," Teresa said as they descended the steps to the sidewalk. "We could just screw instead."

Shriver stopped. Ms. Apple turned and looked up at him from the step below.

"You don't have the panel for another hour," she said. "We could run over to my place. It's nearby. Or—even better—we could go to my office. It's right over there." She nodded toward the school building next door.

Shriver thought of last year's randy author, plowing his way through the faculty.

"I'm very flattered."

"Time's a-wastin'."

She was a pretty woman, he thought, with her flame-colored hair and fleshy lips. But then he thought of Simone—the freckles on her chest, her tiny hands.

"I'm sorry," he said. "I couldn't."

"You got a sweetie?"

"You might say that."

She shrugged. "Okay. I'll walk you over to the Union, if you'd like. You can rest up before the big panel."

She said this as if he had just turned down an offer of iced tea. She walked so quickly along the path between school buildings that he had to double-step to keep up.

"I've never been on a panel before," he said.

"You'll do fine," she assured him. "Just act like you know what you're talking about."

"I suppose so much of life is just that."

He smacked at a mosquito on his hand.

"The first of many," Teresa Apple said.

Chapter Seven

In the ballroom, seven hundred–plus people had gathered for
the panel, creating an aural wash of literary chatter.

"They're all here to see *you*," Ms. Apple told him.

"Please don't say that."

"Shriver!"

T. Wätzczesnam, having changed into a denim suit jacket
over a denim shirt, sauntered over with an ungainly number
of books stacked under his arm.

"Hello again, Teresa," he purred to the graduate student.
"What's shakin'?"

Ms. Apple smirked. "Your hands, Professor."

Sure enough, T.'s hands still shook like a pair of old leather
gloves in a light breeze.

"It's been a pleasure," Teresa said to Shriver, and moved
off to join some friends.

"That gal is a tigress," the cowboy said as he watched her
retreat.

Shriver looked down at his own jittery hands.

T. laughed. "Got snakes in your boots too?"

"I'm just a little nervous."

"Sure you are." Wätzczesnam winked, then patted his
denim jacket pocket and said, "No worries. I got some hair
of the ol' dog right here."

"I'm not sure I—"

"FYI," T. said, "our favorite Sapphic poetess remains MIA."

"Still?"

"I believe the authorities have been alerted."

"Oh my."

"What happened last night, anyway?" the professor asked, one eyebrow askew.

"What do you mean?"

"I seem to recall the young woman lying on your bed when I left your room."

"She was?"

The cowboy shrugged. "I was hoping you'd regale me with the details of her conversion."

"Sorry to let you down."

"You are under no obligation to reveal anything, Shriver. Not to me, anyway. But listen, we should probably head on up to the dais and settle ourselves in."

"They're going ahead with the panel?" Shriver asked. "With Gonquin missing?"

"The show must go on!" T. declared. "Our friend Zebra has agreed to step in."

Shriver followed him toward the front of the room. En route he caught sight of Simone speaking to a very short man in a bright red suit jacket. In a sleeveless blouse and khaki capri pants, she looked as young and fresh as she had the first time he saw her.

Shriver took the seat on T.'s left on the dais. To their right sat Zebra Amphetamine and Basil Rather, gazing down upon the audience like a king and queen. In front of each author was a thin, snakelike microphone. Shriver's mouth had gone dry again, so he drank from the water cup provided. He coughed loudly as the liquid burned his throat. The cup had been filled with whiskey.

The cowboy placed a hand over his microphone and whispered, "I know you're accustomed to the good stuff, Shriver, but I'm living on a professor's salary."

Shriver had intended not to drink today, but he had to admit the stuff hit the spot. He took another, more modest, sip and felt his hands begin to steady. Also on the table in front of him were a blank sheet of paper and a pen, placed there, apparently, by Professor Wätzczesnam, or perhaps by Simone, to help him organize his thoughts.

"Good afternoon," T. announced into the microphone with a voice noticeably smoother than his usual growl. The crowd, previously abuzz, immediately became reverent. "Welcome to today's illustrious panel discussion, about which we are all understandably excited.

"I think our technical difficulties have been ironed out," he continued, casting a glance toward Simone, who crossed her fingers. "Our apologies once again to Basil Rather, whose reading last night was magnificent, even if 'loud roar'd the dreadful thunder.' But anyway, we're now ready to discuss literature, hopefully without all the sound and fury."

He proceeded to briefly introduce Basil Rather and Zebra Amphetamine. Then, glancing over at Shriver, he said, "And the gentleman to my left would need no introduction if only his face were more familiar. But after twenty years we may be forgiven if we do not recognize by sight one of the brightest lights of modern American letters. He is the author of but one novel, but I'd wager that if you asked any major writer sworn to honesty which one book they wished they'd written, it would be *Goat Time*. I could go on and on about this classic tome but will instead limit myself to a brief quote from the revered literary critic Duke Manleyson, who wrote of Mr. Shriver's debut, 'This is the sort of challenging, rude, hilarious, and original novel that any serious author would kill to have penned. I predict that, twenty or thirty years from now, it will still be read and discussed and argued about by anyone bright enough to recognize its importance as a cultural arti-fact. Were its young author to disappear from the face of the earth tomorrow, he would remain a treasured contributor to the starving world of literature.'"

The audience applauded as Shriver drained what remained of his whiskey. Off to the side, he saw Simone clapping. Near her sat Jack Blunt, still busy scribbling away on his dreadful notepad. Beside the door, like a sentry, stood the short man in the red suit coat, his arms folded, scanning the audience.

"Today's theme is reality-slash-illusion," the cowboy an-nounced. "So, to get the ball rolling up here, I guess I'd ask the panel to react to the idea that what we write—the words on the page, whether as intended or as interpreted by the reader—is an illusion. *Or*, is it reality, whether that means actual reality or a constructed reality that is no less real for being constructed in the imagination? Who wants to start?"

Silence.

Shriver kicked himself for not writing down whatever it was that Professor Wätzczesnam had just said. He glanced over at the other panelists, both of whom appeared to be deep in thought. He took up his pen and drew a dark blue question mark, nearly pushing the pen point through the paper. Fi-nally, Basil Rather inhaled theatrically and leaned toward his microphone.

"What I think is this: is not reality an illusion, anyway?" The playwright paused to let this question reverberate. "I think the topic as written on the schedule—'reality-*slash*-illusion'—is wholly appropriate. That slash implies something synonymnal, does it not? Or at least it invites us to take the two terms as able to coexist with one another under the same roof. After all, if I also wrote fiction, like my esteemed colleagues, I would be a 'novelist-*slash*-playwright.' No one would have an argument with that. 'Novelist-*slash*-playwright.' 'Obstetrician-*slash*-gynecologist.' 'AC-*slash*-DC.' 'Reality-*slash*-illusion.' See what I mean?"

"An interesting point," T. said.

Shriver drew thick circles around the question mark.

"Personally, I don't go in for this 'reality is an illusion' bullshit," Zebra Amphetamine declared. "That's a coward's way out. You can always say this moment—this very moment in time, in this place, with these people in this room—is an illusion, because, hey, it's gone now, man. There it went. It's not real anymore, is it? It's now just a memory. And memories, like writers, are notorious liars. So there you have it," she said, leaning back in her seat for emphasis.

Shriver, his head bowed as he drew a horse rearing up on hind legs—the only thing he knew how to draw, having practiced it as a child, based on a sketch he'd seen on a matchbook—heard murmurs of thoughtful admiration from the audience. Though he could sense everyone looking at him, waiting for him to weigh in on this challenging topic, he continued to scribble on the paper: *Dear Ms. LeGros*, he wrote, *Help me!*

"Mr. Shriver?" T. said. "I see you writing down your thoughts there."

Wätzczesnam was poking fun—surely he could see that Shriver had mostly drawn senseless doodles.

"Perhaps," the moderator continued, "you could relate this question to the idea of autobiographical fiction. Many have wondered how closely your work hews to your own life."

Looking out at the undulating sea of faces, Shriver experienced a vertiginous sense of dislocation, as if he had just been dropped into his seat via parachute, having fallen mistakenly from an airplane headed somewhere completely different. He cleared his throat, with no clue as to what he was about to say. Then, while continuing to doodle, he spoke.

"Last night," he said, "from my hotel room, I saw a group of cheerleaders form a human pyramid two stories tall."

The cowboy let out a little cough and squirmed in his seat.

"At the top of this pyramid stood a young girl," Shriver continued, "I'd say about sixteen years old, in an aqua-blue one-piece bathing suit. A lithe brunette, with blue eyes and muscular arms, at once an innocent virgin and a jaded, experienced adult. From my window on the second floor, I could have reached out and touched her face."

Shriver glanced over at Simone, who sat on the edge of her seat. Behind her, Jack Blunt had raised his face from his notepad, waiting for the next word.

"Beyond this lovely young girl, I would not have been able to make out where the prairie met the night sky but for an invisible line where the black earth ended and millions of stars began. Meanwhile, beating against the window screen were a hundred mosquitoes, drawn by the light in my room, or perhaps the smell of blood."

He lifted the cup to his lips. He'd forgotten there was no more whiskey, but he pretended to drink anyway. The room had grown quiet.

"And as all this was happening, a long, slow freight train rolled by, its wheels making that clacking sound that is so reassuring, right in time as it is with our heartbeat."

He saw Simone raise her hand to her heart.

He waited a moment, not sure where to go with all this. The cheerleader, the train, the sky—what did any of this have to do with reality or illusion? He heard someone cough. T. Wätzczesnam squirmed in his seat. Simone looked concerned, as if Shriver might have suffered a stroke. Everyone was waiting. So he leaned closer to the microphone and said, "Or maybe I made it all up," then shrugged in an exaggerated fashion, his hands upturned, his shoulders rising to his ears. He sat back in his chair and resumed doodling.

There was laughter, then some scattered appreciative murmuring.

"Wonderful," T. said, and Shriver was relieved to see Simone smiling.

As the panel discussion continued, Basil Rather spoke of Plato, Homer, Euripides, and Samuel Beckett. Zebra Amphetamine noted the influences of Catullus, Octavia Butler, and the women of the ancient court of Japan. And Shriver covered his paper, front and back, with drawings of horses and question marks. When asked by T. about what writers had influenced his style, he could only come up with "the people who write television programs, especially the news," which elicited smiles and acknowledgment of his eccentric and playful profundity. Later, an audience member asked why he had not written in twenty years. He answered, "It hadn't occurred to me," knowing he could have passed a polygraph exam.

After Professor Wätzczesnam concluded the panel discussion with a quote ("True ease in writing comes from art, not chance, / As those move easiest who have learn'd to dance"), and the audience applauded affectionately, the cowboy turned to Shriver and said, "You're very good at this sort of thing, you sly bastard." As a show of solidarity, the four authors shook hands while still onstage, though Basil Rather, perhaps because of last night's drama, seemed distant, his thin lips white as he pressed them hard together.

"I *also* love TV!" Zebra Amphetamine shouted as she pumped Shriver's hand. "McLuhan said it's a *cool* medium, but I find it *red hot*, don't you?"

"I don't really know."

Simone, he could see, stood talking with T., who was touching her arm in a familiar manner.

"I mean, what is there to fill in?" Ms. Amphetamine asked. "TV fills you up to bursting. I love it!"

She turned and walked away, her earrings swinging with each long stride. Shriver was about to approach Simone when Jack Blunt appeared in front of him.

"You crafty old bugger," the reporter said with a chuckle. "You're putting on quite a performance, aren't you?"

"What do you mean?"

"That whole bit about the cheerleaders, the television shows. You're making yourself out to be some sort of primitive type. Is this a kind of performance piece you're working here? Are you testing people—maybe gathering data for that next big novel we've all been waiting for?"

"I don't know what you're talking about."

"I'll get it out of you yet, Shriver," Blunt promised. "I've got some calls in to New York, your old agent, all the usual suspects—someone's going to crack under the pressure."

He began to walk away, his pen held aloft like a baton, then stopped and turned back.

"Almost forgot." From under his arm he pulled a rolled-up newspaper. "Take a look," he said, unrolling the paper. There, a headline: FAMOUS AUTHOR REAPPEARS, and underneath, in a small but crystal-clear black-and-white photograph, sat Shriver in the booth at the Bloody Duck Saloon. "I think it's a rather nice shot of you," Blunt said. "Very flattering." He cackled and headed off.

Well, that's it, Shriver thought. I'm done for.

Simone appeared at his side, having extricated herself from the cowboy.

"Nicely done," she said, placing a hand on his arm.

"Excuse me?" Her hand—it was so warm.

"The panel," she said.

"Oh, yes. I had absolutely no idea what I was talking about."

She squeezed his forearm and said, "Oh, no. It was great. Everyone's buzzing."

Shriver followed her into the lobby, where he felt everyone's eyes on him. He waited for someone to shout, "Imposter!" Now that his face was in the papers, he needed to confess to Simone right away.

"I was hoping we could have lunch," he told her.

"Oh gosh, I'd like that, I really would, but there's this problem with Gonquin, and . . ."

"Still no word?"

"Nothing. Her friend is going ballistic, the police are talking to people. It's crazy."

"Do they suspect foul play?"

Simone shrugged. "They're going to want to talk to you too."

"To me?"

"I guess you were the last person to see her."

"I was?"

"I'm sorry, I have to go. Edsel will take care of you."

Then she was gone.

Several people approached and asked Shriver to sign copies of *Goat Time*.

"You're a breath of fresh air, sir," one elderly gentleman declared. "I've been coming to this conference for many years, and you hear a lot of hooey at these panels." He cocked his gray head toward Basil Rather nearby. "But you were a real person up there. Thank you."

Two older women appeared.

"Is Jesus Christ your Lord and Savior?" one of them asked.

The other woman frowned and said, "Leave him alone with that stuff, Jillian." She handed Shriver a copy of *Goat Time*. "Please make it out to Jillian and Lillian."

The two women appeared remarkably similar: pale eyes, button noses, even their silver hair was cut in the same style.

Jillian said, "I can see that you're lonely. I used to be lonely before I found Jesus."

Shriver kept his head down and wrote, *To Jillian & Lillian.*

"Jesus fills up your life. Yes, sir. Fills you up more than whiskey. Fills you up more than women. Fills you up more than writing or reading or—"

"Jillian!" the other woman said. "Let the man be."

Shriver wanted to write something clever but was stuck.

Jillian leaned uncomfortably close and whispered, "I know who you are."

"You do?"

"Jillian, I'm warning you," Lillian said.

Feeling suddenly sweaty, Shriver looked at Jillian's face, just inches from his own, and wondered how she could possibly know who he was. Had they met? Surely he would remember her. She was an attractive woman, about sixty, her teeth straight and white, her eyes wide and lively.

"Who am I?" Shriver asked, not at all certain he wanted to know.

"Just a man," she answered. Then she stood up straight and said, "But with the Lord Jesus as your Savior, you could be much, much more!"

Relieved, Shriver wrote, *From just a man*, then signed his name.

"Thank you," Lillian said, taking the book. She grabbed Jillian by her elbow and pulled her away.

"Good luck!" Jillian called over her shoulder. "You'll need it without Jesus!"

Shriver waved as Lillian dragged her off. Perhaps Jillian was right—perhaps he should pray to get out of this mess he'd gotten himself into. As he considered this option, the man in the bright red suit coat quickly approached. He had no book to be signed.

"Mr. Shriver, is it?" Extremely short, he had a trim, wide-shouldered physique, like a teen gymnast. His dark eyes, set far apart, blazed beneath a full head of brown hair so neatly combed that a line of pale skin showed at the part. "Detective Krampus," he said, displaying a shiny badge inside a leather wallet. He then pulled a pencil and a small notebook from his jacket pocket. "I'd like to ask you a few questions about Gonquin Smithee."

"She still hasn't turned up?"

"I understand you were with her late last night."

"Well, there was a whole group of us."

"Where was this?"

"In my hotel room."

"Room number nineteen?"

"That's right," Shriver answered, a little unnerved.

"Who was present?"

"Uh, let's see. It was very late, and everyone had been drinking . . . There was Professor Wätzczesnam . . ."

"Yes," the detective said, scribbling loudly in his notebook.

"Ms. Amphetamine . . ."

"Yes."

"Edsel Nixon, a graduate student . . ."

"Yes."

"Ms. Malarkey-Jones . . ."

"The ample woman?" Krampus asked, displaying a copy of *Harem Girl.*

"Correct. And the folksinger from the café."

"Christo?"

"You seem to know all this, Detective."

"Anyone else in your room last night?"

"And Ms. Smithee, of course."

"That's all?"

"I think so."

"You think so, or you *know* so?"

"I know so."

Shriver then recounted for him the events of the night before.

"And you didn't notice Ms. Smithee's departure?"

"I don't know when she left."

"Did you spend the night together, Mr. Shriver?"

"Are you asking if I slept with Ms. Smithee?"

Krampus raised one thin eyebrow.

"The answer is no," Shriver said.

The detective wrote furiously in his little book.

"If you knew anything about the poor woman," Shriver continued, "you wouldn't need to ask such a question."

"Why do you say 'poor' woman?" Krampus asked.

"I don't know. Obviously she's in some sort of bad situation. You don't just up and leave in the middle of a conference."

"Hm." More scribbling in the notebook. "Any ideas about what happened to her?"

"None whatsoever."

"Did you notice any friction between her and anyone else?"

"Well, she was squabbling with Ms. Labio," Shriver said. He hadn't intended to mention this because, he thought, it might look bad for Ms. Smithee's friend.

"They were fighting?"

"Not *fighting*, I would say."

"A lovers' spat?"

"I suppose so."

"About . . . ?"

"Ms. Labio objected to Ms. Smithee's drinking."

"Was she imbibing a *lot*?"

"She had a few, I'd say."

"Anything else about her behavior last night?"

"Not that I noticed."

"No problems with any of the other authors?"

"I don't think so."

"I was told she took exception to a question you posed to her yesterday."

"Oh. Yes. She didn't like my question, but then last night she told me she'd changed her mind."

"When? While you were together in your hotel room?"

"No. Right here in the lobby. During Mr. Rather's reading."

"You didn't attend Mr. Rather's reading?"

"I left when the sound system started acting up."

"I see."

More scribbling.

"And how did Ms. Smithee get along with Mr. Rather?"

"Okay, I suppose."

"Didn't he accuse her of sabotaging his reading?"

"Not directly."

"Do you think she *did* sabotage the reading?"

"I hadn't considered it. But no, I don't think so. I think it was an accident."

"Did *you* sabotage the reading?"

"Of course not!"

Detective Krampus slid the notebook and pencil into his jacket pocket.

"Thank you, Mr. Shriver. I hope you'll be available for more questioning, if need be."

The little man turned and marched off. Shriver felt a mounting sense of anxiety as he watched the bright red suit coat disappear around a corner. Still, he supposed it was preferable that everyone obsess on Ms. Smithee's disappearance rather than on the scandalous impersonation taking place right under their noses.

"Is that police detective a midget?" Edsel asked.

"Excuse me?"

"Or a dwarf? What's the difference, anyway?"

While his handler attempted to distinguish for himself the difference between a dwarf and a midget—"Which one has the short arms and legs?"—Shriver noticed in his peripheral vision a dark figure over by the exit. His immediate assumption, from years of habit, was that Mr. Bojangles had entered the room. He turned and was about to call out the cat's name when he remembered where he was. There was no Mr. Bojangles, of course, nor any black figure at all. The exit door was empty. He felt a pang of sadness and wondered how the little kitty cat was holding up all alone.

"Do you think there was foul play?" Nixon asked.

"Like what?"

The graduate student shrugged. "I dunno. Murder?"

Since there was some time to kill before Zebra Amphetamine's reading, Edsel Nixon offered to drive Shriver around town, to show him "the few sights worth seeing in our little burg." Shriver accepted, intending to have the young man stop at a liquor store along the way.

They rode beneath a sleek blue dome of sky. The temperature had risen into the eighties. Students traversed the campus in thin T-shirts and short pants, sunglasses hiding their eyes.

Edsel Nixon pointed out the college football stadium and hockey arena. In between these two enormous structures stretched a practice field where hundreds of ponytailed girls in colorful uniforms ran, leaped, and shouted on the grass. As the jeep sputtered past, Shriver watched a pyramid of cheerleaders rise, and at the top stood the brunette girl from the hotel, waving.

Nixon abruptly turned right, just past a frozen custard stand shaped like a giant ice cream cone. Two-story brick buildings lined the town's Main Street, clothing stores and Laundromats and insurance offices topped by apartments with large, old-fashioned windows.

"This is downtown," Nixon said. "That's where we had dinner last night." He pointed out Slander's Restaurant. "Oh my God."

Emerging from the Church of Pornocology was T. Wätzczesnam, his enormous cowboy hat tilted downward to shield his eyes. The cowboy glanced up just as the jeep came up alongside him, as if he had recognized its distinctive rattle.

"What luck!" he hollered. "Where are you boys headed?"

Edsel Nixon braked at the curb. "I'm just showing Mr. Shriver around town."

"Great!" The cowboy, with surprising dexterity, bounded into the backseat. "I suppose you're wondering what I was doing in that den of questionable repute."

"It's none of my business," Nixon said as he steered into the slow flow of traffic.

" 'I am sure no other civilization, not even the Romans,' " the professor quoted in a stentorian manner, " 'has showed such a vast proportion of ignominious and degraded nudity, and ugly, squalid dirty sex. Because,' Nixon, 'no other civilization has driven sex into the underworld, and nudity to the WC.' "

"Is that a quote, sir, or is that your own opinion?"

"Both, my ignorant friend. Both."

"Was it Hugh Hefner?"

"Mr. David Herbert Lawrence, you imbecile!"

"Sorry, sir. And how *was* your visit to the underworld?"

"Illuminating."

"Pull over here, will you?" Shriver said.

"Ah, Shriver"—the cowboy smiled—"you are a mind reader."

In Big Chief's Liquorarium, Shriver and Wätzczesnam picked out a pint of whiskey each. At the counter, Shriver realized he'd left his wallet in his damp suit coat *and* his per diem money at the hotel.

"Mr. Nixon, can I trouble you for a loan of a few dollars? I seem to have misplaced my wallet."

"Of course."

Edsel dug into his pocket and pulled out some crumpled bills. Big Chief grunted thanks and slid the bottle into a brown paper bag.

Half an hour later, the three men sat on the gently sloping banks of the aptly named Black River, watching the murky water rush by. Nearby stood a cluster of trees, their narrow trunks marked by past floods. Shriver and T. took occasional swigs from their bottles while Nixon drank from a can of warm root beer.

"I've always thought it was strange that the river flowed north," Nixon said as a tree limb floated by.

"So, Shriver," Wätzczesnam said, ignoring his student, "have you been interrogated by our diminutive friend in red?"

"I have."

"Your observations?"

"He strikes me as determined."

"Is he a midget or a dwarf?" Nixon asked.

"I believe he is merely stunted," the cowboy answered. "And for your information, a midget *is* a dwarf, only with more proportional features. But then the term 'midget' is out of favor in these dreary, overly sensitive times."

"How do you know all that?"

"I know all, Mr. Nixon. And do not forget it."

During this exchange, Shriver thought he saw something moving among the nearby trees, a blur of black caught out of the corner of his eye. But when he turned to look, nothing was there. Was he suffering a stroke? Hallucinating? Did he miss Mr. B. so much that he imagined him around every corner?

"Any idea about what happened to our friend Ms. Smithee?" Wätzczesnam asked.

"Maybe she just ran away from Ms. Labio," Shriver said.

"Ah, yes. I wouldn't blame her."

A long-legged mosquito landed on Shriver's hand. He smacked it hard and peeled the corpse from his skin.

"That was a male," the cowboy said.

"A male?"

"Only the *female* mosquito bites."

"How can you tell the difference?"

"The males have those long legs. They feed off plants. It's just the ladies you have to be careful of. Words to live by, eh, Shriver?"

"I suppose you're right, T."

" 'Destructive, damnable, deceitful woman!' "

"Was that Otway, Professor?" Edsel Nixon asked.

"Indeed it was."

"I take it you're not a married man, T.?" Shriver asked, emboldened by the whiskey.

The cowboy pushed the lip of his hat back and sighed. Edsel Nixon picked up a stick and tossed it at the river.

"Don't get me wrong, Shriver, I'd love nothing more than to give it a shot, but I'm afraid it's not in the cards for this decrepit old cowhand."

T. gazed at the black water gliding silently by. Shriver seemed to have strummed a deep chord in the man.

"No," T. said, "I long ago came to the conclusion that to be a writer—a true writer—one must sacrifice such conventional comforts as marriage and family. How can you create whole worlds, living and breathing characters—how can you construct plots that pulse with universal truth—and at the same time maintain any kind of meaningful relationship with another person? Both paths demand everything from you. What self-respecting woman would tolerate a man who is chained to his desk for days on end, concocting an alternate reality in a fevered state that has no room for cuddling or cozy chats over dinner? And what novel or story or poem will forgive a man for setting it aside just to attend a dinner party or a piano recital? No! You'd get pulled apart like saltwater taffy, and then neither the art nor the marriage succeeds. You must pick one or the other, Shriver. But then I needn't tell you that."

"What do you mean?"

"Well, it's pretty well-known that your wife . . . Well, it didn't work out, did it?"

"That's well-known?"

"Come, come, old man. You may have crawled into a cave, but you don't write a novel like that without some attention being paid to your sex life."

So the real Shriver was divorced too, Shriver thought. Not so surprising, really, especially given Wätzczesnam's description of a writer's marriage.

"Then again," T. continued, "from that ring on your finger, I see you may have found someone else. Perhaps that's why you haven't written in so long. Tell us: have you been going to the ballet and Little League games?"

"Not at all," Shriver said, covering his wedding band. "I just haven't—"

"You were the real McCoy, Shriver. Few men have written with such fury and precision. I imagine your pen on fire. What doused the flame, if not a woman?"

Shriver did not know what had doused the real Shriver's flame any more than he knew what had doused his own. He hadn't thought of those days in a long time, and when he did he saw only the water mark above his bed—all other images and memories dissolved.

Again, he noticed a blur of black over near the trees. Perhaps some kind of animal, a beaver or a river rat, had clambered up from the water. He got to his feet and stretched. This sudden alteration in perspective gave him a different angle on the trees, and he was able now to see a figure dressed in black running in the opposite direction.

"Did you see that, Edsel?"

"See what, sir?"

Another mosquito, this one more diminutive, landed on Shriver's hand. He slapped it away.

Chapter Eight

"Shriver!"

Jack Blunt ran up to him in the lobby outside the Union ballroom, his eyes bulging with excitement.

"I just spoke to your Mr. Cheadem!" He was so animated that his peltlike toupee had slipped a bit, exposing the pink skin above his left ear.

"Who?"

"Your agent!"

Shriver's stomach went icy cold.

"He says you two haven't communicated in years. He had no idea you were even here until he saw my article."

"He saw the photograph?"

"All he does anymore is deposit your royalty payments, which I imagine are substantial."

If anyone's breath at the conference reeked more of alcohol than Shriver's own, it was Jack Blunt's. Shriver could have done with a drink himself right about now.

"Anyway," the reporter continued, "all is not lost. He'll be here tomorrow in time for your reading."

"What?!"

"This is going to be one hell of a story!" Blunt said as he strutted off.

Shriver made his way to the restroom and into a stall, where he sat on the toilet and gulped down a mouthful of whiskey.

There was no hope now of getting through this thing intact. The genuine Shriver's agent would expose him as a fraud, and he would have to leave town with his head hanging low. There was nothing to do now but go straight to Simone and confess.

He took another deep gulp, went to the mirror, and stared at himself. "Imposter," he said. Then he went out to the ballroom.

Simone stood alone at the front of the room. He had to tell her. Perhaps his honesty would provide him with a sliver of honor in her eyes. But just as Shriver neared her, a young woman—apparently a graduate student—mounted the steps to the dais. Simone saw Shriver coming and placed a finger to her lips, warning him to be silent. Meanwhile, T. Wätzczesnam and Edsel Nixon waved to him from the third row.

"'Stately, kindly, lordly friend / Condescend / Here to sit by me.'"

"Swinburne," came Edsel Nixon's whispered response.

Shriver tiptoed up the aisle and squeezed in between T. and Nixon just as the young woman onstage ostentatiously coughed into the microphone. Simone moved to her usual seat in the front, off to the side. Rarely raising her head from the sheet of paper from which she read, the graduate student began her introduction with a history of her own love of literature—"of *words*," as she put it—and then moved on to her studies here at the college. Prior to coming here, she said, she had never written anything remotely creative, but under the tutelage of various professors—all of whom she named, including Simone—she had blossomed into a person who could hardly stop herself from writing. She wrote from the moment she woke up to the moment she went to sleep. She wrote on notepads, on napkins, in the margins of newspapers and books; she wrote during classes when she was supposed to be listening; she wrote during movies. One time, short of any paper at all, she wrote on the walls of her apartment. She was even writing right now, as she spoke, she said, though it was all in her head. (My goodness, Shriver thought—if that's the dedication required of an author, no wonder they're all so eccentric!) Finally, after ten minutes of talking about herself, the student found her way to the person she was introducing and briefly mentioned that the author was "probably" the same kind of writer as she—"someone who has never stopped, someone born to write, a bottomless well of creativity. Ladies and gentlemen, please welcome Zebra Amphetamine."

The writer's long, metallic earrings swayed with each step up the stairs to the stage. She wore a straight knee-length dress that clung to her thin frame as she walked, as if it were pressed there by a strong wind. After the applause had died down she stood silently at the podium for a moment, her face composed into a serious expression.

Shriver glanced over at Simone, who watched Ms. Amphetamine intently, then something caught his eye: a flash of color over by the entrance. It was Krampus in his electric-red suit coat. The detective appeared to be waving at him, his short arm flapping up and down. Shriver pointed at his own chest and mouthed, *Me?* The detective nodded vigorously and motioned for him to come out to the lobby.

Meanwhile, Ms. Amphetamine shuffled some papers on the podium, preparing to launch into her reading. But when Shriver stood and started toward the door, the writer paused to watch him make his way across the ballroom. Everyone else seemed to be watching as well. The room went completely silent except for the sound of his footsteps and someone's nervous cough. Shriver stooped his shoulders, as if he could make himself less visible, but every eye was on him. He turned back to see Zebra Amphetamine charting his progress. He shrugged and pointed to the doorway, trying to communicate to her that he had been summoned away. Unfortunately, Detective Krampus could not verify this fact, having retreated into the lobby. Shriver continued walking for what seemed like hours, the doorway always several steps away, the echoes of his footsteps growing louder and louder. He glanced over toward Simone, who observed him with an expression of disenchantment. But what could he do? He'd been beckoned by a police official! He felt sweat roll down his spine and pool at the top of his underwear. Then he remembered that his back pocket was bulging with the pint of whiskey, the bottle's neck exposed to all. He could almost feel Simone's eyes on his right buttock, her suspicion that he was a hedonistic drunkard, like all the others, confirmed by what she saw there. Near the ballroom door, along with several other people who had been unable to find a vacant seat, stood the pigtailed Cassandra, who also looked disappointed, her arms folded across her chest like a judge about to pronounce a sentence. It was as if masks had been handed out, there were so many long faces in the room. He was failing everyone today. But then, from her place in an aisle seat near the door, Delta Malarkey-Jones smiled and gave a little wave with the corn dog in her hand. Thank God she remained on his side. Not that it mattered. The real Shriver's agent would be here tomorrow to unmask him. Perhaps he should just keep walking, not even confess to Simone. He could step outside, hail a cab, ride straight to the airport, and take the next flight out of here. As he neared the doorway, he saw that damn photograph flashing across the large screen on the back wall. There sat the real Shriver, in front of those curtains, smiling contentedly. In a flash, he recalled a long-ago birthday. He had been drinking champagne with his wife and some friends. She had drawn the curtains against the glare of the afternoon sun. He remembered how utterly satisfied he had felt that day. Recently married, he had friends, he felt weightless from the champagne, he smelled the aroma of curried vegetables coming from the kitchen, jazz played on the stereo. It was one of those extraordinary rare times when he felt happy without dilution, as if there were nothing wrong anywhere in the world and never would be. But that was so long ago, it might as well have been a dream.

Finally, he entered the quiet of the carpeted lobby. The detective stood near a window.

"I've been reading your book, Mr. Shriver," he said, waving a copy of *Goat Time*. "You certainly have a singular outlook on life."

"I hope this will be quick, Detective."

"Of course. So, tell me—do you remember any more about last night's debauchery?"

"I don't know which debauchery you're referring to."

"How many debaucheries *were* there?" Krampus asked with a girlish chuckle. Shriver noticed for the first time that the detective wore a wispy goatee, so thin that it blended in with his pale skin. "Come now, Mr. Shriver. I've been interviewing the hotel staff, including Miss, uh . . ." He consulted his notebook. "Miss Sue St. Marie Debussy."

"One of the twins?"

"Oh, are they twins?" Krampus asked. "I hadn't noticed."

Was he serious? Shriver wondered.

"Anyway," the detective continued, "Miss Debussy says that Ms. Smithee left a note for you earlier in the evening."

"Yes, that's correct. She wanted me to join her in the hotel bar."

"Did you?"

"No."

"Why not?"

"I was tired."

"Not too tired to throw a party in your room."

"That wasn't my idea," Shriver protested.

"Really?" Krampus scribbled something in his notebook. "Now, refresh my memory. Who was the last person to leave this party, that you recall?"

Shriver had seen enough police programs on television to know that detectives will ask questions over and over again, hoping to trip people up. The problem, as he saw it, was that even the most innocent of characters will get confused if you ask them the same question enough times.

"The last person I saw leave," Shriver answered carefully, "was perhaps Mr. Nixon. Or it may have been the lady next door—Ms. Malarkey-Jones."

"And Ms. Smithee was not with you in your room at that time?"

Shriver pictured the poet passed out on the bed. Maybe it *hadn't* been a dream. "If she was in the room," he said, "she must have been under the bed, because I did not see her."

"Interesting," the detective said, scribbling something into his notebook.

"And how is Ms. Labio holding up?" Shriver asked.

"She is in her hotel room, amply supplied with sedatives."

"I see. Well, Detective, if you'll excuse me."

"Of course. But first . . ." He held out the copy of *Goat Time* and his pen. "If you wouldn't mind?"

Is this what it's like to be a writer? Constantly signing books for people? Shriver took the pen and opened the book to the title page.

"It's an interesting story," Krampus said as Shriver tried to decide what to inscribe. *To Det. Krampus,* he scribbled. "The possible murder of the wife is particularly fascinating."

Best wishes . . .

"Which reminds me," the detective said, "I've been trying to locate *Mrs. Shriver.*"

The pen slipped, creating a long line of ink across the page. "*Mrs. Shriver?*"

"Yes. But I can't seem to track her down."

Shriver composed himself and returned the pen to the page. "That could be because you are under the impression that she remains 'Mrs. Shriver.'"

"Oh? Has she taken another name?"

"I wouldn't know. What does she have to do with this, anyway?"

"Just following a hunch."

Shriver signed the author's name and handed the book over. "There you are."

"Thank you. Oh—and please remain available, just in case I need to speak with you again."

Shriver turned to go, but, remembering the pint of whiskey in his back pocket, and not wishing the detective to see what everyone in the ballroom had just seen, he backed away until Krampus began to make some notes in his little notebook. At that point Shriver turned and ran smack into the closed ballroom doors, his nose making first contact, and then, a split second later, the toe of his shoe. There was a loud bang and the door rattled for a few seconds as Shriver stepped back and put his hand up to his face. The pain radiated out from his nose to his eyes and ears. Exacerbating the sting was the knowledge that, inside the ballroom, seven hundred people were staring at the closed door that, obviously, some fool had just run into.

Krampus burst out laughing. "I just adore slapstick!"

Shriver headed for the restroom. Inside, he looked in the mirror. His nose throbbed red but was not bleeding. He splashed some water on his face and took a swig of whiskey. It bothered him that Krampus was trying to track down his ex-wife. He felt somehow violated. Then he remembered that it wasn't his *own* ex-wife Krampus was looking for, but the ex-wife of the *real* Shriver! He laughed at his own stupidity.

On the other hand, the real Shriver's agent was at this very moment making plans to come here, at which point he would be exposed as a fraud. But he didn't care anymore. His face ached, his rear end was a bruised mess, he was half-drunk and unable to read his own story. It would be a relief to confess and simply go home to Mr. Bojangles.

He returned to the lobby, his nose pulsing, and collapsed into a chair beside the ballroom doors. From inside he heard the sound of hearty applause. A moment later, the doors flew open, and a noisy crowd made its way into the lobby. Immediately, a long line formed at the book table, where people plunked down their money for copies of Zebra Amphetamine's story collections. A few moments later the author emerged from the ballroom, accompanied by Simone and a nimbus of fans praising her reading in loud voices.

Zebra sat down at a small table to sign books. Simone stood nearby, gauging the success of the enterprise with a beaming face. She even smiled at Shriver.

"Shriver!"

T. Wätzczesnam came striding out of the ballroom.

"I've seen the future of literary fiction," he declared, "and it belongs to young Nefertiti over there." He plopped down with a sigh in the next chair. "Honest to God, our day is over.

If you're not young and black and female, you have no hope of getting a book published in this country. And on the basis of that reading, it's just as well. These kids from the ghetto have a fresh voice that's been missing. It's loud, it's angry, it's *real*. People are tired of our dyspeptic white men wandering the suburbs. Oh, 'superfluous lags the veteran on the stage,' Shriver. We old white men are done for."

Shriver rubbed the tip of his tender nose.

"Hey, where'd you run off to, anyway?" T. asked. "Don't tell me it's that irritable bowel syndrome. Goddamn if everyone I know doesn't suffer from that bizarre affliction."

"It wasn't that."

"Well, you sure hustled off in a hurry."

"It was that detective."

"Krampus? What did that little homunculus want?"

"More questions."

"Do you need a lawyer, Shriver?"

"Lord, no."

"Because I know a good one. A real barracuda."

"I don't need a lawyer. I didn't do anything."

"Doesn't matter. Sometimes you need to shoot back just to let them know you mean business."

"No, thanks."

"Of course, my man deals mostly with DUIs and that sort of thing. I'm not sure how he would perform in a more serious criminal case."

"There *is* no criminal case. He was simply asking questions."

"Of course. Still . . ."

The two men sat there watching Zebra Amphetamine autograph copy after copy of her books.

"Are you going to the reception?" the cowboy asked.

"I suppose so. Where is it?"

"Over at the museum. At least there will be booze. Speaking of which." He removed his pint bottle and took a long swig. "Let's track down our Mr. Nixon," he said. "He can ferry us over there in his Jeepster."

Chapter Nine

The current exhibition at the local museum of art was entitled *Slaughter: A Meditation on Carnivorous Consumption* and featured wall-sized color videos of various farm animals in the process of being butchered—a steer getting bashed on the head while gripped in a vise operated by men in cowboy hats; a hog hoisted by its hind hooves into the air and sliced from chin to genitals with a long, sharp blade—all projected above tables laden with trays of pigs in a blanket.

"I don't know how you can eat that," Zebra Amphetamine said. "You're swallowing the murdered flesh of a sentient creature."

"There's nothing else to eat," Edsel Nixon explained, waving toward the empty cheese plate and the tossed-out stems of strawberries.

"I'd rather starve to death," Zebra huffed. "I'm a firm believer in evolution. I think it's our job to move the human race forward and out of the carnivorous age."

"Hear hear!" T. Wätzczesnam cried, a dough-encased wiener held high in his callused hand. "I have loads of faith in your generation."

"If it were up to guys like you, we'd still be swinging from trees by our tails."

"Wouldn't that be fun!" T. said.

Shriver watched Simone standing among a herd of

well-wishers and students over near the video loop of a headless, blood-spouting chicken hopping around a farmyard. She seemed so pleased by the reading that she may even have forgiven him for so rudely walking out.

Though he had considered confessing to Simone his real identity, Shriver was now wavering. He and T. had polished off a bottle or so of wine, and the booze, it seemed—as well as the sight of Simone looking so happy—had fortified his resolve to remain incognito. At least until Mr. Cheadem arrived tomorrow.

He watched her excuse herself from the group and enter one of several gallery alcoves.

"She's not on the market, old boy," T. whispered into his ear.

Shriver, caught, turned the color of pinot noir. "What do you mean? She has a boyfriend?"

"Not exactly." T. laughed, showing wine-stained teeth, and moved off to find another pig in a blanket.

Shriver's face still felt hot. Was he being that obvious? He barely knew this woman, and here he was mooning after her like a virginal schoolboy. And what did T. mean by "Not exactly"?

He finished his current glass of wine and followed Simone into the darkened alcove, where a video of a goose being force-fed through a metal tube played out across an entire wall.

"I came in here to catch my breath, believe it or not," Simone said. She was the only one in the room.

"Oh, sorry," Shriver said. "I can leave."

"No, of course not. Stay, please."

She said it in a way that sounded genuine, not just polite. Shriver suddenly didn't know what to say or do. He realized only now how intoxicated he was.

"Feeling better today?" he finally asked.

"I was until I saw *this*," she said. "I guess I'll never eat foie gras again."

Shriver stared at the floor, trying to think of something interesting to say before she ran from the room and the tortured goose.

"I'm sorry I had to leave Ms. Amphetamine's reading," he said. "Detective Krampus—"

"It's not important, Mr. Shriver."

"No, it is. I wanted to stay, and . . ."

"Yes?" she said.

She had been imbibing a fair amount herself, apparently: her face glowed, her eyes vibrated. It was exciting to see her so wound up.

"I know how important this is to you," he said. "I don't want to disappoint you."

"Well, you sort of *have* disappointed me."

Shriver's stomach lurched. "How so?"

She smiled, ignoring the sight of the goose struggling on-screen. "You haven't exactly lived up to my expectations of a literary superstar."

"Oh. Sorry."

"Don't apologize. I'm *happily* disappointed, if that's possible."

Shriver was surprised by the extent of the relief he felt. His entire body relaxed, as though he had ejected a virus.

"I was looking at your novel again last night," Simone said.

"Really?"

"Yes. It was more . . . interesting than I'd remembered."

The video ended, and the room went dark. Simone was standing so close to him Shriver could smell the wine on her breath. He felt something moving in the air between them, atoms pinging back and forth. Then the video started back up, a man holding a metal tube and approaching the doomed goose.

"Oh, Lord," Simone said. "I can't watch this again." She headed back out to the main gallery, where several students descended upon her.

Shriver rejoined the writers, but he could not concentrate on what they were saying. Had Simone been about to kiss him? Did she like him that much, or had she just drunk too much? He thought of the poet at last year's conference—was this just another case of a crush on a "literary superstar"? To calm himself down, he drank another glass of wine and meditated on Zebra Amphetamine's swaying earrings, which refracted light into little rainbows.

"How can you wear those things?" he asked her. "They look so heavy!"

"These?" She reached up to cup the earrings in her palms. "These are made of tin mined from the dirt of Namibia. They're my good-luck charm and a reminder of the exploitation of my people."

"Don't they hurt your ears?"

"Sure. Just like these photos hurt my eyes. But we all need reminders sometimes."

"Basil, ol' boy!" Wätzczesnam exclaimed as the playwright, accompanied by Ms. Brazir, joined the group. "I thought you were flying back to Gotham today."

"I thought so too. But that mini-cop has ordered us to remain in town until they figure out what happened to our poetess friend."

"Are you a suspect?" Shriver asked.

"It's like a cheap Agatha Christie novel," Rather sniffed, scratching at a welt on his neck. "And then these goddamn mosquitoes."

Seeing Rather paw at his splotchy neck prompted everyone else to rub their various bites.

"Is everyone going to the soiree tonight?" Rather asked.

"Of course!" T. said. "I wouldn't miss that for anything."

"Another soiree?" Shriver asked. "Isn't *this* a soiree?"

"This is obviously your first writers' conference," Rather said.

"Every year," T. explained, "Dr. Keaudeen throws a swanky party for the authors and whoever else tags along. It's wonderfully decadent."

"Who's Dr. Keaudeen?"

"A local gynecologist. Female. She gives beaucoup bucks to the university, so we have to pay attention to her."

"Will there be food?" Shriver asked.

"Tons of it."

"Then I'm in."

"I wonder who will get lucky tonight," T. said.

"What does that mean?" Rather asked.

"Dr. Keaudeen has a habit of seducing writers. Last year it was that mystery writer with the speech impediment. What was his name?"

"Is this bush doctor attractive?" the playwright asked.

"That's the thing. She's not. In fact, she's plug-ugly. But she's rich and charismatic."

"Sounds as though you have had the pleasure, T."

Professor Wätzczesnam became uncharacteristically quiet and downed a good portion of wine.

"Hello, everybody!"

Simone appeared at Shriver's elbow. When she looked up at him her face turned the slightest shade of pink. Shriver turned to see T. watching her, his face like stone.

"I'm still high from that reading, Zebra," Simone said. "How exhilarating!"

"It was a fantastic audience," the young author replied. "It's funny, the farther I get from the projects, the better the response."

"Don't look now," Basil Rather said, "but Hercule Poirot has arrived."

Over by the door, Detective Krampus stood watching over the crowd, smiling crookedly, as if he knew some secret about every single person in the room. *That woman there is having an affair with her dentist. That man has an unlicensed handgun in his car's glove compartment. That fellow is wearing women's underpants.*

"He is a pesky little fellow," T. muttered.

Delta Malarkey-Jones approached the detective and spoke animatedly to him. As she jabbered on, Krampus continued to gaze around the room. When his eyes met Shriver's he nodded almost imperceptibly, as if they had some sort of understanding between them.

"I wonder what happened to poor Gonquin," Simone said.

"She's probably in Vegas," Basil Rather said.

As he snuck a lengthy gaze at Simone's rosy face, Shriver again saw a black-clad figure out of the corner of his eye. He turned quickly to see the figure just as it exited.

"I'll be right back," he said, directing it mostly to Simone, whom he still wanted to talk to. He walked over toward the door.

"Hello, Mr. Shriver," Krampus said through that knowing grin of his.

"Did you see someone leave?"

"When?"

"Just now. Dressed all in black."

"Like Ms. Smithee?" the detective asked, perking up.

"I don't know." That hadn't occurred to him.

Shriver pushed through the door, Krampus right behind him. In the parking lot, a few students sat inside a pickup truck, laughing and drinking beer. Otherwise Shriver saw only empty cars, neatly parked. Simone's slumbering dinosaur took up two spaces off to the side. Mosquitoes buzzed around his ears. He swatted them away as he and Krampus walked around to the rail yard behind the museum, where row after row of freight cars sat rusting on railroad tracks.

"Are you sure you saw her?" Krampus asked. He seemed unbothered by the mosquitoes. He did not wave his arms at them, as Shriver had to do.

"I saw *someone*," Shriver said, peering beneath a row of boxcars. "I don't know who."

"If not Ms. Smithee," the detective said, "perhaps it was the person responsible for her disappearance."

Shriver paused. "You think so?"

"Perhaps he plans to dispatch the writers, one by one."

"Really?"

"Who's next?" Krampus asked. "The great and legendary Shriver?"

Shriver thought about it. The theory made as much sense as any other. Maybe it was some envious would-be author taking out his revenge on those more successful than he. And who was more successful than Shriver?

Krampus laughed. "Really, Mr. Shriver. You don't seem the paranoid type. Tell me—how much have you had to drink today?"

Shriver attempted to display a contemptuous expression, but he wondered if the detective might be right: maybe he was just soused. Krampus smiled and returned to the museum. Shriver then made a halfhearted effort to look beneath the freight cars, but there were hundreds of them; someone could hide quite effectively back here if they wanted to. Plus, it might be dangerous—paranoid or not, Krampus's theory could be correct.

"Shriver!" someone called from the parking lot.

He headed around to the front of the building and arrived in time to see Simone's vehicle pulling away. He waved frantically for her to stop, but she did not see him, or else ignored him.

"Shriver!"

T. Wätzczesnam and Edsel Nixon were climbing into the jeep, madly swatting their arms at the insects.

Shriver ran to the car and, with some difficulty, ascended into the backseat.

"Giddyup, Nixon!" the professor cried out. "Before we get eaten alive!"

Chapter Ten

"I'll drop you off at the hotel," Edsel shouted over the engine noise, "so you can freshen up a bit. Then I'll swing around to pick you up for the party."

"Don't take too long, Shriver," T. said. "Finger foods await!"

Next thing he knew, Shriver was standing at the entrance to the Hotel 19 as the jeep tore off through a cloud of insects. He went straight up to his room and, just as he reached the door, remembered he did not have the key. He rode the elevator back down and, rounding the corner, saw the familiar beehive behind the front desk.

"May I help you?" Charlevoix asked.

"Yes. I left my key in my room. May I have a spare?"

"Oh my," she said. "This has never happened before."

"No one has ever misplaced their key?"

"Not that I know of."

"I find that hard to believe."

"Well, *I've* never heard of it, and I've worked here since forever. Oh my."

"May I have a spare?" Shriver asked again.

"Spare? We pride ourselves on providing the utmost in privacy. If we had a spare, you wouldn't have privacy, now, would you? Not so long as another key was floating around out there."

"But—"

"Why, some nefarious person could use that spare key to sneak into your room and take your things!"

"But what about the maid? Surely she would have a key."

"Of course, the maid has a *master* key. How else would she clean your room?"

"Exactly. Can you tell me where I might find her?"

"Well, I'm sorry, but she's gone for the day."

"And she took the key with her?"

Charlevoix, insulted, narrowed her eyes. "Oh, we trust Luna implicitly, Mr. Shriver."

"Of course, but it just seems impractical to—"

"She's worked here for twenty-five years!"

"Yes, but—"

"She would never abuse her privileges."

Shriver gave up that argument. "So, how do you suggest I get into my room? There are things in there that I need." He thought not just of his keys, but his per diem money, his clothes, and, most of all, his story.

Charlevoix appeared to ponder his question. "I'm going to have to call my big sister," she said. "Perhaps you could wait in the saloon?"

As Shriver started off Charlevoix called him back. "I almost forgot. This was left for you."

She held out a manila envelope with his name written on it in large block letters. Shriver carried it into the Prairie Dog Saloon. The place was dimly lit, with spindly ficus trees and rodeo memorabilia on the walls. Shriver sat at the bar and waved to the bartendress, a skinny college student with blue hair spilling from a too-small straw cowboy hat.

"Whiskey," Shriver said. "Wait—make it a double."

He examined the envelope. It was sealed, and appeared to contain a manuscript of some kind.

His drink arrived. "Please charge this to room nineteen," he told the bartendress, then he downed the drink in one burning gulp.

He started to open the envelope, then hesitated. Detective Krampus's words came to him: *Perhaps he plans to dispatch the writers, one by one.* An absurd idea, probably, but still . . . Who knew what was inside this envelope? Perhaps it contained a threat of some kind, or incriminating photos, or anthrax. No, that was crazy.

"Another?" the bartendress asked.

Shriver was about to answer in the affirmative when he heard a loud car horn beeping from outside the front door of the hotel.

"Maybe later," he said.

/

As Edsel accelerated across campus and T. Wätzczesnam lambasted the "so-called art" on display at the museum — "Honestly, Mr. Nixon, if those unsightly bison were not put on this earth for us to consume, then God has a whole lot of explaining to do"—Shriver sat in the backseat and stared down at the manila envelope in his hands. Perhaps emboldened by the double shot of whiskey, he thought, Oh, what the hell, and tore it open. Inside he found a sheaf of paper. He peeked in at the top sheet and saw these words, typed on an old-fashioned manual typewriter:

THE IMPOSTER

As a tingling sweat broke out on his forehead he pulled the pages from the envelope and tried to read what came next, but the words started to blur.

"What do you have there, Shriver?" T. asked.

"What?" Shriver said, looking up. The cowboy eyed him, one hand clutching his ten-gallon hat to stop the wind from lifting it off and away.

"Is that your new masterpiece, by any chance?" T. asked. "Let me see."

He took hold of the pages with his free hand, but Shriver refused to yield. As they struggled, Edsel Nixon made a sharp turn that nearly lifted the jeep onto two wheels. Startled, both men lost their grip and the pages flew from their hands and out the vehicle.

"No!" Wätzczesnam shouted. "Turn back, Mr. Nixon!"

"It's fine, T.," Shriver said. "It wasn't important."

"Are you sure?"

"Positive. Just some forms to fill out. Keep going, Edsel."

"Will do," his handler said. "We're almost there."

Shriver looked back to see sheets of paper floating, a flock of doves, above a motorcyclist who, distracted, pulled off to the side of the road.

Shriver didn't need to read the story. The point had been made: someone was onto him.

/

Dr. Margaret Keaudeen lived in a large, recently constructed home on the outskirts of town. Cars lined the wide driveway that circled an immaculately kept lawn, each blade of grass glowing in the soft light of dusk. Edsel parked behind Simone's behemoth and the three men leaped from the jeep and made for the front door as mosquitoes buzzed loudly around their heads.

Professor Wätzczesnam flung open the door and entered the two-story-high foyer, followed by Nixon and Shriver.

Conversation and music could be heard from the other side of a padded swinging door straight ahead.

"This way, gentlemen," T. said.

Partygoers milled about the sizable living room, many of their faces familiar from the readings, as classical music floated from speakers built into the ceiling. The walls were covered in vertically striped wallpaper, with fancy gold light fixtures and ornately framed paintings. Large, overstuffed chairs sat atop a plush beige carpet.

"Follow me," T. said as he pushed through the crowd toward a well-stocked bar. He helped himself to a glass of whiskey and poured a glass for Shriver too. Shriver downed his in one gulp and looked around the room for Simone. He had to tell her the truth before it came out. To his right he noticed the entrance to the kitchen, where an army of caterers was preparing finger food. His stomach gurgled loudly.

"Excuse me," he said, pushing off toward the food table. This could be a long night, he reasoned, and he'd need some fortification. En route he was stopped by a tall woman in an elegant linen jacket and matching skirt. She smiled down at him with artificially whitened teeth, her thick lips painted a ruby red.

"Mr. Shriver! So thrilled to meet you!" She thrust out a meaty hand on which sparkled several rings. "Dr. Margaret Keaudeen. Welcome to my home!"

"Very nice to meet you, Doctor," Shriver said, his hand engulfed inside hers. His stomach twisted at the sight of a cracker slathered with some sort of cheese-and-spinach concoction that the gynecologist held aloft in her other hand.

"I'm an alumna of the college," she said. "I loved it so much I feel I must give something back in return, so I throw a little party every year. Plus, I'm simply a nut for literature!"

The top half of her jacket was opened to reveal a lacy blouse that, in turn, showed off the cleavage of her suspiciously firm and rounded breasts. Shriver felt reasonably sure that, were he to touch them, they would be as hard as the breasts of a marble statue.

"You have a lovely home," he told her. "And I'm very excited to partake of the delicious-looking food you've provided."

"Talk to me," she said, taking hold of his elbow and turning him sideways, closer to her, "about your wonderful novel. I haven't quite finished it, but I'm fascinated by what I've read so far. I've written a bit myself, you know—I had a story published in the college literary journal last year—"

"Congratulations."

"Thank you—and I was wondering how you managed to come up with such a marvelous concept."

"Well," Shriver said, his eyes still focused on her uneaten cracker, "I don't really know. It's been so long."

"Oh no, Mr. Shriver. Don't disappoint me. I'm sure you remember."

"Not really."

The doctor devoured the cracker, her teeth making loud crunching sounds as she chewed. With her other hand she still had hold of his elbow in a manner that was strangely intimate.

"Come with me," she said. "I want to show you something." And with her fingers still gripping his arm she directed him down a hallway and into a dark room. He thought of the mystery writer and wondered if their affair began this way.

She turned on a light. Shelves lined the walls from the floor to the very tall ceiling, each shelf crammed with books of all sizes. Shriver felt his sigmoid seize up at the smell of decaying paper.

"This is my favorite room in the house," she said. "I told the architect he could do what he wished with the living room, the kitchen, the bedrooms, but with this room I was to have complete and utter control."

Beside a stone fireplace sat a tall-backed reading chair and standing lamp.

"It's very nice," Shriver said, resting a hand on his lower belly. He could feel his duodenum rumbling, like a kicking fetus at eight months.

Dr. Keaudeen went to a rolling ladder that was attached to the shelves and climbed several steps. She reached out and took down a book. He recognized it as *Goat Time*.

"A first edition," she said as she held it out for him. From a side table she produced a silver pen. "There isn't anything I wouldn't do to get you to sign this." She smiled. A bright green sliver of spinach showed between her otherwise gleaming front teeth.

Nearly doubled over now, Shriver was unable to take the book and pen from her.

"Excuse me," he said, his voice strained, as if talking too loudly would let loose everything from inside his bowels. "I'd be happy to sign it, but first I need to use the facilities, if you don't mind."

Her face showed surprise, but she was not insulted. "Of course. Use the one upstairs. It's much nicer."

She pointed to the door, outside of which he could make out the foyer and a set of marble stairs. He ran.

"Are you all right?" she called out after him.

He scrambled up the marble stairs and found himself in a long dark hallway lined on both sides by closed doors. The first door led to a large closet. The second opened into a guest bedroom. The third room was some sort of recreation room, with a huge television and a Ping-Pong table. In the fourth room he found a small boy sitting in a chair reading a book.

"Hello," the child said. Five or six years old, with well-combed brown hair and freckles on his nose, he wore a long-sleeve shirt and sweater vest. At his feet lay a tuxedo cat. The animal resembled Mr. Bojangles in every particular: the black fur with white socks, the white tummy and chest, even the uneven splash of white under its chin. The cat raised its small head and gazed up at Shriver as if to ask what he was doing here.

"Are you looking for the restroom?" the boy asked. Shriver nodded emphatically. The boy pointed next door. Though Shriver wanted very much to stay and pat the cat's furry little head, he shut the door and moved on.

He entered a vast bedroom, apparently the master suite. He crossed an expanse of white shag carpeting past a king-size bed covered in a crimson comforter and a dozen fluffy, matching pillows. A lamp on the bedside table illuminated the room in a soft pink light. A door in the corner led to a bathroom nearly as large as the bedroom. He almost slipped on the pink marble floor as he made for the commode. With no time to even shut the door, he yanked down his trousers and plunked down on the seat, reigniting the fire of his bruise.

In the peace of the moment, Shriver wondered who the author of "The Imposter" could be and how he knew Shriver's secret. Was he dangerous? Had he done something to Gonquin? Was he some kind of literary serial killer? Shriver groaned. One little error of judgment, he thought, one foolish step out into the world, and I might get *killed* for it? It serves me right, he told himself, for pretending to be a writer.

"Mr. Shriver?" he heard the gynecologist call from the bedroom.

He stood and, with his pants bunched at his ankles, waddled to the still-open bathroom door and shut it.

"Are you okay, Mr. Shriver?"

"Fine!" he called as he sat back down. "*Ouch.*"

"My son says you looked distressed."

"I'm really quite all right."

"Is there anything I can do for you?"

"No, thank you. I'll be back down in a moment."

There was a pause, and then, "Very well."

He finished up, washed his hands, and splashed some water on his face. Several soft-light bulbs lined the mirror, like those in a backstage dressing room. He had rarely seen himself this way—so well lit, without shadows. "How long can you keep this up?" he asked. A pale face with graying whiskers and bloodshot eyes stared back at him.

He opened the door. Dr. Keaudeen sat on the edge of the bed, reading *Goat Time.*

She smiled, as if he'd returned after a very long absence. "I was starting to worry."

"Sorry. My system is a little out of whack. All this excitement, I guess."

She held the book aloft. "I just adore the airplane scene. So amusing."

"Thank you," he said from across the room.

She patted the spot on the bed beside her.

"Don't forget—I would love for you to sign it for me."

"Of course." He wanted to get this over with and go back downstairs to the food. He felt hollowed out, like a Halloween pumpkin. He went to the bed and, without sitting, took the book and pen. He opened the book to the title page and wrote, *To Margaret, Thank you for the lovely soiree.* He signed the author's name and handed it back to her.

"Thank you *so* much!" She set the book down on the bed without reading his inscription. "Now, please, sit here with me for a while and speak to me of literature. It's the least you can do."

She took his hand and, with that surprising strength of hers, pulled him down to sit on the bed, where he nearly toppled over. It was a waterbed. The surface rippled and swayed beneath him.

The doctor laughed. "You have no idea how much this bed weighs, Mr. Shriver. I had to have the floor and walls below specially reinforced to hold it. But it was worth every penny, believe me."

For a long, grueling moment they sat in silence. Shriver stared down at the shag carpet, but he could sense the doctor's eyes boring into him.

"So," he said. "That was your son?"

"Reggie."

"And where is Reggie's father?"

She laughed. "I don't know, and I don't care."

Probably a writer, Shriver thought.

From behind her the doctor produced a bound manuscript.

"This is my novel," she told him. "Will you look at it?"

She thrust it into his lap. Through the clear plastic cover he could make out the title: *Between the Knees*.

"It's about a gynecologist who discovers a deep, dark secret. Oh, I know, I'm writing about someone like me—a vivacious, beautiful physician—but we have to write what we know, don't we? I mean, *your* book is about *you*, isn't it, when you get right down to it?"

He hefted the thick manuscript.

"A patient dies," she continued, "and leaves behind some

mysterious information, a kind of code, if you will, and Dr. Modine—she's the protagonist—must embark on a journey to discover the truth. It's a guaranteed bestseller, I can assure you. There is lots of adventure, sex, and violence. It's got *everything!*"

"Sounds wonderful."

"Will you read it, and tell me what you think? And you must be honest. I know that revision is important when you're writing a novel."

"That's what they say."

"I would be ever so grateful. You must tell me what I can do for you in return."

She leaned toward him, her big, bleached teeth looming, her eyes large and dilated. He could smell nicotine on her, mixed with perfume and perspiration.

Just then, the door creaked open and the tuxedo cat rushed in and leaped onto the bed.

"Mr. B.!" Dr. Keaudeen shouted. "Bad kitty!"

"Mr. B.?"

The cat sniffed at Shriver's hands and began to purr. Shriver ruffled its soft ears and thought of his own Mr. B. back home. The cat then looked up at him with its green eyes, hissed, and swatted at Shriver's hand with claws extended.

"Bad pussy!" Dr. Keaudeen cried. She picked up the cat and tossed it across the room. She then grabbed Shriver's hand to examine it. "He drew blood!"

Three thin red lines had formed on the back of Shriver's hand.

"Let me get a cloth," the doctor said, rushing to the bathroom.

"I'm fine, really," Shriver called to her, though his hand did sting.

"You have to be careful of lymphadenopathy," she called

back over the sound of running water. She returned a moment later with a wet washcloth.

"Lympha *what?*"

"Cat-scratch fever, silly." She covered his hand with the warm cloth. "We may love our kitty-cat friends, but they are little germ factories."

The wet cloth felt soothing on the scratches, which had begun to pulse. Shriver shut his eyes.

"Does that feel nice?" Dr. Keaudeen asked.

"Mm-hmm."

Shriver felt her remove the cloth and then reapply it, but this time the cloth felt different—smoother, warmer. He opened his eyes to see Dr. Keaudeen licking his hand and fingers. He yanked his hand back.

"Oh, darling!" Dr. Keaudeen grunted, grabbing his hand again. She pulled him closer, and the waterbed waves forced him forward until his face landed in her lap. "Yes!" she cried, forcing his head down so that his nose touched her crotch. Before he knew what was happening, she had somehow pulled her skirt up to her waist, leaving Shriver face-to-face with a leopard-print thong. He tried to pull away but the gynecologist gripped his ears and pushed his face deep into the musky triangle.

"Kiss me there, Shriver," she growled. "Please!"

"Mmffpf," he said, arms flailing.

She lay back and the bed heaved and roiled beneath them. Shriver attempted to pull himself up, but the mattress was all give, and he could not find the necessary leverage. Meanwhile, Dr. Keaudeen tugged at his ears and writhed as if his nose were a cattle prod.

Then she grabbed him by the hair—"Oww!" he cried—and yanked his head up toward hers.

"Take me!" she grunted. "Take me *now!*"

Her face was dark pink, her eyes glassy.

"Doctor," he said, but, with nostrils flapping, she pulled his face down and kissed him so forcefully that their teeth clattered together. Her tongue, which tasted as if it had soaked overnight in cheese and tobacco, forced itself into his mouth.

"Mmffpf!"

As he squirmed atop her, unable to roll off with her legs clasped tightly around his sore rear end, Shriver felt something land on his back—four small points of pressure. Just when he'd figured out what was happening, the cat sank its claws through his shirt and into his skin.

"Ouch!" he screamed into Dr. Keaudeen's mouth.

She laughed. "Oh, that's just Mr. B. He likes threesomes." She groaned and ground her crotch against him while keeping his legs pinned.

"*Mr. Shriver!*"

The voice was familiar. Shriver somehow managed to turn his head and saw a flash of blond hair.

"Simone!"

He pushed himself up to see the now-empty bedroom doorway. He heard steps—*angry* steps, somehow—descending the marble staircase.

"Wait!" he shouted. The startled cat leaped from his back. Shriver flopped and rolled his way to the edge of the bed.

"No," Dr. Keaudeen pleaded. "Don't stop now!"

"I'm sorry," he said, clambering over the wooden bed frame and onto solid ground. He felt as though he'd stepped off a rowboat onto a dock. "Simone!" he shouted again.

He ran out of the bedroom into the hall.

"But you forgot my novel!" the doctor cried.

Shriver took the stairs two at a time, nearly slipping on the slick marble, and entered the crowded party room. For a moment no one noticed him, and he took advantage by scanning the room for Simone. There: a blond head exiting through a set of French doors.

Shriver pushed through the crowd.

"Hey, Shriver!" T. hollered.

But Shriver slipped out to the back patio and shut the doors behind him. Something flashed overhead. Lightning? He saw another flash and heard a deep, teeth-chilling buzz. He looked up to see a large insect-killing device mounted on a pole. Flash! *Zzzzzch!* Another mosquito sizzled on an electric coil.

In the blue glow of the bug killer Shriver made out a figure dashing across the grass.

"Simone!"

She turned and in the glow of yet another eviscerated bug he saw her face. Then she disappeared into the darkness. Shriver ran across the patio. As soon as he stepped onto the grass, away from the safety of the bug killer, the mosquitoes descended upon him.

Waving at the bloodsuckers, he ran around the huge house toward the front yard. With each step his hands, his wrists, his neck, his ears prickled beneath the probing sting of a hundred insects. He heard the familiar rumble of Simone's car.

When he reached the front yard he saw the leviathan backing out of the driveway. Shriver ran across the lawn, yelling, "Wait! Wait!" Simone braked and switched gears. Shriver managed to jump onto the foot rail on the passenger side just as Simone accelerated out of the driveway. He held on to the side-view mirror and yelled her name through the closed window.

"And here I was beginning to *like* you," he thought he

heard her say through the glass. Or maybe she said, "Isn't that just *like* you." In any case, he was almost certain he saw tears rolling down her face.

"Please, Simone," he cried, but she ignored him. He held on for three blocks before realizing she really was not going to stop. She made a hard right turn and the wheels jumped a curb. Shriver went sailing and landed hard on the sidewalk.

He lay on the cement, rubbing his now doubly sore behind, and watched Simone's taillights disappear into the night. "Simone," he shouted after her, "I am an imposter!" But she was gone.

"Well," he said to a stop sign, "that didn't work out very well."

On the brief but hair-raising ride, he'd gotten all turned around and was not at all sure which way led back to Dr. Keaudeen's house. On still-shuddering legs he walked a block or so in one direction, but nothing seemed familiar, so he headed in the opposite direction, but that didn't seem right either. Eventually he found himself on a major town road. He walked on for several blocks, then, totally lost, he sat on the curb and rested.

How could he possibly screw this up more? he wondered. Still, there was one silver lining: Simone must have had feelings for him to have reacted that way.

He was consoling himself with this thought when a single sheet of paper, blown by a warm, mosquito-infested breeze, landed at his feet. He picked it up and saw a block of the familiar font. At the top: "The Imposter, page 6." He started to read:

". . . and as he gazed down at the clouds far below, the imposter wondered if . . ."

And then the words turned into little black rivulets, and he was unable to read further. At that moment, he felt like the loneliest man in this harsh, unforgiving universe.

Then he heard the familiar rattle of Edsel Nixon's jeep. He looked up to see the unmistakable vehicle pass through the intersection a block away. He jumped up and ran down the street, waving his arms like a madman. "Edsel!" he shouted, his eyes half-shut as the bugs bounced off his face. At the intersection he turned left. He thought he saw the jeep's taillights, now two or three blocks away. "Edsel!"

He ran on, seeing only a few feet of sidewalk through his slitted eyes. There was no way he was going to catch the jeep. The tiny red taillights were getting smaller. He considered slowing down but feared the loss of blood—at least at his present velocity the insects seemed to have a hard time landing and digging in—so he carried on. But after a few blocks he felt his lungs burning, his legs losing steam. It had been years since he'd run like this—so long ago he couldn't remember.

Walking now, his lungs aching, he felt the mosquitoes latch on to his hands and neck, but he didn't care. In the pale light of the street lamps he saw only a deserted block. An insect buzzed into his open mouth. He gagged and spat it onto the sidewalk.

Wait. He recognized the street. He'd been here before. Across the way stood a familiar building—Slander's Restaurant. He reached the restaurant door and pulled. Locked.

"No!" he cried. Inside, the place was dark, chairs upturned on top of tables. Bugs ricocheted off the windows.

He looked up the street, saw a red neon light: OPEN. He ran to the door. Inside, he found a large room lit by weak fluorescent tubes that hummed across the ceiling.

"Hello." On the far side of the room a young woman sat behind a tall counter reading a book. Shriver took several steps toward her. "Mr. Shriver?" she said. He looked closer. Cassandra, from Teresa Apple's class. "What are *you* doing here?" she asked.

"I'm just taking shelter," he answered, peeling another bug from his tongue.

"Uh-huh. That's a new one."

"No, really. It's the mosquitoes."

"Whatever." She turned back to her book. "Take your time. Let me know if you have any questions."

As he stepped farther into the room he saw that display cases lined the walls, front to back. He paused, taking in the bold titles of the magazines there: *Swank, Cavalier, Stud, Gent, Wet, Slit, Juggs, Hombre, Pump, MiLF, GiLF, 18 & Anxious, Horndog, Hard, Wood, Spunk, Facial, Hole, Hairy Hole, Aureole, Skank, Slut, Teen Slut, Slut Mamas, Boobs, Bodacious Boobs, Tiny Tits, Splooge, Babysitters, Candy Stripers, Teabaggers, Teen Teabaggers, Ho, Dirty Sanchez's House of Ho's, Golden Shower, D Cup, A Cup, Cleveland Steamer, Mammal*—and the endless cover photos of naked flesh.

Shriver's face went warm. He turned away from the magazines only to see, on the opposite wall, row after row of video boxes, all featuring more exposed skin: *Genital Hospital, Anal Babies, On Golden Blonde, Sorest Rump, Foreskins and a Funeral, A Beautiful Behind, Gonad the Barbarian, Anal Babies 2, Schindler's Fist, Free My Willy, Shaving Ryan's Privates, Edward Penishands, A Hard Man Is Good to Find, Million Dollar Boobies, Glad He Ate Her, Legally Boned, Anal Babies 3.*

"You probably think it's pretty funny," Cassandra said from her perch behind the counter. "After all that grief I gave you about your novel being so dirty, huh?" She held up the book she was reading: *Goat Time.*

Shriver turned and headed for the exit. Through a small

window in the door he saw a blizzard of mosquitoes. He couldn't go out there again. His hands, his arms, his neck—they all itched.

"Do you know how much a college education costs now-adays?" Cassandra asked.

He peered up and down the block.

"This is my third job," Cassandra continued. "And it pays better than the other two put together."

Headlights spilled across the pavement, bugs dancing in the beams. A sleek sports car sped past the store, its engine growling remarkably loud, its cloth top down. Inside sat Delta Malarkey-Jones, one pudgy hand on the steering wheel, the other fending off a swarm of bugs.

"Delta!" Shriver cried, pushing open the door. He ran across the sidewalk and into the street. "Delta!" But the roar of her car engine drowned out the sound of his voice. "Stop!" Up ahead, her taillights flared in the dark as she braked at a traffic light.

He ran as fast as he could. When he was about twenty yards away, he saw the side street traffic light turn yellow. Delta's light would turn green any second now. She sat in the con-vertible, waving her thick arms at the marauding bugs.

"*Delta!*"

He reached her just as the light switched to green.

Without bothering to open the door, he jumped into the passenger seat.

"Mr. Shriver?"

"Go!"

Delta applied her considerable weight onto the accelerator and the car jolted forward. Mosquitoes splattered against the windshield.

"I can't get the darn top to go down!" Delta yelled.

Mosquitoes buzzed inside Shriver's ears. He swatted at them, then realized the buzzing sound came from somewhere else. He turned to see a motorcycle fast approaching from behind. The driver wore all black, his face covered by a tinted, insect-flecked helmet visor. It was the man who'd been following him all day, the man who may have done away with Gonquin Smithee!

"Delta," he said, "can you lose that motorcycle?"

She looked into the rearview mirror and smiled. "You betcha." She leaned onto the gas pedal and the little convertible tore down the street. Shriver looked back and saw the motorcycle get smaller. The wheels screeched as Delta took a hard right at a yellow traffic light.

"This is exciting!" she said. "Where do you want to go?"

"There!" Shriver shouted, pointing to a familiar one-story building. Delta swung the wheel and the car caromed into a small parking lot. Shriver sprang from the seat and headed to the door.

Chapter Eleven

Inside, the Bloody Duck was even smokier than yesterday.

"Well, hello there."

From out of the cigarette fog came the alabaster waitress. She took Shriver's hand and led him to the same booth he'd sat in with Blunt. Delta followed close behind and plopped herself down across from him.

The waitress trained her green-apple eyes on Shriver. "What can I get you today?"

He turned to Delta. "I don't have any cash on me. Can you . . . ?"

"Don't you have any plastic?" she asked.

"Plastic?"

"Credit cards! You mean you don't have a credit card?"

"Course I do." Shriver remembered he did have a credit card—sometimes he ordered items for delivery—but he kept it in a drawer at home. "I just don't have it with me."

"We don't accept plastic," the waitress said.

"Oh, all right," Delta said, pulling cash from her purse. "I always bring a big wad to these things anyway. You never know when you're going to be out gallivanting around with some tightwad author."

"Thank you. I'll take a whiskey, please," Shriver told the waitress. "Make it a double."

"And I'll have a Big Wet Screw on the Beach," Delta said.

The waitress blinked. "Uh, I don't think we can make one of those here."

"No problem. How about a shot of to-kill-ya and a beer on the side?"

The waitress turned and disappeared into the mist.

"So," Delta said, "a car chase? What was *that* all about?"

Shriver removed his glasses and covered his face with his hands. "Oh, Delta. I'm in so much trouble."

"What happened?"

Shriver peeked at her through his fingers.

"Tell me!" Delta ordered.

"I was at Dr. Keaudeen's house," he began.

She gasped. "That nympho gynecologist? Did you sleep with her?"

"No! I mean—"

Delta gasped again. "You *did* sleep with her!"

"I didn't sleep with *anybody*."

The waitress materialized, and as she set their drinks on the table, Shriver looked over Delta's shoulder and recognized the graffiti there: NOW THAT I'M ENLIGHTENED, I'M JUST AS MISERABLE AS EVER.

Delta picked up her shot glass. "*Salut.*" Shriver hoisted his tumbler and they both drank. Delta smacked her lips and said, "So, are you going to tell me what happened with Keaudeen or am I going to have to drag it out of you?"

She watched him with eager, bulging eyes.

"That part doesn't matter," he said.

"It matters to *me*."

"What would you say," he said, "if I told you I'm not who you think I am?"

She looked at him closely. He noticed that her eyes were slightly crossed, as if she were staring at her own nose.

"Okay. Then who *are* you?"

"I don't know anymore."

"Is this some kind of existential riddle or something?"

"What I mean is," Shriver said, "I'm not Shriver."

"You're not Shriver?"

"No, I am Shriver, but I'm not the Shriver you think I am."

"Are you drunk already?"

"That's beside the point."

"Well, you're talking nonsense."

"What I mean is, I'm not the Shriver who wrote *Goat Time*."

"Of course you are."

"I'm not."

"Then which Shriver are you?"

"Some *other* Shriver."

She cocked her head. "I don't get it."

"It's a mistake. They got the wrong Shriver."

"Nonsense. The brochure photo . . ."

"That's not even me in that picture!"

"Well, who is it, then?" she asked. "And why'd we have to lose that motorcycle, anyway?"

"I think someone might be trying to kill Shriver."

"Who'd want to kill you?"

"Not *me*! The *real* Shriver."

She thought a moment, then smiled.

"Ah, I get it. You're pulling my leg. This is some kind of stunt. It's just the kind of thing the Shriver in your book would do."

"But it's not *my* book!"

"Sure, sure. Say, have you had a chance to look at *my* book? I really wrote it, by the way. I *am* the real Delta Malarkey-Jones."

"You think I'm crazy," Shriver said.

"You're *all* crazy," she said with a laugh. "Every last one of you."

What did it matter if Delta did or didn't believe him? He had to get to Simone and explain. But for now he would just get drunk. He finished his whiskey in one gulp.

"So, back to Lady Gyno," Delta said.

Shriver wiped at his nose as he recalled the musky perfume of Dr. Keaudeen's thong. "Nothing happened."

Another round appeared on the table. "Gratis," the waitress said before slinking away. The whiskey charged down his gullet and thudded into his belly. A warm chill spread out toward his extremities. Smoke-shrouded specters moved around the bar, murmuring.

"So Keaudeen didn't make a move on you?" Delta asked.

"Yes, *that* happened, but . . ."

"You turned her down?"

"Course I did," Shriver said, his tongue like a dead thing in his mouth. "I'm drunk."

"Well," Delta said, "you may be the first author to escape the jaws of that Venus flytrap."

More drinks appeared. "Where're theez comin' from?" Shriver asked.

"People keep buying you drinks," the waitress said, nodding toward the ghosts on the other side of the smoky room. "Fans."

"But you don' unnerstand," he said. "I'm not the guy."

The waitress looked over at Delta, who said, "He's having a slight identity crisis."

The waitress looked down at Shriver and said, "It's okay. We all have our bad days."

Then she moved off into the fog. Shriver tried to follow

her figure but she was lost among the spirits there. Over near the bar, his back to the bartender, a tall, dark figure lifted a glass in a toast to Shriver before being engulfed in a cloud of smoke. Shriver wondered if perhaps he had died—when he fell off Simone's car?—and this was some way station on the route to heaven. Or maybe he'd been drained of blood by mosquitoes. But no, the itchy lumps on his hands and face could only mean that he was still earthbound.

"I think I'd better get home," he said, thinking not of the Hotel 19 but of his cozy apartment, where Mr. Bojangles waited for him by the door. But the distance between this place and there seemed to him unbridgeable, too far to even contemplate. "Lez go," he mumbled.

He stood and his legs buckled, but Delta held on to him and walked him out to the parking lot. As she poured him into the car, the wind picked up, and a roaring sound filled the air. The mosquitoes, buzzing angrily, were blown away in the maelstrom.

"What on earth?" Shriver said.

From over the rooftops, a helicopter appeared, engine screeching, its floodlights shining down into Shriver's eyes.

Delta climbed in and they screeched out of the lot. Overhead, the copter shuddered and whirred.

"Faster!" Shriver shouted to Delta, convinced now that the black airship was following him.

"I'm trying!" Delta hollered back, but the helicopter remained directly above.

"It's raining!" Shriver cried.

"That's not rain!"

But surely it was rain, he thought, as the wet, oddly scented drops plopped onto his face, and then he saw the moon through the trees, a fat, full, white moon, and stars like the freckles on Simone's chest all across the sky—except for there, directly above, where the helicopter swooped like a dragon.

The car bumped over a curb and there it was, Hotel 19, appearing particularly ominous now, as if all lit up with people waiting to murder him. Delta slammed on the brake and threw the gearshift into park.

He was unable to speak or move. Battery acid coated the back of his throat. Delta climbed out of the car and went around to the passenger side.

"Let me help you, hon'."

She took hold of his arm and, with a powerful tug, pulled him from the seat.

"I dun feel so great," Shriver whimpered.

"No problem. I gotcha."

She walked him toward the entrance. The hotel sign was a neon blur in the sky. Off to the left he glimpsed a large, familiar dark shape, but he could not decipher it. Meanwhile, mosquitoes leaped about his face—he felt one sting his earlobe—but he didn't care anymore.

"Y' know, I'm nod who y' thing I yam," he said.

"Yes, sweetie, I know," Delta said, dragging him toward the entrance.

Unable to keep his increasingly heavy head up, he leaned into her copious bosom for more support.

The automatic doors slid open. The hotel lobby seemed endless, a football field long.

"No, you don' unnerstan'," Shriver said, then he yelled into the lobby: "I'm a imposter!"

"Well, well, well," someone said from the other side of the room. "Look who's here."

There, at the end zone, stood a small figure with yellow hair. Shriver squinted.

"S'moh!" he exclaimed, recognizing her now in the haze. He attempted to stand up straight but was unsuccessful, leaning even harder against the pillar of Delta Malarkey-Jones. As they crossed the endless lobby, Simone eyed the big woman suspiciously. Then she turned a pair of laser eyes to Shriver.

Ecstatic that she had come all this way to see him—to hear his apology—Shriver tried to tell her he loved her, but his dry mouth refused to make a sound.

"I think Mr. Shriver needs to get to bed," Delta said.

Simone's lower lip trembled, but her eyes blazed at Shriver. "Who do you think you are?"

"I dunno," Shriver answered, then belched.

"You're drunk."

"No," he whined, even as he had to lean against Delta just to stay erect.

"I feel so . . . so . . . so *betrayed*," Simone moaned. Her eyes grew moist, reflecting the harsh lobby lights.

"But, S'moh," he said. "Tha' woman. Dr. Keau . . . Dr. Keau . . ."

"Oh, I don't give a damn about *that*," she hissed. "Though it's no surprise to me you'd be so depraved."

"She s'duced me!"

"I *knew* it!" Delta exclaimed.

"Nothing happened!"

"That's not how it looked to *me*," Simone said.

Even in his whiskey-addled state Shriver could detect Simone's jealousy. If he could just convince her that Dr. Keaudeen had ambushed him, he figured, she might back down and give him another shot.

Then, from somewhere nearby—the bar? the restroom?—a man materialized beside Simone.

"Who's this?" Delta asked.

From the way she looked at him, Simone apparently ex-pected Shriver to provide the answer. He took in the man standing next to her: the facial stubble, the aroma of nicotine and whiskey, the eyes raw from reading, the expensive-looking suit jacket and black T-shirt and designer jeans. Shriver became impossibly, unacceptably sober. So this is him, he thought. He tried to say the name, to force the air from his mouth. "Sh . . ." he said. "Shhh . . ."

The man stepped forward, grinning, and extended his hand.

"The name's Shriver," he said. "Pleased to meet you."

Chapter Twelve

Shriver just stared at the hand, then up at the man's face. Look at him, he thought, with that smug expression. He certainly is feeling proud of himself for crawling out of the woodwork and ruining my plan.

"How could you do this to me?" Simone cried.

"Lemme explain."

But she turned away. The real Shriver placed his hand on her quivering shoulder.

"Take your hand off her, you . . . you . . . imposter!" Shriver said.

"Me? *You're* the imposter."

"What the hell is going on?" Delta Malarkey-Jones asked.

"Just calm down, everyone," Simone said, pulling her shoulder away from the real Shriver's hand.

"Tell *him* to calm down," the writer said.

"You keep your hands to your*self*," Shriver countered.

"Mind your own damn business—whatever *that* is," the real Shriver said, moving closer, his face just inches away. Shriver could smell the alcohol on his breath.

"You're drunk," he said.

"*You're* drunk."

Delta stepped up and gave the real Shriver a menacing look. "Careful, pal."

The writer turned to Simone and asked, "Is this the gruesome gal he fornicated with earlier?"

"Hey!" Shriver said. "I didn't fornicate with *anybody*."

"Stop it, all of you!" Simone said.

The two men stood eye to bloodshot eye.

"How do we know you're the real Shriver?" Shriver asked.

"How do we know *you're* the real Shriver?" the real Shriver asked.

"Oh my God," Simone groaned.

"Let's see your driver's license, pal," Delta said.

"Certainly." The real Shriver pulled out his wallet and displayed his license. *Caleb David Shriver*. "Now *yours*."

"My pleasure," Shriver said, before realizing, again, that his wallet was upstairs.

"Well?"

"My wallet is up in my room."

"We can wait."

Shriver blinked.

"What now?" the real Shriver asked.

"I've misplaced my key."

"How *convenient*."

"Never mind," Simone said. She dried her eyes and straightened her spine. "We'll discuss this tomorrow." She glared at Shriver. "And then you'll be going."

"But, Simone—"

"Good night." She turned to the real Shriver. "Let's go, Mr. Shriver."

Grinning triumphantly, the writer followed her to the door.

"Simone!" Shriver called after her. But she did not turn back. He watched her step out into the parking lot, escorting the real Shriver to her car. Where was *he* going? Shriver wondered. Was he staying with Simone?

"What the heck is going on?" Delta asked. "Who was that guy?"

"That was me."

"Everybody's gone bonkers," she said, dragging him toward the elevator.

"Wait," Shriver said. "I need a drink."

"Oh, no."

"Oh, *yes*." Shriver headed across the lobby to the Prairie Dog Saloon and sat at the bar.

"Double whiskey comin' up," the bartendress said.

Delta plopped down next to Shriver with a sigh. "Shot of to-kill-ya."

When the drinks arrived Shriver swallowed his in one gulp and ordered another.

"You sure you want to do that?" Delta asked.

"You're probably right. I should just go after her."

"Who?"

"Simone, of course."

Shriver heard the wheels and pulleys inside Delta's head snap into place.

"You've got a thing for her," she said.

"That man—that other Shriver—he probably has his mitts on her right now."

"You're really smitten."

"She's very susceptible to charming writers," Shriver said.

"You forget, Mr. Shriver. This is my twelfth conference. Professor Cleverly would never fall for another writer."

"*Another* writer?" Shriver said, remembering Simone's story of the short poet. He slammed down his second whiskey and coughed.

"Her first husband was a writer," Delta said. "She supported him for years, and when he finally made it big, he dumped her for his glamorous New York editor."

"He dumped Simone?"

"Like a used paperback."

"What's his name?" Shriver asked. "I'll break his legs."

"Break *whose* legs, Mr. Shriver?"

Detective Krampus appeared at Shriver's elbow. Even in the dim hotel bar his red suit coat vibrated.

"Oh, no one. I was just . . ." He prepared to be arrested—was it a crime to impersonate an author?

"I've been ringing your room for some time now," Krampus said.

"What do you want, Detective?"

"I had a nice chat this evening with one of the cheerleaders in town for the competition. Beautiful young girl. Brunette."

"What about her?" He obviously hasn't heard the news, Shriver thought.

"She said she saw Ms. Smithee in your room last night."

"How could she have seen that? I never had any cheerleader in my room."

"She saw in through the window."

"Through the window?" Shriver pictured the girl standing atop her comrades, defying gravity.

"You told the human pyramid story quite well at the panel today," Krampus said. "We were all enthralled."

"And she said Ms. Smithee was in my room?"

"Indeed. Passed out on your bed, by the sound of it."

"I have no recollection of that."

"Nevertheless," Krampus said, "it is the last-known sighting of our missing poet."

Delta cleared her throat. "Do you honestly think Mr.

Shriver had something to do with Gonquin Smithee's disappearance?"

"I'm just doing my job, Ms. Malarkey-Jones."

"I truly do not remember when she left my room," Shriver said.

"You've said that before, and it is duly noted."

"*I* remember," Delta said.

"You do?" Krampus asked. "But you told me earlier—"

"You jarred my memory, Detective. I remember now that Ms. Smithee left just before I did."

Shriver, like the detective, watched her eyes closely. Was she telling the truth?

"And what time was this?" Krampus asked her, flapping open his notebook.

"No idea. I was pretty sauced."

"But not too sauced to remember her exit."

"Just sauced enough to forget it for about twenty-four hours."

"Interesting," the detective said, writing it all down. "So you were still in the room when the cheerleader saw inside."

"That's right."

Shriver knew then that Delta was lying. He'd been alone when that happened.

"Funny," Krampus said, "she did not mention you being there."

"I may have been in the can."

Krampus waited, as if expecting Delta to recant. But she just sipped at her tequila and smiled.

"Okay, then," he said, shutting the notebook. "I guess that explains that." He started to go, then stopped and turned to Shriver. "By the way, I still haven't been able to locate your former wife."

"Can't help you there," Shriver said.

"Odd how she seems to have dropped off the face of the earth, much like the wife in your masterpiece." He held up his copy of *Goat Time*. "I'm like a bloodhound, Mr. Shriver. I sniff a tantalizing odor, I must follow it. Good night."

When he was gone, Delta finished off her shot of tequila. "This is definitely the strangest conference I've ever been to."

Shriver signaled for another drink. Anything not to think about tomorrow.

Half an hour later, Delta once again had to hold him up as they zigzagged across the lobby. On the elevator, he managed to pull away from her and lean against the wall. He shut his eyes.

"Whydja tell Krampus you were in my room?" he asked as the elevator spun inside his head.

"I didn't like how he was picking on you."

"But you c'd get in big trouble."

"Aw, what's the difference? I know you didn't do anything to that poet."

"But you lied."

"Lied schmied. We all make stuff up. What's the truth anyway? Right?"

"Right."

Next thing Shriver knew, he was outside room nineteen.

"Did you really lose your key?" Delta asked. She patted his pockets.

He pointed at the door.

"In there?"

He nodded.

"Well, I guess you'll have to crash in *my* room."

He tried to resist, but she dragged him along the hallway. From nearby came the sound of tinny music and laughter.

A door creaked open and there stood the willowy brunette cheerleader. She wore a towel as she skipped down the hall to another room, her shoulders brown and soft. She smiled as she passed.

"'Lo," Shriver said, and waved.

Delta opened the door to room twenty. A light went on, and he blinked his eyes. Next time he opened them he lay on the bed, watching the stucco ceiling spin. He moaned and shut his eyes again. Something tugged at his shoes and socks. His feet felt cool and free. A mist came over him. The conference—Simone, the real Shriver, everyone—felt far, far away. Something small but heavy climbed onto his belly and chest.

He clicked his tongue and muttered, "Mizzer Bozhangle."

He reached out his hand to stroke the cat's rabbitlike fur. He felt the soft face, the wirelike whiskers, the thin, cool ears. The kitty purred like a far-off train.

"You're my bez fren," he mumbled, rubbing under the cat's little chin. He was so happy to be home again, in his own bed, with his kitty.

After that—nothing.

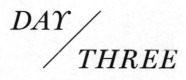

DAY / THREE

Chapter Thirteen

Shriver awakened slowly, his mouth dry, his eyes stuck together. On his chest he felt the familiar warm weight of Mr. Bojangles. Oh, thank God, he thought. It's all been a dream. With some effort he managed to move his arm to stroke the cat's back, but when he touched the animal he felt nothing but smooth flesh. He forced open his eyes only to see darkness. As his eyes adjusted he made out a thin wedge of sunlight over against one wall: curtains. From somewhere far off, he thought he heard someone calling him—"Mr. Shriver?"—before a train horn pierced the darkness.

Realizing where he was, he tried to bolt up in bed like a man awakening from a nightmare, but the considerable arm draped across his chest kept him flat on his back. Dear Lord, he thought as images from last night came to him in short bursts: the whirring helicopter, Detective Krampus's electric jacket, Dr. Keaudeen's leopard-print thong—all seen through a scrim of fluttering insects. Then the distinctive font of a manual typewriter: THE IMPOSTER.

Finally, and most distressingly, he remembered how Simone's eyes had drilled into him as the real Shriver towered next to her in the hotel lobby. He groaned.

Meanwhile, Delta Malarkey-Jones breathed rhythmically beside him, letting out an occasional nose whistle. Shriver tried to delicately lift her arm from his chest, but it was dead weight. Her entire body may as well have been lying across him.

He heard a telephone ringing on the other side of the wall. With some effort he glanced over at the glowing digital clock. It was past eleven. As he set his head back on the pillow he could feel the jelly of his brain sloshing against his cranium.

Again, he thought of Simone's brown eyes compressed into burning slits as he'd clung drunkenly to Delta in the lobby. It had been many years since he'd seen a look of such disappointment on a woman's face. Of course, Simone had been angry about his deception, but she had also been upset, he was sure, to find him in the arms of Dr. Keaudeen. He remembered how she had cried while she drove away from the party. Yes, she must have had feelings for him. For a moment he allowed himself to imagine what might have happened had the real Shriver not appeared, but then his headache returned, along with the image of Simone's searing, coal-hot glare.

Shriver again tried to lift Delta's arm. He started at the wrist, which was relatively light, then moved upward to the bulbous elbow. She remained sound asleep, her breath coming in warm, halitosic puffs against the side of his head. He tried not to look at her, afraid she might not be wearing any clothes beneath the covers. He himself was still in his undershorts and T-shirt, but that was not, by any means, very comforting.

With some effort he managed to hoist her forearm high enough so that he could slip out from beneath it. Once he was free, he lowered the arm gently. Delta grunted and continued sleeping.

When he stood he saw sparks before his eyes and felt a knife push into his forehead. He paused, waiting for the whiskey-poisoned blood to start moving away from his brain. He found his clothes neatly folded on a chair. He quickly slipped into his pants and shirt, then tiptoed to the door in his bare feet. With shoes and socks in his hand, he opened the door slowly, making as little sound as possible. He took one more look around the room, his eyes pounding inside their red sockets. Delta remained passed out in bed. He didn't know if he'd ever see her again. "Farewell," he said to the large lump in the dark. Then he eased the door shut behind him.

He squinted in the unbearably bright hallway as he padded next door to room nineteen. Then he remembered: he had no key.

A door opened behind him.

"Hello."

The cheerleader stood there in her uniform.

"Hi," he said, his voice a dry croak.

She smiled, and he could not make up his mind as to whether it was an innocent smile or a smile that said she knew exactly what had happened last night—whatever *that* was— and was amused by the whole idea.

"I left my key in my room," he told her.

"Oh, I'm sorry."

"That's the least of my troubles, actually." He rubbed the cat-scratch scabs on his hand.

"Oh, you poor thing. Here."

She reached over her shoulder into a backpack shaped like a teddy bear and pulled out a small bottle.

"What happened?" she asked, delicately touching the three red lines on the back of his hand.

"Oh, that was an incident with a cat," he said, shuddering.

"This will help," she said. She took his hand and poured some kind of oil onto the wounds. Then, with tiny but strong fingers, she massaged his hand, front and back.

"I don't know what it is," she said as she pushed her thumbs deep into his palm, "but this stuff really relaxes me. Plus, those darn skeeters don't like it at all."

Shriver's hand felt warm and loose, as though it had been made of stone and was now turning into rubber. Even better, the itching had stopped.

"There," the cheerleader said. "How's that?"

"Lovely. What is that stuff?"

She held up the bottle. "Sunflower oil."

As they rode the elevator together, the cheerleader stood in the corner, smiling, while Shriver slipped on his socks and shoes. In these close confines, she could probably tell he had not showered in several days. He reeked, in fact, and his face was pocked with gray whiskers, his thin hair greasy.

"I'm a little stressed myself today," the girl said. "The semifinals are this afternoon."

"Oh. That's exciting. Congratulations."

She smiled. "It's always been my dream to win the championship."

The door opened on a bevy of cheerleaders.

"Where have you been?" they cried.

"Good luck with the key situation," the brunette said before running down the hallway with her friends.

"Good luck with the semifinals," he shouted at her retreating back.

At the front desk, he found Charlevoix at her usual perch. "Has the maid come in yet?" he asked.

"The maid? Why do you ask, Mr. Shriver?"

"Why, because she has the key," he said.

"What key?"

"The key to my room, of course."

As she stared up at him with a puzzled expression he realized that this was the sister, Sue St. Marie. He quickly explained the situation.

"Oh my," she said. "That's never happened here."

"Yes, I know. So, the maid?"

"Right. Let's see." She checked a printed schedule. "Luna *was* on duty this morning."

"What do you mean, '*was*' on duty?"

"Went home early. Tummy trouble."

"Oh, Lord," Shriver said.

"Maybe you should have some breakfast at the saloon while I call my little sister."

"Mr. Shriver!"

Edsel Nixon approached the front desk.

"I've been trying to call you," he said. "What's going on?"

"I don't know."

"You don't know? Some guy showed up last night and he says he's *you*."

"Oh, that. Yes, I've met him."

"Who is he?"

"He's Shriver, I guess."

"I don't understand."

"We'll talk about it later," Shriver said. "Right now I need to get into my room. I locked myself out."

Sue St. Marie hung up the telephone.

"I'll have to leave a message with maintenance," she said. "Lord only knows where he is."

"How long will it be?"

She shrugged. "We might have to change the lock on the door."

"Maybe we should grab some breakfast?" Edsel Nixon suggested.

In the saloon, Shriver ordered his favorite, oatmeal and a

side of toast. He made this breakfast for himself every day back home. Taking in the aroma of oats and milk, he longed for his tiny kitchen, the decrepit gas stove, the old toaster. Mostly he longed for a bath. He could feel every speck of grime and sweat on his body.

"Have you talked to Simone today?" he asked Nixon.

"Mm-hmm," Nixon said, avoiding his eyes.

"Did she tell you about the party last night?"

"She mentioned something . . . " Edsel's voice trailed off in embarrassment.

"I swear to God, Mr. Nixon, I did not sleep with—"

Edsel put up his hand to end the conversation. "Things happen, Mr. Shriver."

"Not *that* thing!"

Edsel waved the topic away and dug into his raisin bran. Parched, Shriver drank from a thimble-sized glass of watery orange juice, then took a bite of food and nearly gagged. The oatmeal tasted gummy no matter how much milk he poured over it.

"So, who *is* this guy who's pretending to be you?" Nixon asked.

Shriver sighed and set down his spoon. "Does everyone know about it?"

"It's the talk of the town."

"Does anyone believe him?"

"Hard to say."

"Simone?"

"She sounded upset when I spoke to her."

Shriver leaned in and asked, "Was he there?" though he was afraid of the answer.

"Who?"

"The other Shriver."

"Where?"

"At Simone's house."

"She didn't say."

In between two of the potted ferns that cordoned off the saloon from the main lobby, Shriver saw a dark blur.

"Don't look now," he said, "but there's someone spying on us."

Edsel Nixon glanced around the lobby, but the figure by the ferns had disappeared.

"He's gone," Shriver said.

"Who was it?"

"Remember yesterday by the river?" Shriver asked. "This person has been following me at least since then. He dresses in black and rides a motorcycle. I think it might be—"

"This imposter fellow?"

"I never considered that." Maybe the real Shriver had been here all along, Shriver thought.

"What I don't get," Edsel said, "is why anyone would go to the trouble of coming all the way out here just to pretend to be *you*."

For a moment, Shriver considered confessing to Edsel Nixon, but the expression on the young man's face was so earnest and trusting that he couldn't bear to tell him the truth.

"I don't get it either," he said.

Light glinted off the hotel's front door as it opened on the far side of the lobby. In walked Simone with the real Shriver.

"Uh-oh."

Simone looked tired, her shoulders hunched beneath a simple blue blouse. But even in this state, with her hair disheveled and bags beneath her eyes, she glowed. The real Shriver, meanwhile, gave off a curious aura of unkempt cool.

"Is that him?" Edsel Nixon asked.

"Don't tell them I'm here," Shriver said, slipping beneath the table.

"But—"

"Shhh!"

From beneath the table he heard Simone call out from across the room: "Edsel!"

Shriver watched Edsel's feet twitch. He felt bad asking his handler to lie for him. The poor lad didn't have a dishonest bone in his body.

"Have you seen him?" Simone asked, closer now.

"Seen who?"

Two sets of feet appeared beneath the tablecloth: tasseled black loafers and a sensible pair of pale blue pumps. Shriver thought they were standing a little too close together.

"You know who," Simone said, her voice uncharacteristically hard and authoritative. "Now, where is he?"

Edsel hesitated. *Please*, Shriver thought.

"That's probably his porridge," the real Shriver noted.

Did he say *porridge*? How pretentious!

"Well?" Simone said. "Is it his, Edsel?"

"Yes," the student confessed. Shriver froze and sent a telepathic message: *Don't tell them I'm here, Mr. Nixon!*

"Where is he, Edsel?" Simone asked.

Shriver held his breath. Edsel's feet tapped like a jazz drummer's.

The real Shriver spoke up: "Come now, Mr. . . . ."

"Nixon."

"You're kidding. *Edsel Nixon?*"

"I know what you're thinking," Edsel said. "You're thinking, 'This must be the most unfortunately named—'"

"What I'm thinking," the writer said, "is that your parents must be sadists."

Edsel Nixon's feet ceased their tapping. Shriver could sense the boy's resolve hardening.

"Now," the real Shriver said, "where is this imposter?"

"I don't know."

"Edsel," Simone said.

"He left a while ago."

"Well, where was he going?"

"He didn't say."

The writer sighed. "He's no help. Let's go check the room."

"Fine," Simone said. "I'll speak with you later, Edsel."

Nixon said nothing, but his feet started tapping again, even more than before. Shriver watched the two pairs of shoes move off.

"All clear," Edsel said after a while.

Shriver climbed back onto his chair. "Thank you."

"I don't like that guy," his handler said.

/

A few moments later, Shriver and Nixon watched from behind a fern as Simone and the writer headed out to the parking lot. Shriver detected no outward signs of intimacy between the two—no touching or other clues—but still worried that Simone would, in her weakened state, be susceptible to seduction.

"Let's see if we can find a way into your room," Edsel said.

Shriver followed him to the reception desk.

"Oh," Sue St. Marie said, "that lady from the college was looking for you, Mr. Shriver."

"I know."

"She says you have to be out of your room by checkout time."

"When is that?"

She checked her watch. "Half an hour ago."

"First I need to get *into* my room," he reminded her.

"Oh—right. I did get in touch with our maintenance guy." She searched through some message notes on the desk.

"What did he say?" Edsel asked.

"Here it is." She read the note to herself, then said, "He's out sick today, actually."

"First the maid is sick, now the maintenance guy?"

"What can I tell you? Don't eat the mozzarella sticks in the saloon."

Shriver wanted to weep. He didn't so much care about his clothes, but he desperately wanted to retrieve his story before he was run out of town. He'd worked too hard on it to leave it in that decrepit hotel room.

"I'm very sorry about this," Sue St. Marie said.

"Is there any way to break in?" Edsel Nixon asked her.

"Well, you can knock the door down with a battering ram. Or you could try to pick the lock, but then you don't strike me as the cat burglar type."

"How about the window?" Edsel asked.

She mulled it over. "If it's unlocked, that would work. You'd just need a ladder."

Edsel turned to Shriver. "Is your window open?"

"I don't remember."

He knew that, at one point the other night, the window had been open as he watched the cheerleaders construct their pyramid. But had he locked it afterward?

Sue St. Marie directed them to the maintenance room in the basement. There, among the tools and saws and gloves and scattered copies of *Teen Ho*, they found a long aluminum extension ladder. They each grabbed an end and hobbled up the stairs to the lobby and out the front door. They lugged the ladder around to the back of the hotel, where they were immediately set upon by mosquitoes. Oddly enough, none attacked Shriver's hand, where the cheerleader had applied the soothing oil.

Far out on the expanse of grass, halfway toward the railroad tracks, the cheerleaders practiced their hyperkinetic drills in preparation for the semifinals. High-pitched shouts of *Red hot! We're red hot! R-E-D-H-O-T!* floated above the prairie as Shriver and Nixon ferried the ladder across the field. When they finally set it down, Shriver's fingers were numb with divots.

"Which room?" Edsel asked, staring up at the identical windows.

"Nineteen."

They counted the windows from the end of the building until they estimated which one was Shriver's. It was not open, but from this angle, they couldn't tell if it was locked. With some difficulty, they hoisted the ladder up and extended it until it reached the second floor.

"Here," Edsel said, holding out a rusty box cutter he'd picked up in the maintenance room. "To cut through the screen."

"Me?" Shriver had expected the young man to climb up the ladder.

Edsel looked at the ground. "Afraid of heights," he said.

Shriver slid the box cutter into his back pocket and approached the ladder, which, despite its weight, now struck him as thin and insubstantial. He put his hands on a rung and tested the ladder's sturdiness. It seemed strong enough, though there was some give. Edsel stepped forward and, with one hand, took hold of the ladder from underneath, to stabilize it. With his other hand he continued to swipe at the marauding mosquitoes.

Shriver began to climb. The ladder shuddered under his weight. He was only two feet above the ground and already he felt vertiginous. From far behind him he heard the cheerleaders chanting: *We're too hot to handle, there's no doubt! We're too hot to handle, we'll knock you out!* He ascended, one rung at a time, as mosquitoes buzzed around his face.

"Is the window locked?" Edsel asked.

Shriver, who had been staring straight ahead, glanced up. "Can't tell yet," he answered through clenched teeth.

The sun beat down on his head. With each step the ladder shivered, despite Edsel's hold upon it, and each vibration made its way into Shriver's bones. The box cutter weighed ten pounds in his pocket.

At the top he took a deep breath. The window appeared to be open a half inch. Through the glass he could see only the thick curtain.

"It's open!" he tried to shout, though it came out a thin whine.

"Cut the screen out," Edsel called up to him.

As Shriver slowly reached back to retrieve the box cutter from his pocket, he stared up at the deep bowl of clear blue sky overhead. Somewhere on the other side were billions of planets spinning in their rutted orbits, impossibly cold and empty, and oblivious to this quaking man on an aluminum ladder. What difference would it make if he plunged to the ground and landed on the blade of the box cutter? By the same token, what did it matter that he was not the real Shriver, but an imposter bumbling through a pointless charade? Paradoxically, the thought that his actions meant so little in the grand scheme of things gave him strength. His head cleared; his hands grew calm and steady. With the mental clarity of a surgeon, he decided he would seek out Simone to confess his story. Perhaps she would even forgive him before sending him on his way.

Gimme an S! the cheerleaders cheered. *Gimme an H!*

Bolstered by his newfound optimism, he pulled on the window frame until it opened out all the way.

Gimme an R! Gimme an I!

He opened the blade and began to slice the edge of the screen.

Gimme a V! Gimme an E!

He felt his foot slip and the box cutter flopped from his hand like a fish and fell to the ground below.

Gimme an R!

Then his other foot slipped.

Shriver! Shriver! SHRIVER!!!

He plummeted the length of the ladder, his feet *thuk-thuk-thukking* at each rung, his arms flailing at blank air, and then, before he knew what had happened, he landed on his back, his lungs emptied of all oxygen, the blue sky clouded by swarming insects that may or may not have been real.

"Mr. Shriver! Are you all right?"

Edsel Nixon's normally tranquil face, now twisted into a fearful mask, floated above him. Then the sky filled with other faces, pink-cheeked cherubs with their hair neatly swept back into ponytails. There among them was an angel, surely, with a face as familiar as that seen in old Italian frescoes.

"Are you okay, mister?" the angel asked.

"Aw, he just got the wind knocked outta him," another cherub declared.

A hand, light as a feather, alighted on his chest.

"Breathe," the angel chanted. "Breathe."

With each incandescent syllable uttered by this vision, Shriver's lungs expanded a little more, until he could finally pull in a satisfying breath. Soon the faces came into sharp focus, their cupid-bow lips smacking with bubblegum, their eyes grown bored now that the foolish grown-up was out of danger.

"Thank you," he whispered to the brunette, whose smile made the sun look ridiculous.

Tiny, powerful hands took hold of his arms, his wrists and hands, and pulled him onto his unstable feet. By the time he'd shaken the blinking lights from his eyes the girls had returned, antelope-like, to their practice field, and Edsel Nixon was nowhere to be seen.

"I'm in!"

The graduate student waved from the open window. The mesh screen hung loose at the edges, like a flap of skin.

There was a bloodcurdling screech, and Edsel vanished. Suddenly, his feet and legs appeared out the window. Behind him, barely discernible in the darkened room, loomed a large pink figure.

"Where are you going?" Delta Malarkey-Jones shouted from the open window. She draped the black curtain before herself like a toga. "Come back!"

Edsel scrambled to the ground. "I guess we aimed for the wrong room," he said, wiping himself off.

"Was that *you* who screamed, Mr. Nixon?"

"She caught me off guard," the boy replied, a little defensively.

"Sorry," Shriver called up to Delta with a hesitant wave.

"Don't be," she laughed. "You made my day!"

/

After moving the ladder over to the appropriate room, Edsel Nixon bravely climbed up again, only to find the window closed and locked tight.

Leaving the ladder angled against the building, they moped their way back to the lobby, where Sue St. Marie informed them that the afternoon maid was due in around two.

"And she has the only other key with her?" Shriver asked. "There is no master key in the building?"

The clerk looked at him blankly from beneath her towering beehive. "Sorry. I guess we need to rethink our security policy."

Shriver leaned against the counter and put his head in his hands. Just a few moments ago, when he'd been gazing up at the limitless sky, he had felt so strong and invincible. Now he felt defeated, done for.

"Oh!" Sue St. Marie exclaimed. "I almost forgot. Someone left this for you, Mr. Shriver." She held up a manila envelope marked "SHRIVER."

"Who was it?" Shriver asked. "Was he tall? In dark clothes?"

"You'll have to ask my little sister," she said. "It was here when I arrived this morning."

Shriver turned to Edsel Nixon and said, "I need a drink."

As Shriver and Edsel headed to the saloon, Jack Blunt came bounding across the lobby, looking almost as disheveled as Shriver in a brown corduroy jacket and checked shirt, his toupee only partially affixed to his scalp.

"Hey, you!" he said. "I don't know who the hell you are, and I sure as hell don't know why you did what you did, but I want to thank you."

"Thank me? What for?"

"For handing me the literary story of the year! This is going to be on front pages all over the world!"

"It is?"

Blunt laughed, exhaling a waft of whiskey breath. " 'Reclusive author comes out of hiding, then turns out to be an imposter, in turn prompting the *real* reclusive author to come out of hiding.' Man, that is golden!"

"Excuse me," Edsel Nixon said. "I'm wondering, since you're one of the few people to have met the real Shriver— why didn't *you* know this man here was an imposter?"

"Hey, it's been twenty years. People change. The guy says he's Shriver, he looks reasonably like him—hey, I bought it. So sue me."

Shriver turned to Edsel. "I really need that drink."

"Hey," Blunt said, "I'm headed to the airport to pick up your agent." He laughed. "Listen to me. I mean, the *real* Shriver's agent. Maybe you could come along."

"I don't think so."

"Oh, come on. I'll play nice. I want your side of the story. You know—what motivated you, how you did it, all that good stuff."

"No, thank you."

"This is your chance. You could be famous too. The next Clifford Irving. Maybe even get a book deal!"

Edsel Nixon stepped forward, positioning himself between Shriver and Blunt. "He said no. Now leave him alone."

Shriver could have hugged the boy.

"Fine, okay," the reporter said, backing away. "But listen, if you change your mind, Mr. . . . uh . . . What *is* your name, anyway?"

"It's *Shriver*."

Blunt laughed again. "Tell that to the fellow in *there*," he said, gesturing toward the saloon. Then, with a wave and a wink, he headed out the door.

Inside the saloon, Shriver and Nixon found the real Shriver at the bar, nursing a glass of whiskey.

"You," the real Shriver said.

"Let's get out of here," Edsel said, pulling on Shriver's elbow.

Shriver turned to the real Shriver. "Where's Simone?"

"She's very busy," the writer said. "Damage control and all that."

Shriver could see that the man was drunk.

"Come on, Mr. Shriver," Edsel said.

"Wait for me outside," Shriver told him.

"But—"

"Please, Edsel."

His handler sighed, turned, and left the saloon.

Shriver approached his rival.

"What can I getcha?" the blue-haired bartendress asked.

"Give him one of these," the real Shriver said, holding up his glass. "On me."

"No thanks," Shriver said.

The real Shriver shrugged. "Suit yourself." He finished his drink and ordered another.

"Careful," Shriver said. "You have a reading later on."

"Piece of cake," the man said.

"What are you going to read, may I ask?"

"Oh, an excerpt from my masterpiece, I suppose. Any suggestions?"

"I'm afraid I can't help you there."

The real Shriver smiled. "No? How about the motel scene?" he asked. "Or the honeymoon scene? Remember writing that?"

Shriver looked away.

"Or the scene on the airplane?" the writer continued. "Which would be best, *Shriver*? You wrote the goddamn thing, after all."

He had a point, Shriver had to admit.

"Tell me," the real Shriver said. "What happens in chapter two?"

"I don't know."

"Caleb arrives in Oregon. How about chapter five?"

"I don't know."

"That's the art museum scene. Chapter fifteen?"

"I don't know."

"The wedding. Don't you even know your own goddamn book, man?"

There was something off about this, Shriver decided, but he didn't know what.

"Chapter eleven, the fireworks scene," the writer said. "Or chapter six—the first time you and your wife make love."

He had to get out of here, but first . . .

"Stay away from Simone," Shriver said, trying to sound calm.

The writer swiveled toward him on the bar stool. "Whatever do you mean?"

"I mean, leave her alone."

The real Shriver tossed some coins onto the bar and wobbled to his feet. "Lovely girl, our Simone. I think you might've stood a chance, if only . . ."

"If only what?"

The man laughed. "If only I hadn't come along."

Shriver considered slugging him, but the writer was tall and rangy, not to mention drunk. How would it look if he got into a fistfight and lost, especially given all that had happened?

"Now, if you'll excuse me," the writer said, "I've got a date to keep."

Shriver watched him exit the saloon.

"Well, what do you want to do now?" Edsel Nixon asked, suddenly beside him.

Chapter Fourteen

Shriver lay in Edsel Nixon's claw-footed bathtub, warm water up to his neck, frothy bubbles tickling his nose.

"Everything okay in there?" Edsel called from the hallway.

"Perfect," Shriver answered. "Thank you."

The bathroom itself was enormous, as large as Shriver's bedroom back east, with black and white floor tiles and an old-fashioned freestanding sink. The rest of the apartment was to scale, with a spacious kitchen overlooking a vast living room, and a bedroom large enough that the queen-size bed appeared small. Nixon had bashfully conducted a tour, apologizing for what he called messiness, though Shriver had never seen a more orderly home in his life. The hardwood floors were spotless, the antique tables shiny. Nixon's desk—where he worked on his thesis—was neatly arranged, with two piles of paper stacked squarely into boxes. Shriver decided that the place had been decorated by a woman. He had never seen curtains and towels and wall hangings so well coordinated, and the kitchen was simply too organized to have been planned by a lone bachelor. He looked for clues of a woman's presence as he was shown around the place but saw no brassieres on a doorknob, no ladies' magazines on the nightstand. Only here in the bathroom were there a few feminine products, such as bath oil and bubble crystals.

Cleansed of dirt and grime, he felt like a new man already.

He had gargled for a full five minutes with Nixon's citrus-flavored mouthwash and had shaved with a triple-bladed razor and a magnifying mirror connected to the side of the tub. If only he had a fresh set of clothes. His malodorous shirt and trousers lay folded neatly on the commode. On top lay the unopened manila envelope, reminding Shriver of his sins.

As he rested his head back on the edge of the tub, Shriver replayed the scene from the saloon in his mind. He heard the real Shriver's derisive laugh. Could Simone fall for such an arrogant person? Delta didn't think she would succumb to another writer, but she was clearly vulnerable, and there was that poet last year . . .

Soft sunlight filtered through the gauzy window curtain. Shriver gazed up to see a poster tacked onto the ceiling: a field of tall grass, a forest in the distance, all beneath a blue sky dotted with cottony clouds. Near the bottom of this picture, obscured by the tall grass, he saw a dark smudge. He squinted. Was that an animal lurking in the grass? A panther? Shriver sat up, sending a small wave of foamy water over the lip of the tub, and stared. The bucolic scene was now somehow menacing. His heart beat rapidly in his ears.

"Here's a towel," Edsel Nixon said from the other side of the partially open door. A hand appeared, setting a fluffy, powder-blue towel on the edge of the sink.

Shriver continued to gape at the picture.

"Where'd you get this poster on the ceiling, Mr. Nixon?"

"Oh, that," came Edsel's calm voice from the hallway. "That was here when I moved in. I've been meaning to take it down, but for some reason I never have."

Shriver blinked and the black creature seemed to disappear. He lay back and shut his eyes. Just a few more minutes, he thought. Then I'll dry off, get dressed, retrieve my things, and fly home. Never mind Simone. She would never understand his predicament. Hell, *I* don't even understand, he thought.

He heard the melodious ring of a doorbell, followed by a familiar rumbling voice coming from the front room.

"Where is he?" T. Wätzczesnam asked.

Shriver froze and held his breath.

"I haven't seen him," Nixon said, sounding stricken.

"They told me at the hotel that he left with you." T. sounded steamed.

Shriver watched a drop of water form on the tip of the spigot, plumping itself until too heavy to hang on anymore. It fell in slow motion onto a bubble-free patch of water. *Plop.*

"What was that?" the cowboy asked, his voice growing louder as he entered the hallway. "He's here, isn't he?"

"Professor," Edsel pleaded.

Shriver inhaled and immersed himself beneath the thick bubbles. From above he could make out a few watery syllables but no words.

This is quite pleasant, he thought. Enveloped in warm water, his senses dulled, he wished he could stay here forever. He recalled a program about a shipwreck he'd seen on public television. Apparently, there is a reflex among drowning mammals that slows the heart rate and shifts blood flow so that the brain receives more oxygen than normal. Amazing how the body reacts to trauma, he'd thought at the time. Even now he was sure he could feel the blood coursing to his brain.

Then he felt a hand grab him by the hair and tug him to the surface.

"Shriver!"

Shriver coughed and heaved and wiped the bubbles from his eyes. T. knelt by the tub, his weathered face just inches away.

"What're you gonna do about this imposter?" the cowboy asked, each syllable arriving with a sour whiff of whiskey.

Shriver could not speak. He was still sucking oxygen into his deprived lungs.

"Do you know that charlatan stayed at your sweetheart's house last night?"

"He did?" Shriver croaked. "I knew it!"

"I thought that would arouse your interest."

"You don't think—" Was that why the real Shriver had laughed like that back at the saloon?

"Anything is possible," T. said. "I hate to tell you this—I know how sweet you are on our Professor Cleverly—but last year she did succumb to the charms of an admittedly charismatic but decidedly second-rate poet."

"I know all about that, T."

"You know about the poet?"

"I know about the poet. And the first husband."

The cowboy sat on the clothes and envelope atop the commode. "That woman broke my heart, Shriver."

"*Your* heart? You mean—?"

"I know, I know. 'It is thought a disgrace to love unrequited,' Shriver. 'But the great will see that true love cannot be unrequited.'"

"So when you said she was not on the market—?"

"Wishful thinking on my part, old boy."

"I'm sorry, T."

"Not a problem, Shriver. Your feelings for my dear Simone are entirely understandable. Later on we can shoot at each other with pistols. At the moment, my concern is purely literary. We have an imposter in our midst, and we must stop him!"

"But, T.," Shriver said, "he's not an imposter."

"What does *that* mean?"

"*I'm* the imposter."

T. did a double take. "Explain yourself, sir."

"I didn't write *Goat Time*."

"Of course you did."

"That other Shriver wrote it."

T. turned to Edsel. "What on earth is he talking about, Nixon?"

The graduate student shrugged.

"I got the invitation by mistake," Shriver explained. "And for some idiotic reason, I decided to come anyway. I don't know why. Maybe I was lonely. Maybe I was looking for something meaningful."

T. stared at him for a moment, not blinking his bloodshot eyes. Then his face cracked open into a grin and he laughed.

"Oh, this is rich!"

Shriver laughed with him. It felt so good to tell the truth. "Crazy, isn't it?"

T. bent over and convulsed, tears forming in his eyes. "You are one clever son of a bitch."

"Not really," Shriver said. "Just stupid."

"You know, when I heard about that charlatan this morning, I was ready to believe him for two reasons. One, I could see how my dear Simone was growing fond of you, and I was jealous, I admit it."

"Wait," Shriver said. "Simone was growing fond of me?"

"But the other reason," T. barreled on, "was your blasted modesty. I've never in all my years met a writer—a real, bona fide *writer*—who didn't think his shit smelled like eau de cologne. But you, Shriver, a giant among us, you skulk around like some insecure graduate school poet just dreading the moment when someone's going to tell you to put away your quill and take up haberdashery. I can't believe you've *always* been like this. What the hell happened to you?"

"You don't believe me, do you?"

T. sighed and stood up from his perch. "You didn't come here because you're lonely, Shriver. You came here because, goddamn it, you're a writer."

"But, T.—"

"Don't 'but' me, sir. You're the real deal, Shriver. I feel it in these tired old bones. Now, get your ass outta that tub and go reclaim your good name."

Chapter Fifteen

Seated in Edsel Nixon's shuddering jeep, stopped at an insufferably long-lasting red light, Shriver swatted at the mosquitoes that swarmed around his head. The graduate student shifted into neutral and revved the engine, as if the noise might keep the insects at bay.

Professor Wätzczesnam had left before Shriver got dressed, swearing he'd track down "that goddamn imposter" while Shriver returned to the hotel for his story and some clean clothes.

"You have a reading to give today, Shriver," T. had said. "You don't want to stink up the joint with those rank rags."

"But what about the *real* Shriver?" Shriver asked him.

"You mean the *fake* Shriver? Don't worry—we'll take care of him."

Then he was gone.

The intersection formed a gray X in the middle of an oppressively flat stretch of prairie. A mile south, the town water tower and clumps of various campus buildings nestled beneath a blanket of rich blue sky.

As they sat there the shrill buzz of mosquitoes intensified and Shriver swatted helplessly at them until he realized too late that it was not the sound of insects at all: a motorcycle was fast approaching the jeep from behind. Shriver tensed. As the motorcycle pulled up alongside, he ducked, waiting for something—a bullet?—but the driver just waved, then tore ahead through the red light.

"That guy has the right idea," Edsel said. He shifted into drive and peeled out.

Shriver could hardly breathe. He felt like he'd lost what little control he'd ever had of his destiny and was now being jostled and pulled around like a character in a novel. He appreciated that Edsel Nixon and Professor Wätzczesnam believed in him and wanted to help him, but he really needed to get out of this place.

"Mr. Nixon," he said, "this is what's going to happen. We're going to the hotel, where I'll gather my things, and then you'll drive me straight to the airport."

"But the imposter—"

"Never mind him."

"But Professor Wätzczesnam said—" The poor boy looked crushed. "What about your good name?"

"That's just it, Edsel. My name is no good. It's certainly not worth getting killed for."

"*Killed*, sir?"

"Look what happened to Ms. Smithee! I'm done here. I want to go home."

A moment later, a disappointed Edsel Nixon turned into the hotel parking lot. "I'll drop you off," he said, "so you can run inside without getting bitten too badly."

"You are a gentleman, Mr. Nixon."

The jeep screeched to a halt at the front door, but Shriver stayed put.

"Mr. Shriver?" Edsel said.

At the far end of the parking lot sat the black motorcycle.

"Sir?" Edsel said.

"Do me a favor, Mr. Nixon."

"Of course."

"If something happens to me . . ." He turned to his handler, who watched him with curious, concerned eyes. "Please tell Professor Cleverly that . . ."

"Tell her what, sir?"

"Tell her I said thank you."

Shriver leaped out and ran to the entrance. The lobby was deserted but for the telltale beehive behind the counter. But as he made his way to the desk he noticed Jack Blunt just inside the saloon entrance. The reporter, facing the other way and speaking with someone, had not seen him, and Shriver wanted to keep it that way.

He quietly asked Sue St. Marie if the afternoon maid had arrived.

"I think so," she replied. "She should be up on the third floor somewhere right now. You can go try to find her if you want."

"Thank you."

As he turned to go, the receptionist said, "Oh— some gentlemen have been looking for you, Mr. Shriver."

He glanced toward the saloon, where Blunt remained with his back turned. "Can you do me a favor, Sue St. Marie?"

She grinned and pointed at her name tag: CHARLEVOIX.

"I'm so sorry," Shriver said. "I can't keep you two straight."

"No problem, Mr. Shriver. What can I do for you?"

"Those gentlemen in the saloon? Don't tell them I'm here."

With that he ran around the corner and jammed a finger at the elevator button. The door did not open. The light showed the car stopped at the third floor. From behind him Shriver could hear Blunt talking to someone in the lobby. Nearby was a door marked STAIRS. He pushed through and ran up to the third floor.

The maid's cart sat parked in the hallway, loaded down with cleaning equipment and supplies, but none of the room doors were open. She had either stepped away or was in any of twenty rooms on the floor.

He put an ear to the door nearest the maid's cart. Nothing. He went to the next door. No sound. From inside the next room he thought he heard the rustling of sheets. He knocked gently at the door. The rustling continued. He knocked again, this time a little louder. The rustling stopped. He heard a man's voice. He was about to step away when the door cracked open, revealing a sliver of Basil Rather in a royal blue silk robe. He held the door so that Shriver could see only one of his eyes.

"Well, well, if it isn't our own Victor Lustig, come to sell us the Eiffel Tower."

"Victor *who*?"

"What is it you want?" Rather asked.

"I'm looking for the maid."

"Can't help you there, old boy."

"I've locked myself out, you see, and she's the only one with a master key."

Rather gazed down his long, straight nose and said, "What would you like *me* to do about it?"

The playwright peered back into the room for a moment, opening the door an inch or so more, so that Shriver saw the flash of a pale green maid's outfit.

"Is that the maid in there?" he asked.

"Of course not."

"Who's that in the room with you?"

"Who?"

"That's what *I'm* asking."

"Please, Shriver. I'm very busy."

He made to shut the door but Shriver inserted his foot in the doorway.

"What do you think you're doing?" Rather asked.

"I know the maid is in there!"

Shriver forced the door open and pushed inside. Near the window, in a pale green maid's costume, barefoot and holding a feather duster, stood Ms. Brazir. A large rubber phallus poked from the front of the skirt, like the head of a snake from under a rug.

"Oh," Shriver said.

"Are you happy now?" Basil Rather asked.

"I thought you were the maid," Shriver explained.

The three of them stood there for an awkward moment until Rather cleared his throat and held the door open for Shriver's exit.

"Sorry," Shriver said.

The playwright sniffed contemptuously and slammed the door behind him.

There was still no sign of the real maid. Afraid to barge into any more rooms—Lord only knew what he might encounter!—Shriver waited in the hallway for an interminable amount of time, then took the stairway down to the second floor, but the maid was not there either. He was afraid to go back to the lobby for fear of running into Jack Blunt—or the motorcycle man in black—but there was no choice. He had to find that maid. Just as he reached the stairway door, the elevator arrived. From inside came girls' voices. Before Shriver could disappear into the stairwell, several cheerleaders, still in their uniforms, their hair slick with sweat, burst into the hall like freed ponies.

"We won the semifinals!" the brunette squealed.

"That's wonderful," Shriver said.

She paused, letting the other girls continue down the hall. "Feeling better?" she asked. "That was a nasty spill you took on that ladder."

"Well, I can breathe."

"That's half the battle, isn't it?"

"I must keep that in mind," Shriver said.

The girl skipped down the hall.

"Congratulations," Shriver called out to her. "On the semifinals."

"Thanks. But we still have to win the finals."

A door swung open and the girls disappeared into their room.

Shriver took the stairs to the first floor. At the bottom, he cracked the door open. No one at the elevator. He stepped out and poked his head around the corner. No sign of Blunt or the agent in the lobby. He took a breath and walked quickly over to the desk.

"Those gentlemen keep asking for you!" Charlevoix practically shouted.

"Shhh!"

"They're in the saloon," she stage-whispered.

"I can't find the maid," he told her.

"She's not on the third floor?"

"Her cart is, but there's no sign of her."

"Maybe she took a break."

"Where does she take her break?"

The desk clerk leaned forward and said, "Why are we whispering?"

"Is there a room where the maids go?"

"There's a locker room."

"Where's that?"

"It's for employees only."

"Never mind," he said, and scooted around the corner to the elevators. Maybe the maid had returned to the third floor. He pressed the button. Just before the elevator door opened, Edsel Nixon appeared from around the corner. Shriver waved him forward, but Nixon looked back over his shoulder, toward the lobby, as if someone was speaking to him. It sounded like Blunt.

"Have you seen our infamous so-called Mr. *Shriver*?" came the reporter's voice.

Shriver waved frantically, pleading with the graduate student to reply in the negative.

"Uh, I'm looking for him also," Edsel told Blunt.

Shriver blew him a kiss and then stepped into the elevator just before the doors rolled shut.

As the elevator ascended, Shriver leaned against the wall, his heart thumping in his ears. If he ever got out of this, he would never leave his apartment again.

The door opened at the third floor. The maid's cart was now gone. Shriver jumped back on the elevator and went down to the second floor. Rounding the corner, he saw the man in black sitting on the floor, waiting, just outside room nineteen. Shriver stopped and turned back, but not before the man saw him. Shriver ran into the stairwell and back up to the third floor. From the landing he watched as the man tore down the stairs to the first floor.

After a moment, Shriver returned to the second floor. He opened the door just as the elevator whirred into motion. Someone was coming. He backed into the stairwell again and waited.

"It's room nineteen," he heard Jack Blunt say as he exited the elevator. Shriver peeked through the door to see another man accompany Blunt around the corner, followed by Detective Krampus. What was going on? Why was Krampus here? Had he come to arrest him?

A moment later Shriver heard a knock from down the hall, followed by Krampus calling out, "Open up, Mr. Shriver!"

"Doesn't seem to be anyone there," someone said in a deep voice.

"He's in there," Blunt said. "I can hear the son of a bitch breathing."

"Mr. Shriver, I really must speak with you," Krampus shouted.

Shriver pounded down the stairs and burst through the lobby door. He ran past the front desk, where Charlevoix called out, "You certainly are popular here!"

He sped toward the entrance. As he got near, the doors slid open automatically. He skidded to a stop just outside. He scanned the lot. Behind him, through the glass, he watched as Jack Blunt and another man—the agent, Mr. Cheadem, apparently—came around the corner from the stairway, followed by Krampus. On the other side of the lobby, emerging from the saloon, came the tall man in black.

This is it, Shriver thought. I'm done for.

Just then he heard the distinctive clip-clop of horseshoes on pavement. Across the parking lot galloped Walter with T. Wätczesnam astride his sloped back. Shriver held up his arm, as if hailing a cab.

"Yee haw!" the cowboy hollered, waving his ten-gallon hat.

Shriver looked back to see the men running through the hotel lobby toward the door. Nixon, lagging behind, signaled frantically for Shriver to run.

The cowboy steered Walter up to the hotel entrance.

"Climb aboard, Shriver!"

Shriver looked back again. The men had almost reached the door.

"Time's a-wastin', buddy," T. said, holding out his knobby, weather-beaten hand. Shriver took hold, and, with surprising strength, T. pulled him up onto the horse, where Shriver settled in behind him on the saddle.

"Giddyup!" T. roared, and Walter tore out of the parking lot.

Chapter Sixteen

Walter ran at a full gallop, each stride sending Shriver's sore rump in the air and then back down against the hard back edge of the saddle. He had never ridden a horse before. Amazed and terrified by the animal's power, he clutched at T.'s denim jacket as they hurtled down the campus's main drag. Students waved and shouted hello, apparently accustomed to seeing the cowboy professor around town on his trusty steed.

"Hold on, Shriver!" T. cried as he abruptly steered the horse around a sharp corner onto a wide side street.

"Where are we going?"

"To a party!"

They rode past several old, solidly built homes with well-cared-for lawns before slowing and turning up a long gravel driveway. The drive was lined with cars parked beneath a double row of massive trees that formed a green tunnel overhead. Among the cars, Shriver noticed, was Simone's giant vehicle. At the end of the drive stood a white house with tall columns. To Shriver the place looked like a plantation house or the home of the warden in a chain-gang movie.

They rode right up to the front steps and T. pulled the reins. "Whoa!" The horse snorted and came to a stop.

"Where are we?" Shriver asked.

"This is the house of our outrageously overcompensated college president."

Mosquitoes descended upon them as they dismounted.

"Good boy," T. said, patting the horse on its powerful flank. The animal snorted and flicked its tail at the ruthless insects.

At the bottom of the steps leading up to the wide, columned porch, the cowboy produced a flask and offered it to Shriver.

"No thanks, T."

T. looked taken aback. "Very prudent of you, Shriver." Then he took a long pull, screwed up his face into a pleased grimace, and pushed through the pulsing wall of mosquitoes to the front door.

"Are you sure I should be here, T.?" Shriver asked, rubbing at his saddle sores.

The cowboy snorted, sounding remarkably like Walter the horse. "Of course you should be here, Shriver. This party's for *you*."

He lifted a heavy brass knocker and banged it against the door. Shriver looked back down the long driveway, estimating how long it would take to run down its length and back to the hotel.

As they waited, there came a shrill noise from the far end of the porch: another insect zapper. *Zzzzzzch!*

"Amazing contraption," T. said. "I'd like to strap one to my back."

As the bug killer zapped away, the door swung open and a black-jacketed servant appeared.

"We're here for the soiree," T. said.

The servant, a stoop-shouldered older gentleman, consulted a clipboard. "Your names, sir?"

"My name is T. Wätzczesnam, Ph.D., and this here is the party's honoree, Mr. Shriver."

The servant checked off T.'s name on the list, then paused. "It seems Mr. Shriver has already arrived."

"Nonsense," T. said. "*This* is Mr. Shriver."

"T.," Shriver said.

"According to the list, sir—"

"Damn your list, man."

"T., please."

"Sir," the servant said, puffing out his fragile-looking chest.

"Out of our way!" The cowboy pushed past the man, nearly knocking him over. "Come on, Shriver. Let's settle this once and for all."

Apologizing to the shocked servant, Shriver followed T. inside. They passed into a wood-paneled hall with a wide staircase. T. turned left through an arch into a large room full of people chatting and drinking wine. Over by the tall windows, Christo, Delta's musician friend, played "Somewhere over the Rainbow" on a grand piano. Nearby stood Simone and the real Shriver speaking to a squat man with silver hair and a matching handlebar mustache. When Shriver followed T. into the room, a few faces turned and stared, then, like a wave, other faces turned and stared, the wave coursing through the crowd until it washed up at the back, where Simone's face went hard and red. By now, the room had grown silent except for the piano, which the oblivious young man continued to play.

Simone detached herself from the triangle and pushed through the room. She'd changed into an elegant white dress with spaghetti straps. The freckles on her chest and shoulders glowed with rage.

"You've got a lot of nerve," she said through clenched teeth.

"Simone, dear," T. said, but she ignored him and marched straight up to Shriver.

"I hoped you'd left town by now," she said, "with your tail between your legs."

Shriver did not know what to say. He glanced around the room, hoping to see a friendly face, but no one smiled— except for the real Shriver, whose grin was of the well-fed-canary type.

"So," Simone said, "what have you got to say for yourself?"

Shriver cleared his throat. "I'd like to apologize."

"What the hell for?" T. asked.

"No, T.," Shriver said, "I need to say this." He paused, trying to figure out what it was he needed to say. Simone waited with a skeptical expression. "I came here under false pretenses," he started.

"Nonsense!" T. cried.

Simone wheeled toward the cowboy. "Will you pipe down, you blithering old drunk?"

Wätzczesnam stepped back, as if she had struck him across the face, but it worked: he shut up. And so did the piano player, who stopped in the middle of a verse.

Simone turned back to Shriver. "Say what you need to say and go."

"Of course."

Looking at all these glasses of wine, Shriver wanted more than anything to have a drink. No—he wanted more than anything to be somewhere else. No again—he wanted to be somewhere else *and* drunk. But here he was, sober, in a predicament of his own manufacturing, and he swore he would exit as gracefully as possible.

"First of all, I'd like to say what a privilege it's been to be here with you all these past few days. With Mr. Rather, Ms. Amphetamine, with Ms. Smithee, wherever she is. I'd especially like to thank Professor Wätzczesnam, and my intrepid handler, Mr. Nixon, who I wish was here, for their generosity and support."

"Hear! Hear!" T. said, lifting a glass of wine from a passing waiter's tray.

"You have treated me with such undeserved respect and courtesy. I will always remember you fondly."

Simone sighed dramatically. "Are you finished?"

The real Shriver, who had remained beside the piano, now moved through the crowd and stood inappropriately close to Simone. To Shriver this smacked of some kind of territorial signal: *This woman belongs to* me. The writer also appeared intoxicated as he swayed on unsteady legs, his eyes glassy and unfocused. Shriver felt his face burn, but he was glad to see Simone take a small step away, as if she too were uncomfortable with his proximity.

"Most of all," Shriver continued, "I'd like to thank *you*, Professor Cleverly, for presenting me with the opportunity to meet these lovely people."

Simone rolled her eyes.

"And I want to say how profoundly sorry I am for—"

"Wait!"

Through the arch came Gonquin Smithee, followed by Edsel Nixon.

"Thank God!" Simone said, running to the poet. "Where have you been?"

Gonquin, waving a sheaf of yellow paper, sidestepped Simone and approached Shriver. "This," she said, holding out the pages, "is wonderful."

"Is that my story?" Shriver took the pages in his hand. It felt like being reunited with a child. "But how did you get it?"

"Guess where she was," Edsel Nixon said, beaming. "She was in your room this whole time."

"I passed out under your bed, then woke up yesterday morning after you'd gone," Gonquin explained. "I really didn't want to face Majora, so I stayed and spent all day composing a slew of new poems—all from the point of view of my father." She pulled several pages of hotel stationery from her pockets. "I think it's my best work."

"You've been there since yesterday?" Simone asked.

"When Shriver didn't come back last night, I figured I'd stay another day." She turned to Shriver and added, "I spent half the night reading your story. I think I read it five times."

Simone directed a withering look at Shriver. "He didn't return to his room last night?"

"I was locked out," he explained, thrilled by her jealousy.

"When those men knocked on the door to room nineteen this afternoon," Edsel said, "Ms. Smithee climbed out the window and down the ladder we left there."

"When men pound on the door," Gonquin said, "my instinct is to run the other way."

"Does Detective Krampus know about this?" Shriver asked.

"Detective *who?*" the poet said.

The real Shriver stepped forward, again positioning himself beside Simone. Swaying slightly, he extended a hand to Gonquin. "Ms. Smithee, so pleased you turned up."

"Who's this?" the poet asked Shriver, ignoring the man's hand.

"This is Mr. Shriver," Simone told her.

"I don't understand." Gonquin looked to Shriver for an explanation.

"It's a long story," he said.

"Don't you think it's time you left?" Simone asked him.

"Leave?" Gonquin said. "Why would he leave?"

"Ms. Smithee—"

"This is the best story I've read in a long, long time," the poet said, grabbing the papers back from Shriver. "You can't make him leave now."

"You don't understand," Simone said.

"Damn right, I don't."

Looking at Shriver as she spoke to Ms. Smithee, Simone said, "This man is *not* Shriver."

"Of course he is."

"Hear! hear!" T. interjected as he helped himself to another glass of wine.

Simone addressed Shriver. "Perhaps you'd like to explain this to Ms. Smithee."

All eyes turned to Shriver. He licked his dry lips. "Well," he began.

The doorbell rang.

"Now what?" Simone said.

Excited voices were heard from the hall before in rushed Jack Blunt and another man, a portly young fellow with a double chin that spilled over his shirt collar.

"Greetings, everyone," Blunt said, his toupee still askew. "May I introduce Donald Cheadem, Mr. Shriver's agent."

Mr. Cheadem walked directly up to Shriver and offered his hand. "How do you do, Mr. Shriver?"

"No!" cried Simone and the real Shriver in unison.

Startled, Cheadem stepped back, as if to begin again. The real Shriver stepped forward. "*I* am Shriver."

"Oh, so sorry," the agent said.

"Wait a second," Gonquin Smithee said. "You're Shriver's agent, and yet you don't know what he looks like?"

"We only met the one time," Cheadem said as the real Shriver pumped his hand, "and that was twenty years ago."

"Good to see you again," the real Shriver said.

"I was only fifteen years old at the time," the agent continued. "My *father* was Mr. Shriver's original agent, you see."

"That's right," the writer said. "I remember now."

At this point, Shriver considered running. Nothing good was going to happen here. He'd been exposed as an imposter, Simone loathed him, and he had retrieved his story. It was time to go home, before he got thrown in jail—or lynched. With this in mind, he backed away toward the front hall.

"And how *is* your old man?" the real Shriver asked Mr. Cheadem.

"I thought you knew," the agent said. "My father passed away ten years ago."

Just as Shriver had reached the arch that led to the hall, the front door burst open again and in marched Detective Krampus.

"Nobody move!"

"What's going on?" Simone asked.

"Will Mr. Shriver please step forward?" the detective said.

Some in the room turned to our Shriver, some to the other Shriver. Neither man made a move.

"Well?" Krampus said. "Is no one here the author of this novel?" He held up a copy of *Goat Time*.

Shriver watched the real Shriver, whose eyes darted about the room.

"*This* is Mr. Shriver," Simone said, indicating the man beside her.

"Is that so?" Krampus asked.

"Of course it is," Simone answered just as Gonquin Smithee said, "Of course not."

"Ms. Smithee?" Detective Krampus said, just now noticing the poet. "Is that you? Where on earth have you been?"

"Oh, around," she said.

"But—"

"I'll explain later," Shriver told Krampus.

The detective digested this, then turned back to the real Shriver. "Well—*are* you Shriver?"

"Go on, Caleb," Simone said. "Tell him."

Caleb? Shriver thought. She's calling him *Caleb?*

The silver-haired man with the voluminous mustache pushed through the stunned group and addressed Krampus.

"Detective, my name is Horace Wimple, and I am the president of the college and current resident of this home."

"How do you do, Mr. President."

"Frankly, I'm a little confused."

"Of course. Let me explain. This man"—Krampus gestured toward the real Shriver—"is wanted in three states for fraud."

Simone let out a cry of anguish.

"I knew it!" T. hollered.

Shriver too had known something was off. The man was simply too familiar with his own novel.

In shock, no one made a move when the real Shriver bolted from the room.

"Caleb!" Simone shouted when the front door slammed.

"Simone!" Shriver called, following her into the hall.

Simone opened the door and, on the front porch, restrained by two uniformed police officers, the real Shriver squirmed and cursed.

"Let him go!" Simone ordered, but the officers held tightly to the struggling writer.

"You can take him away," Krampus said to the men.

As a crowd gathered behind her, Simone confronted the diminutive detective. "This is outrageous! Where are you taking Mr. Shriver?"

"That is *not* Mr. Shriver," Krampus said.

"But I *am* Shriver!" the man shouted as the officers steered him down the steps. "*He's* the imposter! Not me!"

"Detective," Horace Wimple said, "can you please explain all this?"

"For the past several years," Krampus said, "this man has assumed the identities of several important people, including a bank president, a member of Congress, and an airline pilot."

"Good Lord," Horace Wimple said. "Why?"

"Apparently, it's a desperate bid for attention. Particularly"—here he cleared his throat and made a show of looking away from Simone—"*female* attention. Just last month he pretended to be a casting director for a reality television program about women exhibitionists."

Simone gasped.

Then, just as the not-real Shriver was being forced into the police vehicle, he tore free from his captors and dashed down the driveway.

"Stop him!" Detective Krampus yelled as the two officers gave chase. But the man was surprisingly quick and disappeared around the corner well ahead of the policemen.

Krampus, cursing his men, tore down the driveway in pursuit. The partygoers, oblivious to the cloud of voracious mosquitoes that descended upon them, spilled out onto the porch and watched the little man dash around the corner and disappear.

Zzzzch! went the insect zapper.

T. Wätzczesnam, full wineglass in hand, patted Shriver on the back and said, sadly, "I believe this singular situation has me stumped for an appropriate bit of verse."

"May I have a word?" Simone asked Shriver, escorting him into another room off the hall, Mr. Wimple's office, apparently. There was a desk, a file cabinet, and shelves lined with books. Shriver's lower bowel puckered at the smell of decaying paper.

"I'm sorry about all this," Shriver said.

"Never mind that. I want you to look me in the eye and tell me who you are."

"Simone—"

"Oh, will you please just do it," she said, starting to tear up. "I don't know which end is up anymore, and I could use a little certainty here."

Shriver removed his handkerchief and handed it to her. She thanked him and wiped her eyes. Then she glanced down at the hanky and let out a little gasp.

"What is it?" Shriver asked.

"The handkerchief." She held it out to him, unfolded. "*CRS*. That's you?"

He nodded.

Her face relaxed into a smile. "Oh, thank God." She handed the handkerchief back to him.

"You keep it," he said.

T. entered and cleared his throat. "I hate to interrupt this tender moment, but we have a reading to go to."

"You still want me to read?" Shriver asked.

Simone touched his arm. "Everyone here would understand if you decided not to go ahead with it, after the way we've treated you."

"Oh, he's reading," Gonquin Smithee said from the doorway, the yellow pages in her hand. "Right, T.?"

The cowboy approached Shriver and said, sotto voce, his whiskey-and-wine breath curling Shriver's nose hairs, "There's about eight hundred people in that ballroom waiting for you, old man. Don't bail on us now."

Shriver looked over at Simone. She nodded. His duodenum whined.

Edsel Nixon stepped forward. "Here," he said, handing Shriver the manila envelope. "You left it in the jeep."

"I need to use the restroom," Shriver said.

Chapter Seventeen

Shriver rode with Simone to the College Union. The whole way he toed the precipice of confessing the truth, but now that everyone once again believed he was the actual Shriver, he wasn't sure what the truth *was*. He'd been sure, after all, that the other Shriver was the real thing, and look how *that* turned out.

"I am just so profoundly embarrassed," Simone said for the seventh or eighth time. "To have fallen for that . . . *liar*."

Shriver watched her skin turn red with shame every time she said it, and he had to wonder what had transpired between her and the imposter. Had she . . . ?

"I should have known better," she said. "Even for a writer he was full of himself."

"Simone . . ."

"It just burns me up that he got away," she continued. "I'd love to see him in shackles. Do they execute people for this kind of thing? Of course they don't—I know that—but I sure wish they did. I'd like to pull the switch myself, or whatever it is they do nowadays."

"You look lovely," Shriver said.

"Excuse me?"

"In that dress, I mean. Lovely."

She blushed an even richer shade of red, if that were possible. "Why, thank you."

She drove in silence now, his compliment having dammed for a moment the torrent of shame.

He took out his story and straightened the papers on the still-unopened manila envelope atop his knees. There was the opening line: "The water mark appeared on my ceiling on the rainy day my wife walked out on me." So far, so good. "At first it was just a spot, approximately the size of a quarter, directly above the bed where I lay weeping." His heart beat rapidly as he read on.

He read the first page, then the second. He laughed. They were good, the words, and the story was good. What was it Gonquin Smithee had said? She had pronounced it "wonderful." *Wonderful!*

Simone pulled into the Union parking lot and shut off the engine. "Well, here we are."

Shriver gulped. "Yes."

"The culmination of the whole conference."

"Don't tell me *that*."

"The final event, after all that planning."

"Oh, boy."

"Everybody's been talking about this reading for months."

"Simone."

"And to think I nearly ruined it."

"Please . . ."

"To think I made a fool of the conference and the college, and dragged you through the mud in the process."

"No . . ."

"As for me, I'll be lucky to keep my job after all this. I'll never get tenure now."

"I'll speak to Mr. Wimple."

"And even if they keep me on as an adjunct, surely they'll have someone else organize next year's conference."

"They'd be crazy to let you go."

"That's sweet of you to say." She sighed. "I'm sorry I doubted you."

"Simone, you don't have to—"

"No, I can't say it enough. I think I was just so disappointed at the thought of . . . of you and . . ."

"You mean Dr. Keaudeen? I told you, Simone—"

She turned squarely toward him. "Tell me nothing happened."

"Nothing happened," Shriver said.

"So you were up in her bedroom because . . . ?"

"Because I needed to use the restroom."

Simone's face wrinkled into a quizzical expression. "And you were on her bed because . . . ?"

"She was showing me her novel."

Simone leaned in. "And you were writhing on top of her because . . . ?"

Shriver thought hard. This was not easy to explain. "Because she's stronger than me?"

Simone smiled. "You know, as hard as those answers are to swallow, they're so absurd that they must be true."

Shriver felt the air return to his lungs. "It's absolutely true. Plus, have you ever tried to climb out of a waterbed? It's like quicksand!"

"I'll take your word for it. Anyway, that whole . . . *tableau* put me in a state of shock, and I felt vulnerable, and then that bastard caught me off guard."

"Say no more, Simone. I understand."

"Thanks."

They sat silently for a moment. To accumulate courage, Shriver made a fist, the way one makes a fist to pump blood to a vein for a needle.

"Did you . . . ?" he began.

"Did I what?"

"You and . . . ?"

"Me and who?"

"Did you and . . . ?" He couldn't say it.

She tilted her head, trying to understand. Then it came to her.

"Are you serious?"

"I just wondered."

"Who do you think I am?"

"Well, the way he was acting. And there was that poet you mentioned last year."

"I wouldn't sleep with him if you paid me."

"You mean the poet? Or—"

"He was so arrogant. So full of himself."

"Never mind."

"I can't believe you asked that. I've *had it* with egomaniacal writers."

"I understand."

"You guys with your epic novels and big advances and throngs of groupies and sycophants, you just march out here to the hinterlands and expect everyone to fall to their knees and grovel while you drink and screw your way through the week, and—"

It wasn't easy, because he had to hoist himself up and over the wide armrest that divided the front seats, and then he had to bend his face down toward hers as he balanced himself by grabbing the steering wheel with one hand and the headrest in the other, but he somehow managed it smoothly and swiftly so that she remained off guard even as his lips met hers. Still, she continued talking for a moment, her angry words filling his mouth until they finally softened into a moan that he felt deep in his own ear bones. Now that he was a writer, Shriver took note of this and other details: the hair standing up on his arms, the tingle where his spine met his skull, the taste of cheap white wine on her tongue, the smell of sweat and powder. He had always dreamed of kissing Tina LeGros of the Channel 17 Action News Team, but this—this was so much better.

Then he heard the car door creak open, and before he could disengage from Simone—for who would ever want to voluntarily pull away from those lips?—a hand grabbed him by his collar and yanked him out of the car and onto the pavement.

Shriver heard Simone scream as fists rained down on his head and shoulders. He squeezed his eyes shut and held up his arms to fend them off.

"Damn you, you son of a bitch," someone grunted.

"Thaddeus!" Simone cried out. "Stop!"

The punches slowed in frequency and strength, and then stopped altogether. Shriver looked up to see T. Wätzczesnam bent over him, his eyes rimmed red, tears rolling down his ruddy cheeks.

"T.?" Shriver tasted blood. Mosquitoes, smelling food, swarmed around him.

The cowboy collapsed onto his knees and bellowed, "I loved her so much," as a long glob of snot poured from his nose. "And now she loves *you.*"

"*Loves* me?"

"Oh, don't be an ass, Shriver," T. said, the words coming out in choked syllables.

By now Simone had run around the huge car and was pounding the cowboy on his ten-gallon hat.

"You idiot!" she yelled while T. made no attempt to defend himself.

"No, Simone," Shriver said, reaching up and grabbing her arms.

"Oh my God!" she cried out. "Your nose is bleeding!"

She took out his handkerchief from her purse and pushed it against his nose.

"I'm okay," he told her.

"Look what you did," she screamed at Professor Wätz-czesnam.

"I'm sorry," the cowboy blubbered.

"I'm fine, Simone," Shriver said. "You go on inside. I'll be there in a minute."

"Are you sure?"

"Go on. I promise I'm okay."

She gave T. one last shove before she turned and walked up the stairs to the Union.

Shriver sat there on the pavement for a few moments while the cowboy leaned into his shoulder, the tears flowing out of him. Finally, T. caught his breath, wiped his nose, and pulled away a little.

"It's not fair," he said, a tiny note of belligerence returning to his voice. "You get all the kudos for one book that no one has even finished."

"If it makes you feel any better, T., I don't think I deserve it either."

"And then you get the *girl*."

"I deserve that even less."

The cowboy reached into his pocket and produced his bottle of whiskey. "Ah, hell," he said. "Let's toast to your success."

"You toast for me, T."

"Don't tell me you've climbed on the wagon."

"For today, anyway."

"Well then, here's to my beautiful Simone."

T. took a long swig, coughed, and climbed to his feet. He reached down and offered Shriver his hand. "Come on, Shriver. Let's get your face cleaned up."

Shriver took his friend's hand and stood.

"Ah, I feel much better now, old man," Wätzczesnam said, helping Shriver up the steps. "It's been a coon's age since I bloodied a man's nose."

"I'd say I'm glad to be of help, T., but . . ."

"As the poet says, 'A ruddy drop of manly blood / The surging sea outweighs.'"

/

The ballroom was at full capacity, with a standing-room-only crowd gathered at the back. People pointed and murmured when they saw Shriver enter. His nose had finally stopped bleeding, but he could still taste blood, along with Simone, on his tongue.

"I'll say a few words first," Simone said as she escorted him up the steps and onto the stage, "and then Mr. Cheadem is going to introduce you." Smiling, she gestured toward the chairs on the dais. "Have a seat, *Mr. Shriver.*"

He sat and gazed out upon the throng. On the table was a Styrofoam cup. He lifted it to his nose—water—and drank.

"Ladies and gentlemen," Simone began, "welcome to the final and, dare I say, most highly anticipated event of this year's wildly successful and, well, just plain *wild* conference. I'm very pleased that this special occasion has brought to us a notable personage from the New York literary world, who will be making the formal introduction today. So, please welcome Mr. Donald Cheadem."

The audience applauded respectfully as the agent ambled

toward the stage. He climbed the stairs, shook hands with Professor Cleverly, then took his place at the podium. Shriver watched Simone return to her usual seat. Next to her sat Horace Wimple, his silver hair reflecting the fluorescent light.

"Ladies and gentlemen," Mr. Cheadem began, "I cannot tell you how honored I am to be here today to say a few words about this great man to my left."

Shriver felt a numbness spread from his toes straight up to the top of his head as Cheadem spoke. Afraid to look at the audience while the agent continued, he stared down at the yellow papers in his hands.

"I've only met Mr. Shriver once in my life, but the memory of it is quite vivid. I was about fifteen years old and spending the day at my father's office—my father being the late Donald Cheadem Sr., Mr. Shriver's first and only agent—when in came this disheveled gentleman wearing a look of great distraction. Much like the expression he's wearing today."

The audience laughed.

"My father said, 'Donald, meet Mr. Shriver, the best writer you'll ever know.' Now, coming from my father, that was saying quite a lot. I shook the great writer's hand, then was immediately sent on an errand while the two men talked about the upcoming publication of Mr. Shriver's novel. I never saw the man again until today, but I never forgot my father's pride at having represented him. He even gave me a copy of the manuscript, something he never did, and I read the novel more than once that summer. Can anyone ever forget the great characters in that book—Caleb; his wife, Sarah; Sal the doorman; even that amazing cat of theirs? These people were as real to me as my own relatives and neighbors. Then there were the unforgettable scenes of love and heartache and comedy. My father was especially tickled by Mr. Shriver's reconstruction of one of his own memories as a private in the army on a troop train headed from New Jersey to San Francisco. Dad had told the story to Mr. Shriver over drinks one night, unaware that it would be immortalized in print soon after. Warning: never tell a writer anything unless you are willing to let it go."

More laughter.

"So, here we are, twenty years on, my father gone, and after two decades of silence, Mr. Shriver suddenly appears with manuscript in hand. For the life of me, I cannot think of a more exciting event in the world of literature than this reading today. We are witnessing history here, ladies and gentlemen. So, without further ado, please welcome . . ."

Shriver felt his face go cold, while, at the same time, sweat rolled down his spine. He heard what sounded like waves crashing onto a beach, and he looked up to see more than seven hundred faces looking at him, each person banging their hands together in applause. Donald Cheadem, also clapping, stood aside from the podium. Shriver was supposed to stand, but he felt too heavy, and the feeling had not yet returned to his legs. It was like one of those dreams he sometimes had, where he absolutely had to get from here to there to rescue Mr. Bojangles from a rampaging serial cat killer but could not move without the greatest of effort, and then only in slow motion. The applause intensified. He tried to smile, to show his appreciation, as he swiveled in his chair, dragging his leaden legs. He placed a hand on the table and, using what little strength he had in his arms, lifted himself to his feet. More applause. He felt like Lazarus.

Mr. Cheadem shook his hand, then stepped down from the stage and returned to his seat next to Jack Blunt. Shriver leaned against the podium, praying that it would not tip over.

The applause slowly died down. Above the heads of those standing in the back, the photograph of Shriver loomed large on the screen. The window, the living room, the curtains.

"Thank you," he tried to say, but it came out a wheeze. He cleared his throat and repeated, "*Thank you*," this time more audibly.

He set his story on the podium in front of him.

The audience seemed to be holding its breath. Someone took a flash photograph, raising bright white spots on the yellow writing paper. Shriver rubbed his eyes.

"I'm going to read something new," he announced. He looked down at the pages. There at the top, obscuring the title, a perfectly round bloodstain, and next to it, a smear of chocolate. The words underneath, so clear just moments ago in the car, began to blur, little blue raindrops rolling across the paper. His heart slipped from its place behind his ribs to somewhere lower, below his large intestine. He looked up. Each face in the audience was as sharply defined as that of a Vermeer model. He saw Delta Malarkey-Jones in the fourth row, a proud smile on her face. He saw Edsel Nixon a few seats away, his pale, smooth countenance like that of a child. He saw Cassandra, in a tight tank top, her eyes blinking seductively. He saw Basil Rather and Ms. Brazir, and, just behind them, Gonquin Smithee. He saw Zebra Amphetamine, a lonely dark face in a sea of pale skin. He saw Teresa Apple, in a clingy sweater top, her bosom high and almost accusatory. He saw Dr. Keaudeen, her taut face made even tauter by her blinding grin. He saw Charlevoix and Sue St. Marie, their twin beehives thrusting upward to block the views of the people sitting behind them. He saw the willowy brunette cheerleader, standing radiant and tall in the back. He saw all those who had requested autographs over the past two days, clutching their books to their chests. He saw Detective Krampus, inscrutable as ever, enter the ballroom through the door.

Standing in the very back, far enough away that Shriver wasn't sure he was seeing correctly, he thought he could make out his old friend Vinnie the doorman, and, next to him, Blotto. In the delivery boy's arms lay a small black-and-white animal, its tail flapping contentedly. Shriver blinked and they were gone.

He looked down again at his papers. They were covered in blue ants, marching off the podium in revolt. What on earth was he going to do? He glanced up at Simone in the front row. Her head cocked to the side, she looked up at him with an expression of intense concentration, as if the next words he spoke would decide for her the future. Shriver felt panic spreading across his face like a rash. Simone's eyes widened as she took this in. She uncrossed her legs and leaned forward. She appeared to consider rushing up onto the stage, then thought better. Instead, she held out her hands, subtly, as if to say, *Take it easy, hold on, you will be all right.*

He shut his eyes. He saw his room: the bed, the white walls, the portrait of Tina LeGros, the mahogany bureau. Mr. Bojangles lay nearby, his black fur rising and falling with his steady breathing. And there, on the ceiling, the water mark. Then, he spoke:

" 'The watermark appeared on my ceiling on the rainy day my wife walked out on me,' " he said in a clear, strong voice. And he went on from there, seeing the water mark as clear as day, and remembering, word for word, all he had written just a few days ago while lying on his bed.

Chapter Eighteen

The applause seemed to last forever.

Shriver, his tongue as dry as cardboard, the glass of water long empty, stood with his hands gripping the sides of the podium as if he might otherwise fall backward. Before him roiled a sea of clapping hands and upturned faces. Edsel Nixon applauded. Delta Malarkey-Jones applauded. Even Detective Krampus applauded. Jack Blunt was clapping, also, and Mr. Cheadem, the agent, smiled broadly as he brought his meaty palms together. Still, Shriver avoided glancing over at Simone. What if she was not clapping? What if she was clapping only halfheartedly, her eyes cast down toward the floor?

As the applause finally started to thin, T. Wätzczesnam appeared at his side, a tight grin on his face.

"Well done, old boy," the cowboy said into his ear. Leading with his elbow, he edged his way to the microphone. "Thank you, Mr. Shriver," he announced. "That was truly wonderful. Now, if there are any questions . . ."

Dozens of hands shot up into the air. T. happily took charge. "Yes?" he said, pointing to a young woman in the third row.

"That was great," the woman said. "So different in tone from your novel. It's as if it were written by a different person!"

"Thanks," Shriver said. "It was."

"What have you been doing these past twenty years?"

"Not much." There was some laughter. More hands shot up.

"Is this the beginning of a new novel?" a man asked.

"I hadn't thought about it," Shriver said. "Maybe it is."

"Do you write your first draft on a computer or by hand?" someone asked.

"I don't own a computer," Shriver said to the amazed crowd.

He answered their questions for almost an hour, and at the fifty-nine-minute mark he began to relax. He was getting away with this. These people *still* thought he was the real Shriver. He could say almost anything and they would buy it.

Finally, T. stepped in and said, "We have time for just one more question."

An arm, sheathed in black leather, rose up from the throng. "I have a question."

He stood up—Vlad, the waiter/student. He was dressed all in black, and Shriver now made the connection: it was Vlad who'd been following him everywhere. His heart pinballed around inside his rib cage.

"Your story," Vlad said, "is about a man deserted by his wife, who also takes their young son, and the man's distress at the loss."

He paused. After a moment, Professor Wätzczesnam stepped up to the microphone. "We all heard the story, young man. Do you have a *question*?"

"I'm wondering," Vlad said, after some thought, "how autobiographical is this story?"

The room became absolutely quiet but for the soft hum of the microphone.

"How *true* is it?" Vlad went on, as if to fill the void.

Shriver looked at all the faces in the room, all the eyes

focused solely on him. He looked at Simone in the front row, who seemed to be holding her breath. Then he glanced down at the story he'd written, and the words were as clear as the minute hairs on the back of his cat-scratched hand: *The water mark appeared on my ceiling on the rainy day my wife walked out on me.*

The audience started to stir, waiting for Shriver's answer. Finally, he leaned into the microphone and said, "Any good writing is true. Even when it's made up."

A few audience members murmured, then there came the sound of general approval. Simone grinned and T. clapped Shriver on the back. Vlad nodded and sat down, and Shriver thought, Yes, perhaps I really *am* a writer.

T. approached the microphone and announced, "Mr. Shriver will now be signing books, so you can get a little one-on-one time with him out in the lobby." There was more applause, and Shriver smiled and waved until the audience members finally stood and started filing out of the ballroom.

"Well, Shriver," the cowboy said, "you are certainly Big Man on Campus."

"You really think so?" He looked around for Simone, who had left her seat.

"There's a boatload of people out there waiting for you," Edsel Nixon said from the bottom of the platform stairs.

"Have you seen Simone?"

"I'm sure she's around here somewhere."

Out in the lobby, a long line snaked around the corner, each person clutching a copy of *Goat Time* to his or her chest. Many others mingled around the book table. But Simone was not among them.

"This way," Edsel said, escorting Shriver over to a small table and chair.

"Mr. Shriver!"

Donald Cheadem rushed over, accompanied by Jack Blunt.

"Well done," the agent said, grabbing Shriver's hand and pumping it. "If only my father had been here to see that!"

"Thank you."

"Listen—since I took over the business, and since I've been the one depositing your checks for the past ten years, I feel I can technically lay claim to being your agent. And I would love to get together and discuss this story of yours. Is there more?"

"Uh, I'm not sure."

"Well, I'm certain we could get a significant book deal, if there is. And then there's the ancillary rights—"

"Ancillary?"

"If we play our cards right we might even get you on *Oprah*."

"Really?" Shriver said, getting excited. "I *love* Oprah!"

"Let's figure it out, shall we? Can we meet for dinner?"

"Tonight?"

"No good? How about breakfast first thing tomorrow?"

"I don't know . . ."

"Or we could meet back East. At my office. Or at your apartment. Wherever you'd like."

"Yes. That would be fine."

"Excellent! Here's my card." He handed Shriver a business card: *Cheadem Agency, Donald Cheadem Jr.* "You promise to call me?"

"Okay."

"Oh!" Cheadem laughed. "You don't have a telephone, do you? Well, we'll work something out." He pumped Shriver's hand again before starting off.

"What just happened?" Shriver asked.

"Who said life doesn't have a second act?" Edsel Nixon said.

"Well," Jack Blunt said, lingering behind, "I suppose I'm on the long list of boneheads who owe you an apology."

"Not at all."

"I'd like to make it up to you, if I could. How about that interview?"

"You've got your story, Mr. Blunt. Let's not get too greedy."

"I'll pin you down one of these days, Shriver."

"I don't doubt it."

The reporter started off.

"Oh, Mr. Blunt," Shriver said. He pointed to the man's cockeyed toupee. Blunt reached up and adjusted it, then followed Mr. Cheadem out the door.

Shriver went on to sign books for more than an hour, only half listening as each person complimented him and asked that he make the inscription out to Frank or David or Jane. He mechanically opened the books and signed his name with an increasingly indecipherable flourish, all while thinking only of Simone.

The second-to-last person in line handed him a copy of *Goat Time*.

"Please make it out to Caleb," the tall man with a cap and bushy mustache said.

"Caleb?"

The man winked and pulled the mustache partially from his face. The other Shriver!

"What are *you* doing here?" Shriver glanced across the lobby to where Detective Krampus stood chatting, notebook in hand, with Gonquin Smithee.

"I might ask you the same thing," the man replied.

"I have no idea what you mean," Shriver said, realizing he did not sound very convincing.

The man leaned down and said, "Don't worry. I'm not going to make any trouble. I just wanted you to know there's no hard feelings."

"Is that so?"

"Let's just say the better man won," the imposter said. "You're pretty good at this." He opened the book to the title page. "Your signature, sir."

Shriver wrote, *To Caleb*, and signed his name.

As he went to shut the book, he came upon the book's epigraph, two italicized lines alone on the page:

> *Now that I'm enlightened, I'm just as miserable as ever.*
> *—Japanese monk*

"Thanks," the man said when Shriver handed back the book, and he quickly headed off.

Shriver stood and tried to get the attention of Krampus— *The imposter*, he wanted to shout, *he's getting away!*—but the detective was still busy talking with Gonquin. The fake Shriver had disappeared into the crowd anyway, and what did it really matter?

He turned back to see one last person in line: Vlad. The boy smiled bashfully, and seemed so sincere, his face so open, that Shriver wondered how he could have assigned such dark motives to his actions.

"So, Vlad," Shriver said, "that was *you* following me around?"

Vlad nodded reluctantly, as if admitting to a misdemeanor. "Did you get the story I left for you?"

"I did," Shriver said. "Twice."

"Sorry. I just wanted to—I don't know—*connect*."

"Connect?" Shriver said. "I thought you were out to kill me."

"Kill you?"

"I know. Crazy, isn't it?"

"I just wanted to meet my father," Vlad said. "And show him my work."

"Yes, and about your story . . ." Shriver shook his head, as if to get rid of a ringing sound in his ears. "Wait. Did you say—?"

"It's true, Mr. Shriver," Detective Krampus said, appearing from behind the student. "I never was able to track down your ex-wife, but I did manage to locate some relatives of hers, and though they were reluctant to reveal it, they told me your son was enrolled at the college here."

He gestured toward Vlad, who grinned and swayed on his long legs.

"Vlad is your son?" Edsel Nixon, suddenly beside Shriver, asked. "What a crazy coincidence."

"Not really," Krampus said. "Young Vladimir here was on the conference committee. He was the first to float Mr. Shriver's name as a guest writer. And that's where they got the photograph—from Vlad."

Shriver stared at the boy. He could detect a vague resemblance to his younger self. Tall and thin, with jet-black hair and a prominent nose. Is that why he'd looked so familiar?

Then it came to Shriver: This was not *his* son. This was the son of the *real* Shriver!

He tried to speak, but the words collided in his throat.

"This must be a very emotional moment for you," Krampus said.

"I . . . I . . ."

"We understand," Krampus said. Then, to Edsel Nixon: "Perhaps we should leave these two alone for a moment."

He and Edsel wandered toward the far end of the lobby.

Shriver and Vlad stood several feet apart, each of them looking anywhere but at the other.

"I don't know what to say," Shriver managed to whisper.

"I've been wanting to talk to you about it," Vlad said. "At the restaurant, the readings, after the writing class—it just never seemed to be the right time."

Shriver's eyes wandered the lobby as if searching there for another way to tell this young man the truth. But there was only one way.

"Son," he said, and immediately regretted using the word. "I mean, *Vlad*—the thing is, I'm *not* your father."

"I know what you're saying."

"You do?"

"But just because you weren't there for me when I was growing up doesn't mean you're not my dad."

"*No.* I mean, that's not what I mean—"

"It's okay. I don't blame you."

"But . . ."

While Shriver cast about for what to say next, Vlad stepped up and wrapped his long arms around him.

"I love you, Dad."

Shriver's arms hung limp at his sides while the boy squeezed him tightly.

"It's funny," Vlad said. "At first I wasn't convinced you were my father. You just didn't act the way I thought he'd act."

"How did you think your father would act?"

"Like an asshole. A big shot. Actually, like that other guy who *pretended* to be you. He fit the bill pretty good."

"Maybe he *is* your father."

"I considered that. But then I decided that, even if he was, I'd rather *you* were my dad."

"And if I'm not?"

"Oh, you *are*. I'm convinced of it."

"I'm very . . . touched, Vlad."

"That was a beautiful story you read, by the way."

"Thanks."

"And you're right. It was the truth."

At the far end of the lobby, Simone emerged from a side door, accompanied by Mr. Wimple.

"So," Vlad said, "have you read my story?"

"Your story?" Shriver watched Simone say good-bye to the college president, who then exited the building.

" 'The Imposter,' " Vlad said.

Simone's face betrayed no emotion. If she'd just been fired, she wasn't letting on.

"Oh, I'm sorry, Vlad. I've been kind of . . . distracted. But I promise I will read it."

"I really want to know what you think."

"Of course."

Simone saw him and waved, her face still impassive.

"Well, I guess I'll see you at the party," Vlad said.

"Party?"

"The end-of-conference bash."

"Oh, right."

Vlad hugged him again and whispered in his ear: "Accept who you are." Then he loped off, his long legs striding confidently across the lobby. Shriver watched him go and wondered how on earth—and when—he would tell the boy the truth.

"Are you okay?" Simone asked.

"Life just keeps getting stranger and stranger," Shriver said.

"I know exactly what you mean."

"Why? What did Wimple say?"

"He said there's a new position about to open up in the English department."

"Simone," Shriver said. "I'm so sorry."

"Don't be."

"This is all my fault."

"You don't understand. He didn't fire me."

"He didn't? Then . . . ?"

"He wants to hire *you*."

"Me?"

"We need a writing professor."

"Yeah, but *me*?"

"Why *not* you?"

"What do *I* know about writing?"

"Just everything."

"But . . ."

"You don't want the job?" She looked crestfallen.

Just when he thought things couldn't get crazier. After three days of wanting desperately to escape this labyrinth, he was now being drawn farther into it.

"I'm just so surprised," he said.

"Just don't say no yet," Simone told him. "That's all I ask."

"Okay."

She smiled and grabbed his hand. "Come on. We have one more party to go to."

Shriver didn't move.

"What's wrong?" Simone asked.

"I don't know if I can take another party."

She laughed. "I understand. No party, then."

Shriver saw a promising turn in the labyrinth. "Thank you."

"So what shall we do instead?"

DAY / FOUR

Chapter Nineteen

When Shriver woke up, he knew exactly where he was. There was the bright stripe of sunlight between the thick curtains. There, on the wall, hung the painting of a cow in a field. From off in the distance came the now-familiar howl of a freight train rolling across the prairie. He lay in the hotel bed and smiled, remembering his dream. Simone had been here beside him, her skin smooth and warm and lightly filmed with sweat. Her head lay on his shoulder, her yellow hair bunched up on the pillow.

"I remember now," he had said to her in the dream.

"Remember what?"

"Who I am."

"Who *are* you?"

That was when he woke up. He couldn't remember what he was about to say to her, but he knew now that it didn't matter. The dream spoke of other, more important things. He sighed and shut his eyes. His flight was scheduled for later this morning. Simone would pick him up and take him to the airport. She was still waiting for his answer about the teaching job.

Last night they had gone out to dinner, just the two of them. No parties, no whiskey, no Shriver fans, no drama. It was the first time he'd really relaxed in days. He'd let go of the need to tell her the truth about himself, that he was not the real Shriver. He had tried to tell Professor Wätzczesnam, Delta Malarkey-Jones, Edsel Nixon, and no one had believed him. On the contrary, Horace Wimple had extended a formal invitation to join the college faculty, Mr. Cheadem wanted to meet to discuss future projects, and Vlad seemed content to have the father he'd always wanted. He might even go on *Oprah*! As far as Shriver could tell, whether or not he was the *real* Shriver seemed irrelevant now. If he'd gained anything from this ridiculous charade, in fact, it was the sense that he really was a writer. Maybe he could even do it again, write more stories, or even a novel. He could base it on this very experience: a sad, lonely man is mistakenly invited to a prestigious conference, where he falls in love with the event's organizer. He could name his protagonist after himself, just like the real Shriver did. But this novel would end happily, with the beautiful professor and the imposter united.

At dinner, Simone had done her best to make this a reality. She spoke of the charms of campus life, the thrill of teaching, the lure of various local attractions.

"What about the mosquitoes?" he asked.

"That's only for a week or so out of the year."

"And the twenty-below winters?"

"You get used to it."

He could see that she knew he was only pretending to resist.

"Where would I live?"

"I already have a place for you."

"I have a cat."

"Oh. I'm allergic to cats," she said. Then, "But I suppose they have pills for that."

She told him how much he would be paid. It wasn't so much, she explained, considering that he was such a celebrity, and that his teaching there would increase the college's profile dramatically, but it was all the college could afford. He felt a twinge of guilt, knowing that he would be making money on the back of some other man—the real Shriver, wherever *he* was—but the feeling did not last long.

After dinner, Simone drove him to the hotel.

"I think I'm going to sell this damn car," she said. "My ex bought it, and I've always hated it. Time to start a new chapter."

"I know what you mean," Shriver said as he went to twist his wedding ring around his finger. "Oh my God!"

"What is it?"

"My ring. It's gone!" His finger was bare.

"It fell off?" Simone asked. "Just like that?"

Shriver shrugged. "I never even noticed." It must have been all that oil the cheerleader had applied. He held up his left hand, surprised by the sense of freedom he felt. He waved his hand around. It seemed . . . lighter.

"It must be a sign," Simone said.

Shriver wondered when it had fallen off. It could have been anywhere—the hotel, Edsel's tub, the parking lot where T. ambushed him. Wherever it was, he didn't care.

At the hotel, he asked her if she'd like to come in for a drink.

"It's so late," she said. "And it's been a long, weird day."

He was sure she could sense his disappointment.

"Besides," she said, "how else am I to lure you here for that job?"

They both blushed.

"I want to thank you," Shriver said after a moment.

"For what?"

"I feel like you saved my life."

"Aw, no. I just gave you a reason to leave the house."

"You say that as if it's a small thing."

She leaned across the wide armrest and kissed him. Again, a jolt of electricity sparked up and down his vertebrae. Then she pulled back.

"I'll pick you up at nine," she said.

He climbed down from the vehicle amid a swirl of mosquitoes. He stood there unbothered while they attacked him, and waved as Simone drove off.

In the lobby he heard raucous laughter coming from the Prairie Dog Saloon. Gonquin Smithee, Basil Rather, and Zebra Amphetamine called to him from their stools.

"Shriver!" the playwright yelled. "Where've you been?"

"We missed you at the party," Gonquin said.

"Join us for a nightcap," Basil demanded.

"It's very late," Shriver said.

"C'mon!" Zebra said. "Just one!"

"Please," Gonquin said. "One last snort before we all head off in different directions."

"Well, okay. But I'm going to have a ginger ale."

He stayed up for another hour, laughing with the three writers as they recounted various events at the conference.

"Here's to Shriver!" Basil Rather said, hoisting a glass of wine.

"To Shriver!" the others chimed in.

He was surprised to find that he would miss them. How long had it been since he'd missed anyone? Twenty years, at least.

"Where is Ms. Labio?" he asked Gonquin.

"Oh, she left town. Said she couldn't bear to see me betray 'the cause.'"

"Which cause is that?"

"I dunno. The full-scale demolition of the patriarchal construct?"

"Hey," Basil said. "You know what I'm going to do when I get home? I'm going to reread *Goat Time*. And this time I'm going to read the whole thing!"

When the bar closed they headed to their rooms, all four of them crowding onto the elevator, where they suddenly became quiet. Shriver, the only one staying on the second floor, said good-bye when the doors slid open, and wished them all well. Gonquin Smithee gave him a hug. Zebra Amphetamine did also. Basil Rather extended his narrow, long-fingered hand.

"See you at the next conference," Gonquin said as the doors started to close. "There's always another one right around the corner!"

When he got to his room, Shriver remembered he did not have his key. He laughed, and went back down to the lobby, where Charlevoix—he was pretty sure it was Charlevoix—had a new one waiting for him.

"We were able to change the lock," she told him. "Sorry for the inconvenience."

"No problem. It was an adventure."

When he finally got back into his room, he found a copy of *Goat Time* on the desk, perhaps left by Gonquin, or one of the others who had partied there the other night. He carried it to the bed and lay down. He opened the book to chapter one. He read the first page, then read it again. The words, which had scrambled and melted when he tried to read it two days ago, cohered into decipherable symbols, but still he could make no sense of them. It seemed to be about an angry young man on an airplane, but he wasn't sure about that. There were a lot of big words and fancy metaphors. Half the page was italicized. And yes, it was written in the second person. Maybe I'm just not smart enough, he thought. Well, he'd have to smarten up if he was going to continue pretending to be the real Shriver. He made one more stab at it, but his eyelids soon grew heavy, and he fell asleep.

/

By the time the telephone rang, Shriver was up, bathed, and dressed.

"Good morning," Simone said on the phone. "I'm downstairs."

"On my way."

He slipped into his dry but wrinkled jacket and grabbed his bag. At the door he turned back. He took in the paintings, the old TV, the raggedy carpet. Through the window he could see a train bisect the prairie. On the bedside table sat *Goat Time*. He was about to retrieve it but then thought better. Maybe twenty years ago it would have meant something to him, but now it failed to move him. He opened the door.

In the hall, just outside the door, he found a small jar labeled "Sunflower Oil." Attached was a note:

Dear Mr. Shriver [the "i" was dotted with a heart],
    I hope this will keep you relaxed.

xo

P.S. We lost the finals, but that's OK. We made it to the end—that's what counts!

/

Shriver found Simone in the lobby talking to the clerk. In a pair of faded jeans and a white blouse, she looked like a country girl, ready for anything.

"Hi," he said, hoping for another kiss.

"What is this all about?" she asked, her face stern. She handed over a copy of his bill.

"What?"

"Look at it."

He saw the room charges, the tax, and there, at the bottom, the miscellaneous items. They included two movies: *Glad He Ate Her* and *On Golden Blonde*.

"I d-d-don't understand," he said. "I didn't even turn the TV on."

Simone laughed. "It was Gonquin!" she said. "While she was hiding out in your room." She grabbed the bill from his hand. "Don't worry. I'll clear this up. Thank you, Sue St. Marie," she said to the clerk.

"Anytime." Sue St. Marie produced a copy of *Goat Time*. "Could you sign it for me and my sister, Mr. Shriver?"

"Of course."

To Sue St. Marie and Charlevoix, he wrote. *Love your hair.*

"We better get crackin'," Simone said, grabbing his suitcase.

"Please, Simone. Let me carry that."

"You don't want to miss your flight," she said, dragging the suitcase across the lobby floor.

Before he could stop her, she was out the door and tossing his bag into the backseat of her car.

"Climb aboard!"

Shriver opened the car door and pulled himself up into the behemoth one last time.

As Simone shifted into gear, the clip-clop sound of horse hooves heralded the arrival of T. Wätzczesnam.

"Whoa!" the cowboy cried, pulling Walter up alongside the passenger window. "Well, well," he said, "if it isn't our local power couple."

"Mr. Shriver has a plane to catch," Simone told him.

"I understand you may be joining our disreputable faculty, Shriver," T. said. "'Slumming' is the word that comes to mind."

"I haven't quite decided, T."

"Well, I'd be most honored to share our ramshackle faculty lounge with you."

"I appreciate that."

"Oh—here," T. said, producing a thin volume from his denim pocket. "In case you need something to read on the airplane."

He handed the book over: *At Home on the Range*, by T. Wätzczesnam.

"I'm much obliged."

"Don't mention it."

"We have to get going," Simone announced.

"She's a slave driver, Shriver," T. said. "You've been warned."

With that, the cowboy tipped his hat, shouted, "Giddyup!" and rode off toward the campus.

Shriver opened the book. On the title page, in childlike block letters, T. had written:

To Shriver, Please accept this dull product of a scoffer's pen, from one writer to another. Yours in kindly inebriation,

T.W.

/

They drove with the windows down, the crisp morning air cool on Shriver's face.

"Did they spray this morning?" he asked. He hadn't seen or felt one mosquito.

"No need. It's over. At least until next year."

Shriver watched the little town recede in the side-view mirror. Ahead was endless prairie and sky. Huge, fluffy clouds hung motionless in the blue air.

"It is beautiful here," he said.

"I think you'll like it."

He turned to her. "Who said I'm taking the job?"

She looked over at him and grinned.

Was it only three days ago that Simone had driven him in the opposite direction, toward the hotel and the campus—toward his future?

As they drove silently along, Shriver glanced down and saw a copy of *Goat Time* on the floor. "Oh, is this your copy?" he asked. "I'll sign it for you."

"Oh, that's okay," Simone said, reaching to grab the book from him.

"Don't be silly." Shriver opened the book to the title page.

"No—" Simone said as Shriver took in the inscription there:

To Simone, Best wishes, and the signature.

"Sorry," she said. "I really did think he was—"

" 'Best wishes'? That's the best that weasel could come up with? For *you*?"

Simone laughed. "I know. Lame, right?"

Shriver tore the page from the book and wrote, above the epigraph, *My dearest Simone*. Then, from the epigraph he scratched out *I'm as miserable as ever* and wrote, *I'm as happy as ever, thanks to you*, and signed his name.

"Here we are," Simone announced as she pulled into the airport's short-term parking lot.

"I'll wait in the car," came a familiar voice from the backseat.

Shriver turned to see Edsel Nixon. "Mr. Nixon, you continue to amaze me."

Nixon's eyes started to shine with water. "I just wanted to say, before you go, it's been an honor to be your handler, Mr. Shriver."

Shriver extended his hand into the backseat, where Edsel took hold of it firmly. "The honor has been all mine, young man."

Simone opened her door, and before Shriver could negotiate the steep climb down to the pavement, she had his bag out and was hauling it toward the terminal.

"Do you promise to call me when you get back home?" she asked as he scrambled to catch up with her.

"I don't have a telephone, remember?"

"Call from a pay phone. Collect."

"I promise."

"And then buy yourself a telephone."

"Okay."

"The semester starts on September fifth," Simone told him, "but you need to be here at least a week before that so we can sort everything out."

They joined the check-in line, not saying anything.

"You don't have to wait here with me," Shriver said.

"I want to."

"Good."

He checked his bag and received his boarding pass. They walked together toward the security area.

"They won't let me through," Simone said. "Not without a boarding pass."

"Then I'll wait right here."

Simone stood close to Shriver. Neither of them said anything. She put her arm around his waist and leaned her head against him. He ran his fingers through her yellow hair.

After a while, the boarding announcement came over the loudspeaker.

"You'd better go," she said, but he couldn't move. He wondered if he had to leave at all. Why couldn't he just stay here? He had nothing back home; none of his furniture or possessions meant anything to him. Then he remembered Mr. Bojangles. He needed to retrieve his little friend. His heart thumped at the thought of Mr. B.'s furry face. Won't he be happy when I walk in the door?

"Good-bye, Simone."

"Good-bye."

He leaned over and kissed her firmly on the lips. It was like falling into a warm pool. He kept kissing her, not wanting to get out of the water for fear the air would be too cold.

"G'bye," she mumbled, laughing.

He finally pulled away. "So long."

He entered the security lane and made his way through the metal detector. No beep.

At the gate, he turned back, but Simone was gone. He felt a stab of panic go through him. Where was she?

"Your ticket, sir?"

He handed a uniformed woman his boarding pass. After glancing back once more—still no Simone—he walked out onto the tarmac toward the metal stairway.

He didn't know why such a small thing—that one last look—was so important, but it was. He felt like he'd been abandoned at the last, most crucial moment.

"Caleb!"

She stood behind a fence separating the tarmac from the parking lot. She waved. He waved back. She was shouting to him, but he couldn't hear her over the noise of the airplane engine. He squinted, trying to read her lips.

I love you?

He wasn't sure, but he waved back at her and shouted, "I love you too!"

Then, with Delta Malarkey-Jones's memoir tucked under one arm, and T.'s novel and Vlad's story under the other, he boarded the plane and headed home.

THE END

Acknowledgments

The author wishes to thank the Connecticut Commission on Culture and Tourism for the generous artist fellowship grant that helped support the writing of this book.

Thanks also to Matthew Carnicelli for being the first to believe in Shriver.

Extra thanks to Stephanie Dickinson and Rob Cook at Rain Mountain Press for first ushering Shriver into the world.

Huge thanks to John Gosslee for taking Shriver to the big party, where the great Sally Kim waited with open arms. Thank you, Sally, and thanks to your team at Touchstone, especially Elaine Wilson.

Special thanks to Michael Maren for seeing how Shriver could bust off these pages.

Finally, thanks to all my colleagues who lie awake at night wondering if they are really writers. Rest assured, you are.

SHRIVER

When lonely Shriver receives a letter inviting him to attend a prestigious literary conference, he doesn't realize he's been confused for a famous, reclusive, Salinger-like author of the same name. He decides to attend and, once there, he is feted, fawned over, and featured at stuffy literary panels and readings by admirers who believe he is the famed novelist. Tensions begin to mount when one of the authors in attendance mysteriously goes missing, and the "real" Shriver (or so he claims to be) suddenly appears to stake his claim among the literati. The ensuing calamity forces Shriver to question everything he thought he knew, come face-to-face with his past, and fight for his future.

For Discussion

1. *Shriver* pokes fun at the pretensions of contemporary writing culture by satirizing the superficiality of literary conferences—however, do you think there can be value to conferences of this sort? Do you think the academic culture around writing, such as an MFA program or a conference like the one Shriver attends, is important, unnecessary, or somewhere in between?

2. Much of Shriver's past is obscured, whether purposefully left out by the author or blurred in Shriver's own mind. If

you had to guess, how would you fill in the gaps of Shriver's past life? Why do you think the author intentionally made Shriver's history mostly a mystery?

3. So many of the characters in *Shriver* are heightened versions of real people, almost cartoonish in their buffoonery, right down to their very names (Professors Wätzczesnam and Cleverly, Delta Malarkey-Jones). Would you classify *Shriver* as satire in the classical sense, akin to Jonathan Swift's work? How do you think exaggeration and hyperbole of character is projected by Shriver's perspective, and how does it set him apart from those who surround him?

4. *Shriver* begins with the following H. L. Mencken quote: "A writer is always admired most, not by those who have read him, but by those who have merely heard of him." Do you agree with this? Have you ever found yourself in a situation where you've pretended to have read a book that you actually haven't? If so, why?

5. Discuss the impetus behind Shriver going to the conference, despite considering the invitation a mistake. Have you ever been mistaken for someone else, and gone along with it? Would you have done so in Shriver's situation?

6. When Delta presents Shriver with an old photograph supposedly of himself, he struggles to see a resemblance. How much of one's identity do you feel is self-made versus informed by one's surroundings? How does Shriver struggle with his own identity as he is confronted with others' opinions about him?

7. At a bar, Shriver sees the phrase, "Now that I'm enlightened, I'm just as miserable as ever" scratched into the wood of a seatback in a booth. Why do you think the author chose this phrase, and why does Shriver encounter it at this particular moment? How do you relate to this phrase—does it ring true?

8. The protagonist of *Goat Time* is also named Shriver. Think about the three Shrivers that exist within the book—our protagonist, *Goat Time*'s protagonist, and the real Shriver—how do they coexist, in both reality and fiction?

9. Shriver's life before the conference seems ruled by comfortable routine: soup, baths, and Mr. Bojangles. How is his preferred way of life disrupted by the chaos of the conference and the trauma of Gonquin Smithee's disappearance, and how does it affect his creativity? How are his physical inhibitions (inability to read words, tummy troubles at even the smell of books) related to his writing of "The Water Mark," and how is his creative flow slowly unstoppered? What most inspires creativity in your own life?

10. Who do you think is the real Shriver after all? Why?

A Conversation with Chris Belden

You've taught creative writing through the Bronx Writers-Corps in underserved areas, as well as at a maximum-security prison—how do your experiences there compare with Shriver's experience at this writer's conference, and with teaching a class of MFA students?

Teaching creative writing at a maximum-security prison is the most rewarding thing I've ever done on a professional level. The students are enthusiastic, motivated, and grateful. I've always believed that writing can change your life, and with inmates it's even more apparent than with "civilians." These convicted criminals are learning to express themselves in a productive, nonviolent way. Teaching at the MFA level is obviously a different experience—for one thing, the students are allowed to leave the building when we're done—but in some ways the two are remarkably similar: both sets of students share their writing for purposes of discussion, and in both venues we are trying to communicate story, feeling, character, mood, etc., through language. As for how this compares with Shriver's experience, there's not much overlap for me—except that, like Shriver, I am considered an authority (the "writer/ expert") in a teaching environment. Interestingly, I've become much more comfortable with this role in the classroom than I have in the outside world, where I still expect to be dismissed as a wannabe.

Why do we meet Shriver at this particular point in his life?

The simple answer is that, as in all dramatic stories, we start where things are beginning to change. As a writer—whether of fiction, creative nonfiction, plays, or screenplays—you have to ask yourself, "Why is today any different from any other day for my protagonist?" For Shriver, [this] is the day he steps out into the world, when he pretends to be someone he doesn't think he is, or could ever be. Everything is about to change for him—he just doesn't know how.

You're not only a writer, you also studied film and are a musician. How do these three art forms compare and contrast in your mind? How do you decide to tell a story through the format of a novel, versus that of a song or movie? How do they interrelate?

Not to be a smart-aleck, but the difference is mainly one of space and time. A song, like a poem or postcard, must communicate a story in a brief amount of time and words. A film, though it might be based on a script [that is] 120 pages long, is digested in two hours. A novel, in contrast, has all the time it requires to tell a story. The technical differences are there simply to accommodate the format. Rhyme and melody in a song help make up for the fact that the story is being told so quickly, without the kind of detail or nuance that a novel can have. A film script must consist mostly of action and dialogue—any psychological motivation must be shown via these two conduits instead of through the interior monologue that novels can use. In a novel the writer is free to do whatever he or she wants, which is both liberating and constricting (too much freedom can lead to a lack of focus). But [a] story is the common element in all three disciplines.

Though this is not your first novel, it is the first with a Big Five publisher in New York. How has your experience compared to Shriver's, if at all?

Any time I am taken seriously as a writer, I feel like an imposter. In fact, the genesis of *Shriver* was a writers' conference to which I was invited, at which I sat on panels, spoke to students, gave a reading, and was treated like a "real" writer. At the time I had self-published one book and had had a few stories accepted at small literary journals, and here I was sharing the limelight with a National Book Award–winner, a beloved poet, and the author of a couple of *New York Times* bestsellers. I was so discombobulated that I eventually created an alter ego, Shriver (which, of course, means "writer"), who really is an imposter in a similar situation. It's ironic, to say the least, that it's this creation that has garnered me the most success as a writer.

You yourself have an MFA in creative writing—where do you stand in the constant tug-of-war of whether it is necessary or even harmful for a young writer to attend an MFA program? What would you say to an aspiring young writer asking if he or she should consider attending a writing program?

First of all, strike the word "young" from the question because I have met many "older" people who have attended MFA programs, some of whom are very talented but have not previously had the opportunity to practice their craft and get their work seen. In any case, I think if you are serious about writing and want to improve your craft, an MFA program is an ideal environment to do so. Is it for everybody who wants to write? Of course not. Some lucky people already have trusted readers and a well-developed routine of writing, but many others would benefit from the structure of an MFA program. Like Tobias Wolff, I don't believe you can teach a person to be a great writer—those people have an innate talent—but I do think you can teach a person to be a better editor and a better reader, and this might help turn a good writer into a great one. But most of all, an MFA program provides a community for writers. Writing is lonely, hard, and frustrating. If you have an opportunity to hang out with people in the same boat, it can inspire you to keep returning to that blank page, which is the hardest part of being a writer.

Enhance Your Book Club

1. Chris Belden is also a screenwriter. Imagine *Shriver* as a movie—devise a cast of famous actors to play the main characters, and even write a scene to act out among your group.

2. Famously reclusive authors include J.D. Salinger, Elena Ferrante, Harper Lee, Thomas Pynchon, and more. Go around the room and list things you've heard about these or other enigmatic authors, or impressions you've had based on the cult of personality (or lack thereof) surrounding them. Then, read one of their books for your next meeting and do some research on them—how does your experience of their writing compare to your perception of them and the mystery that surrounds them?

3. At your next meeting, take a stab at being a writer yourself! Share a piece of your own writing with the group, and have others reflect on how your personal writing sheds light on your identity.